DRAGON'S FUTURE

BOOK 1 OF DRAGON COURAGE

KANDI J WYATT

Cover Design by Amalia Chitulescu
Edited by Christina Lepre

*This is a work of fiction. Names, characters, places, brands, media, and incidents are either the product of the author's
imagination or are used fictitiously. Any resemblance to similarly named places or to persons living or deceased is
unintentional.*

PRINT ISBN 978-1533212351
Library of Congress Control Number: 2015910446

ACKNOWLEDGMENTS

I want to say thank you to the people who made this book possible; without them, it wouldn't have come into being as it is now. First, to my daughter Dawnya, for being the inspiration for Duskya. Second, to my Lord and Savior for giving me the words and creativity for this series. A special thanks goes out to my youngest son for sitting and listening to all the books, eager for every line and twist to the plot.

The books would have just stayed in my computer or in a binder if it wasn't for the South Coast Writer's Conference and Tess Thompson who encouraged me to submit to Booktrope. Once in Booktrope, I found a wonderful team willing to make the Dragon Courage series the best it could be: Pam Labbe, my book manager, who helped me with the ins and outs of social media; and Christina Lepre, who took my words and made them even better! Amalia Chitulescu, for making an amazing cover. I love your art, Amy. Then there's Vicki Sly who caught all those little errors. Thanks for proofing this, Vicki. Finally, thanks to Galit Breen for adding me and the Dragon Courage series to the UPdrift imprint. Thanks for seeing what my work could be, and for having the same vision I did — books that kids love to read, and that parents *want* them to read. Even though Booktrope is no more, the friends I made along the way gave me the courage to republish *Dragon's Future*. This second edition was made possible with the encouragement of my author friends in Fellowship of Fantasy and Book Nerd Paradise.

To David and Robin,
because you asked,
"Are you going to publish it?"
Here it is guys.

CONTENTS

PROLOGUE

IT WAS a special day, and Ruskya couldn't be late for the procession. He doubted that he would be chosen, but one never knew with dragons. The hatchlings were in their second winter. At their coming-of-age, all the younglings of Woolpren village who had seen ten winters would parade before them. It was up to the dragons to decide if any of the children were worthy enough to become riders. Ruskya smiled at the thought. Every child of Woolpren dreamed of becoming a dragon rider, but in reality, only a select few were picked. No one from his family had ever been chosen.

He turned to survey himself in the mirror of his lofted bedroom. What he saw in the dim light shining through the lone high window was not impressive. He was short for his ten winters, and skinny. Many people said he would blow away like a tumbleweed in the summer wind; yet he had managed somehow to survive for ten winters. His sister, Duskya, was the opposite: tall, dark, and slender—just like Ma. She wasn't skin and bones like him. How they could be twins still mystified him.

"Are you going to stand there and admire yourself all day, or are we going to go see the hatchlings?" Duskya demanded. "I know we don't have a chance of being picked, but we can at least say that we saw them," she added in a softer tone.

She too dreamed of becoming a dragon rider, but knew it was beyond them. Although the dragons were the ones who selected the riders, it often appeared they only picked the children of rulers or the wealthy. It was said that they chose them because of their elegant gowns. With this in mind, the twin's mother Meredyth had carefully gathered wool for the past ten summers. She had cleaned it, spun it, and then woven it into cloth and sewn the tunics for her offspring to wear for their one opportunity of becoming dragon riders. Duskya took one last look at herself and her brother in the mirror and then turned.

"Let's go make Ma proud of us," she stated and climbed down the ladder. Ruskya followed behind her.

Meredyth was waiting for them as they descended, her face etched with concern; yet, a hint of expectation glinted from her pale blue eyes. She wiped a stray wisp of gray hair from her face. "Ruskya, you've dillydallied too long. You'll be late if you don't run. Go!" She urged them out the door and down the lane of the canyon to the procession grounds.

Their steps made soft thudding noises as they ran, the ground hard-packed from many seasons of feet passing along that way. The ice of winter had not yet frozen it, but the nip in the air said it wouldn't be far off. The twins ran down the open canyon pathway, passing without seeing the familiar doors and windows that towered up the canyon face on either side of them. All the doors were shut and no lights shone from the windows, for everyone was at the procession grounds. Even those who had no children of age were there to see which younglings would be chosen. There were five dragons who were of age and would be in the procession this winter. With that many dragons available, the children were hopeful, though, they all knew that the dragons did not have to pick a youngling each year. There were two dragons that had seen as many winters as Ruskya and Duskya who had not yet selected any rider. They had been part of the procession for the last eight winters and while many believed they would never choose riders, others thought that they were waiting for just the right younglings.

The twins soon found themselves at the procession grounds. The crowd was not as thick as one would expect, for many people were looking down from their windows or rooftops, two to four stories above the canyon floor, to get a better view. Yet because the canyon bottled down before opening into a bowl at the procession grounds, there was still a press of people to move through. Duskya took the lead and started to push her way closer to the front where they could see. As she pushed past one adult, he grabbed her by the shoulder and turned her around.

"Look here," he started to scold and then stopped. "Duskya and Ruskya!" he exclaimed. "Why are you not up there yet? Come with me. There are two dragons that have not decided on a youngling and will not go away. It is as if they are waiting for some more younglings to materialize. The rider is trying to tell them that there are no more choices. He will be surprised to see you two."

The man started to clear the way to the front with shouts of "clear the way, prospective dragon riders coming through." Duskya could tell that her brother wanted to hide and run. He hated this type of attention, but she basked in it. Neither of the two really thought for a moment that anything would happen when they reached the front, but Duskya felt proud and important. At least for a little while, she could let the dream be real. With the man's help, they were soon up front. There he stopped and pushed the younglings forward. They had to walk the rest of the way on their own.

The twins both halted for a heartbeat while they realized the enormousness of the moment. Before them was a line of younglings, all who had seen ten winters, and in front of them, where the ground sloped into a bowl out of the twin's view, were the hatchlings. Suddenly, Ruskya heard a male voice call to him.

"Ruskya, come. I have been waiting for you. Please, come forward."

Ruskya looked around and couldn't see who was talking, but the voice was a calm comfort that seemed to give him the courage to take Duskya's hand and move forward to the line of younglings.

"Ruskya, thank you. You cannot imagine how long it has seemed as my sister and I have waited for you and your sister."

"You have a sister, too?"

"I do, and soon you will meet her, but first you must come join the other younglings."

As the voice spoke, Ruskya and Duskya arrived at the line. Ruskya looked around but still couldn't seem to see who was talking to him. Then he looked forward and caught sight of the dragons. His breath caught in his throat, and his heart seemed to skip a beat.

Standing before him were three dragons. One seemed enormous—a royal blue dragon with a solemn rider sitting atop him, surveying the scene. The other two were large but not as big, and blue, but of a lighter shade than the older and larger dragon. One was a pastel shade with streaks that looked like ice showing through. The other was the color of the sky with silver strokes spreading throughout its body. The two small dragons stepped forward. Just as Ruskya was about to step back, the voice called to him again.

"Ruskya, don't be afraid. I want to meet you. Please, come forward."

Ruskya paused, still looking around dazedly, and wondering where the voice was coming from, yet willing to go meet this person who could inspire courage in him. He took Duskya's hand and stepped forward.

* * *

The dragon rider surveyed the scene from the top of his perch on his dragon, the sunlight highlighting his sandy-blond hair. He had tried to talk sense into the two young dragons, but they had been insistent that there were more younglings to come. Then suddenly, two younglings appeared. They both wore the black wool of the procession, but each had a different shade of blue trim on their tunics. The boy wore a pastel color that matched the dragon Wyeth. The girl wore trim the color of the sky that was identical to the color of Wyeth's sister, Wryn. He marveled that a mother would have chosen those colors for her children.

As he considered these things, he noticed the boy take the girl's hand and step forward. The surprised look on the girl's face caused the rider to look closer. What was happening here? Often after being chosen, a youngling would gain courage that wasn't ordinarily there. Yet, this youngling had not been selected yet. Could that be what was going on now? Had Wyeth and Wryn known about these two younglings somehow? One never really knew with dragons, especially these two. He watched as the boy walked confidently up to Wyeth, paused, and then gave Wyeth's leg a hug. The girl had let go of her brother's hand and proceeded to give Wryn's leg a hug.

"Well, Wyden," the rider addressed his own dragon. "It looks like we've found our newest riders."

"I sense something different about them," Wyden responded.

Glendyn nodded as he urged his dragon forward and then called out to the people around, "Behold, the dragons have chosen. Blessed be those who were selected, and blessed be the village of their birth."

The crowd gave the traditional response, "Blessed be the dragons and those who have been chosen," and then slowly dispersed back to their abodes.

*　*　*

Ruskya was oblivious to the others around him. He was simply basking in the sound of the dragon's voice. He had just learned the creature's name when a hand was placed on his shoulder. Ruskya looked up into the dragon rider's face. Dark blue eyes gazed down at him from a severe fair-skinned face, examining him and weighing his worth. Ruskya at first felt shy and unworthy, and then he heard Wyeth give him encouragement. He was sure that the rider also heard the dragon's words, but the rider didn't respond. He continued to look at Ruskya, taking in his skinny form and short stature. Ruskya again sensed that he wasn't worthy to be a rider, when a warm breath of air touched the nape of his neck, and he smelled rosemary and pine needles. He had smelled it many winters ago when his da was still around and he would sit on his lap. A part of him wondered who his da was—Ruskya didn't even know his name, but the smell was enough to make him feel safe and secure. Ruskya straightened his back and took a step toward the dragon rider. He bowed to the man and then straightened, not waiting for the traditional response. He knew he was on equal footing with this rider, even though he was a youngling. The man's face broke into a large, friendly smile relieving the severity that had been there before. He bowed in return and turned to Duskya.

Duskya came forward and immediately bowed to the rider. She, too, did not wait for him to bow before standing back up. She stared at him, taking in his gaze and seeming to give it right back. Ruskya was amazed at the forwardness of his sister. She always had been the courageous one, but this almost seemed rude. The rider, however, didn't seem to mind. He allowed Duskya to weigh him. She sensed him reach out with some unnamed senses toward her. It was as if he was trying to see if she measured up. When both the young and old rider had finished weighing each other and seemed to find what they sought, the older one stepped back.

"May I introduce myself?" the rider queried. Upon receiving nods from both of the twins he continued. "My name is Glendyn. This is my dragon, Wyden."

The two looked up at the royal blue dragon. He seemed enormous to them, especially compared to Wyeth and Wryn. Ruskya heard Duskya greet the dragon. If he hadn't been looking directly at her, he would have sworn she had talked, but her lips did not move. He gazed at her in amazement, until he heard Wyeth call to him.

"Do not be surprised, or show your astonishment. You, too, can talk with me without using your voice. Try greeting Wyden. He is waiting for you. If you wait much longer, he may consider you just an ordinary youngling."

Ruskya looked back at Wyeth, and upon receiving a slight nod from the dragon, he returned his gaze to Wyden and bowed. While he bowed he thought, "Greetings, honored dragon. May your flight be blessed."

Wyden seemed pleased as he answered, "And you, respected rider. May your dragon bring you fortune."

Ruskya stood up straight and looked at Wyden's eyes. They seemed to sparkle. He also noticed they were the same color blue as Glendyn's. Ruskya then remembered that the rider was still standing waiting for his attention. He turned around, coloring slightly.

"Honored rider, may your dragon bring you fortune," Ruskya said with a slight bow. He saw the shock that quickly passed across Glendyn's face before he could conceal it, and heard the chuckle of approval from Wyeth. He stood up taller.

"Well, I see you have been trained well, young one. Whom do I have the privilege of meeting?"

Duskya stepped forward, "Honored rider, I am Duskya, and this is my brother, Ruskya."

After a slight pause during which he seemed to look more closely at them, Glendyn answered, "I am honored to meet such younglings. Will you please take me to your parents so that I can receive their consent?"

Duskya did not miss a beat before she answered, "Our father is no longer with us; it is just our mother, but come, I will take you to her."

Ruskya called to Wyeth, "Will that be okay with you, Wyeth? I don't want to leave you here alone."

"Go on, young one," Wyeth assured him. "I will be fine. Greet your mother for me; assure her I will take care of you."

Ruskya smiled and turned to Duskya who also had paused before moving on. He nodded to her, and they moved out with Glendyn following.

* * *

Glendyn noticed the icy blue sparkles that lingered on the boy. He still couldn't believe that Wyeth had sprayed the boy with a small amount of dragon courage. Glendyn knew this was what had given the boy the nerve to step forward, but he still wondered about these two. Their names were familiar, and they knew the proper greeting of a dragon rider. Beyond that, their mother had known what colors to add to their processional tunics.

As they tread down the well-worn trail, Glendyn thought back to his own trip home to get his mother's approval. He remembered the excitement and trepidation that accompanied it. He pondered the twins' confidence and wondered what else was going on with these two young dragon riders. He again considered their names, but cast it aside as coincidence, although it would possibly explain how their mother knew what colors to use.

Before he knew it, they had stopped in front of a doorway. Glendyn looked around with shock and wonder. It had been a very long time since he had been here; Ardyn had been gone for seven winters. There was no reason for the family to still live here; yet doubt played through his mind, and he felt a nagging sense that fate was playing with him. He tried to ignore these feelings, and to convince himself that it had to be someone else's home.

The girl pushed open the door and entered the small dwelling. She and the boy rushed to their mother and started to tell their tale. Glendyn distracted himself with the simple surroundings and avoided looking at the mother, not wanting to believe that Ardyn's twins were the riders that Wyeth and Wryn had chosen. He saw a typical canyon home with dining and cooking areas close to each other and a large hearth with a fire blazing on it, a living area farther back, and a bedroom off to one side. A ladder at the back of the abode led up to a loft. Finally, he heard the voice he had not heard in seven winters give commands to the children.

"All right, go upstairs and gather your things into two piles on the bed.

You don't need to worry about tunics or trousers, but underthings, and anything that you want to remind you of home. I will go through it all and put it into a rucksack for you. Now, go on."

She patted them both on the head and pushed them toward the ladder. Then she turned and pulled the iron that held the kettle out of the fire. With practiced ease, she reached up into the familiar nook and withdrew a mug and a small tin, from which she gathered some tea leaves and dropped them into the mug. Motioning for Glendyn to sit down at the table, she poured water into the mug and set it in front of him along with a crock of sugar, then sat down herself at the other side of the small table.

They both sat in silence for a few minutes, listening to the twins chattering upstairs. The smell of the tea transported Glendyn to a time he had thought lost forever. He marveled at fate. How did the dragons know that Ardyn's younglings would be there today? How did they know to wait? How did Ardyn's widow know which colors to add to the trim of the tunics? Glendyn shook his head. There was no way of knowing. He looked up into her pale blue eyes and saw the pain that had been hidden along with the hope.

"Meredyth," Glendyn spoke in a whisper, emotion choking his voice, "I will fully understand if you decline the honor—" he began, but Meredyth cut him short.

"No, Glendyn," she whispered, "I accept with joy the honor of dragon riders in my family. Even though my husband cannot join in the joy, it was his hope that both of the twins would be chosen as riders."

Glendyn nodded. He knew of Ardyn's wild dreams, but it seemed as if those dreams were coming true before his eyes. If only Ardyn could be here to see it. Glendyn blinked the moisture from his eyes and looked at Meredyth.

"I will take responsibility for them as if they were my own," he pledged. At Meredyth's look of surprise, he added, "I vow it. Upon Wyden, my dragon, I will do all in my power to train your children to be the best dragon riders they can be. They will bring honor to the memory of their father."

Meredyth reached for Glendyn's hand and squeezed it, unable to say anything through the tears streaming down her cheeks. She nodded at him, then released his hand and stood. Wiping her cheeks with her apron, she headed up the ladder to sort her younglings' belongings.

Glendyn sat and stared into the fire. "Wyden," he called to his dragon, "I don't know if it was a good thing or not, but I just swore to protect these two."

"It was a good thing," the dragon's gravelly voice came to him. "They are different than most younglings. They were already communicating between each other and their dragons."

"They were?" Glendyn said with surprise. "How did they do that?"

"I am not sure. The girl and Wryn had it figured out before the boy, but the boy caught on without any training. The girl spoke to me, and he heard and wondered. Wyeth explained that he could do so also. He greeted me in the traditional way. Who are they?"

"Their father has been gone a long time from among the riders. His name was Ardyn."

"Ardyn," Wyden seemed to mull the name through his mind. "That would explain a lot."

Glendyn didn't need to say anything else. He gazed into the fire until Meredyth returned with the twins. He stood, and she started to speak.

"Honored rider, I entrust you with the training and upbringing of my younglings," her soft familiar voice repeated the traditional greeting. "May they fly true and brave."

Glendyn admired her courage and replied, "Respected mother, I will endeavor to bring them up and to train them to be honored riders. May your home know peace and fulfillment from your sacrifice. I will keep my promise," he added, and received a warm smile of thanks from Meredyth, her pale gray eyes moist with unshed tears. He turned and added, "Come, younglings, you have a lot to learn. I hear you are already learning many things. I believe great things are in store for you both."

After the twins received a final hug from their mother, he led them from their home and into their new lives as dragon riders.

CHAPTER 1: A NEW RIDER

"COME ON, DUSKYA," Ruskya called to his twin through the mind link they shared. "I'll race you back to the canyon, and this time Wyeth and I will win!"

"Yeah, right, brother," Duskya responded, as her dark hair blew in the wind behind her. She refused to cut it short or tie it back as was the custom of female riders. She loved to let it whip in her face. If she couldn't see, she would let Wryn see for her, or use her senses from the dragon bond to find danger around them.

"There's no way that you can win. Wryn is just faster. We ride as one when I shut my eyes."

"Sure you do, but I also can do that. Glendyn has taught me just as well as you these past fifteen winters."

"Yes, but Wryn's faster."

"Well, then maybe we will have to find an advantage and take it," Ruskya replied with a laugh as he felt the wind pick up under Wyeth's wings. He focused to block his sister out of his thoughts and urged his dragon to catch the updraft. The dragon responded in kind, and soon they were soaring over the desert floor. The sagebrush and rocks below were unrecognizable lumps of brown and green. When the updraft petered out, Ruskya shielded his thoughts again from his sister and, using dragon senses, searched for another air advantage for Wyeth. Duskya had been correct in assessing that Wryn was faster. Just as Duskya was larger than Ruskya, Wyeth was smaller than his sister. The shorter wingspan made for slower flying, so Ruskya had to find other advantages that his twin didn't even bother to look for. Finding what he was seeking, Ruskya guided Wyeth down. As if on a wild roller coaster ride, the dragon dropped lower, and with a cry of glee, Ruskya guided Wyeth to the canyon floor before Wryn.

"See, sister? I can do it! I don't need to have the faster dragon in order to beat you," Ruskya called in triumph so all could hear.

Duskya brought Wryn in for a graceful landing. As she dismounted, she bowed to her brother, "Honored rider," she exclaimed, "you have bested me."

Ruskya beamed at his sister. "Honored rider, you honor me in allowing me to best you."

A rush of surprise swept through the other riders, who had gathered to see the twins land. It was rare for a rider to admit defeat, and to have that admission turned back on the rider as a compliment was even rarer. Even after fifteen winters, the dragon riders still were unsure about these twins. They were different from the others. As younglings, they had seemed more advanced than other riders their age. They were friendly enough, but very private; they rarely allowed others into their conversations. It also didn't help that Glendyn had shown special attention in training them. While they seemed to fit in better with the older riders, the older riders didn't exactly want younglings as best friends.

A cheer went up from the young riders who had gathered. The twins bowed and dismissed Wyeth and Wryn to their perches up in the crags then headed to their rooms. On the way, a youngling who had been in the colony just two winters approached the twins.

"Honored riders," he interrupted them and paused to think of the proper wording, "Respected rider, Glendyn, requests your presence for the evening meal. He has returned from the procession with a single youngling."

"Thank you, youngling. It looks like you may have someone to keep you company," Duskya answered. "Tell the honored rider that we will join him and the new youngling."

Ruskya hid a smile at the attempted traditional responses the youngling had used. He remembered what it was like to be a youngling, but he couldn't relate to how these newer ones couldn't seem to keep the responses straight. He knew that Glendyn had been concerned about the dwindling number of younglings, a by-product of the fact that the dragons were not hatching as regularly. The winter the twins were chosen was the last winter where five younglings had joined the dragon rider colony. In the winters since, only five riders had been chosen altogether.

Glendyn wasn't the oldest rider, but he was in charge of training the younglings. With fewer younglings to train, there was less for him to do.

The twins showed up a bit early at Glendyn's that evening. The older man met them at the door and invited them into the cooking area.

"Welcome, honored riders," he greeted them.

"And you, honored rider," Duskya responded. "May your dragon have flown straight and true today."

Glendyn smiled, "I came back with a youngling for our one dragon. That is always a good day." He paused, and then switched gears. "I've been thinking. I can't explain why, but I think it's important that you two keep working on trying to communicate with other humans the way you communicate with each other."

"Glendyn, I don't understand," Duskya said, her silvery eyes flashing with impatience. "We have tried this before, and it seems to only work with us."

"I know, young one, but please keep trying. Maybe if you try again, it will work. Just humor an old rider on this."

"We can only keep trying, Glendyn," Ruskya said, running his hand through his blond hair. "So, does this youngling show promise?

"I can say that he reminds me of one of the more promising younglings we had several winters ago," Glendyn answered, with a twinkle in his royal blue eyes.

"So the youngling's a boy," Duskya commented as she brushed a stray strand of dark hair behind an ear.

"Yes, you will meet him shortly. I had Coryn take the boy to get his garb. I thought that after dinner, Ruskya could escort him to his quarters."

"Certainly, Glendyn," the young rider replied.

A knock at the door interrupted any further conversation. Glendyn answered the door and returned with a skinny towheaded boy. Underneath his obvious timidity seemed to lurk a courage that could be teased out. Ruskya was surprised to see that the boy reminded him of himself as a youngling. Could Glendyn have been giving him a compliment?

"Respected rider," Glendyn started, "I present to you Honored Riders Duskya and Ruskya."

The boy stepped forward and greeted Duskya, "It is an honor to meet you," the youngling paused trying to find the right words. Ruskya thought, "honored rider" toward the boy. The boy finished with a sheepish, "honored rider."

Duskya stepped forward and observed the boy. Ruskya could feel her trying to use her dragon senses to test the boy's character. The youngling stood there looking back at her. Ruskya was amazed and wondered where the boy was gaining his courage.

When Duskya was done, she bowed to the youngling and said, "The honor was mine, respected rider, may your dragon fly true."

"Thank you, honored rider," the youngling replied.

Ruskya thought toward the boy, "May your dragon fly true," but the boy did not respond.

Now it was Ruskya's turn to examine the boy and see why the dragon had chosen him. He had done this before, and each time he had seen different qualities in the riders. This, however, was the first that he had been impressed before the examination.

Ruskya stepped forward and looked the boy in the eyes. The youngling's sincere green eyes met his gaze. Ruskya first tried his dragon senses, and he saw what he had expected: a timid, yet willing-to-be brave young lad who seemed to be trained in courtesy. He decided to do as Glendyn had suggested and reached out toward the boy with his thoughts. He didn't expect anything to happen, so when he saw a glow emanating from the youngling, creating a halo effect, he thought it was from the fire behind the boy.

He stepped back, bowed and said, "It was an honor to meet you, respected rider. May your dragon fly true."

As the boy started to reply, Ruskya thought the correct answer toward him.

"May your dragon fly true," the youngling replied.

Ruskya felt his sister's surprise that the youngling had caught on so quickly when he had just stumbled over his reply to her. Ruskya smiled assurance at the boy.

Glendyn stepped forward and continued the introductions. "Honored Riders Duskya and Ruskya, I present to you respected rider, Kyn. May your dragons fly true."

All three replied, "May your dragon fly true."

Glendyn led them over to the table, where they sat down. He served the meal of roast lamb, rolls, greens with dressing, and goat's milk. Each procession day the riders celebrated with lamb. The new youngling would have a small meal with Glendyn and a select few riders that the older man chose. The other riders would celebrate in their own way together. Often it would be enough to overwhelm a young one who had just been uprooted from his or her home.

As they ate, Glendyn and Duskya asked questions, and Kyn talked about his home. He was the youngest of five children. His parents owned a store where the villagers could trade for things they could not make on their own. While they talked, Ruskya just listened. He liked the youngling's voice. It had a soothing manner to it. Ruskya thought it would be good for calming a dragon or any other animal in distress.

Toward the end of the meal, Ruskya decided to do as Glendyn had suggested. He reached out and focused his thoughts toward his mentor. With a shock, he immediately saw his own father sitting beside a fire warming his hands. Duskya felt the shock wave also and sent a query mentally toward him.

"I'm fine," he responded, then tried again.

This time he was ready for the image of his father. He heard Glendyn say, "But what happens if the dragons disappear? Won't the villagers revolt?"

"No, Glendyn," Ruskya's father replied, "I think they will be relieved. Although it is my heart's desire that the twins become riders, when I see them in Meredyth's arms, I wonder if I can truly tear them away from her like that."

"Ruskya!" Duskya's insistent voice in his head blended with Glendyn's spoken voice. "Are you okay?" she added.

"Ruskya, did you not hear what I said?" Glendyn asked.

"I am sorry, honored rider," Ruskya replied with a flush. "I missed that."

"It's all right." Glendyn's dark eyes regarded his young friend. "I just asked if you would take on the responsibility of training respected rider, Kyn."

Ruskya was shocked. Him? Train another rider? He would be honored, but was he ready? He knew the response was up to him. He cleared his head and his throat and replied, "The honor would be mine, honored rider. I will train this youngling in the art of dragon riding, and all the duties and responsibilities that it entails. This I vow by Wyeth, my dragon."

Glendyn answered, "I hear your vow. Respected rider, Kyn, do you accept the training offered by Honored Rider Ruskya?"

Kyn timidly replied, "I do. This I vow by Wylen, my dragon."

"Good job, Kyn," Ruskya thought toward the boy.

"Honored Rider Ruskya, I hold you responsible for the training of this youngling. May your dragon fly true and straight in this endeavor. I understand, because of your close relationship with your sister, that she will be an intricate part of this youngling's training. I trust both of your judgment to train him well. If you have any questions, please come to me. Now, it is time to send you all off to bed. It has been a long day for both youngling and honored rider. I bid you all good night."

"Duskya, can you take Kyn home? I need to talk with Glendyn," Ruskya thought toward his sister. "I'll explain later."

"Good eve, honored rider," Kyn bade their host. "May your rest be with peace this night."

"And you, youngling," Glendyn responded.

Ruskya waited until his sister and Kyn had gone. "Glendyn, may I come back and talk with you tonight? I will explain why I did not hear your request the first time. Will that be okay? I can't guarantee how much later it will be because I will have to get Kyn settled. Would it be okay for him to stay with me for now?"

Glendyn smiled. "Yes to both of your questions. I knew there was something, but it was not the time to talk about it with the youngling present. I also think it is best for him to stay with you since there are no other younglings for him to interact with. Now, go on and return as soon as you think it wise."

"Thank you, honored rider," Ruskya replied in all seriousness. He truly did look up to Glendyn and value his advice. Even if he was shocked that Glendyn knew his father. Why hadn't his friend and mentor told him?

"Wyeth," Ruskya called, "did you follow all that happened?"

"No, I just know you are confused. Let me see your memories, and I will know. I cannot guarantee that I will know how to advise you, though."

"Before I do that, would you be willing to breathe dragon courage on

Kyn? Glendyn asked me to train him. I think it would help him. I know it wouldn't be the same as it would be from his own dragon, but I don't think Wylen is old enough."

"You are right. I will try. I don't think it would hurt to try. Now, let me see your memories."

With that, Ruskya gave Wyeth free rein of his thoughts and memories of the night. Soon the dragon knew what all had happened, and Ruskya had joined his sister and the youngling.

"Thank you, Duskya for escorting our youngling for me," Ruskya said.

"It was an honor, brother. I will bid you both good eve. May your rest be with peace this night."

"And to you," Ruskya and Kyn replied. Duskya bowed and entered her abode.

The twins had chosen dwellings away from the main hustle and bustle of the rider colony. They enjoyed being closer to their dragons. It also meant they were not too far away from Glendyn. Ruskya escorted Kyn on toward his home.

"You will be staying with me, youngling. Does that sound okay with you?" Ruskya asked.

"I am honored, honored rider," Kyn replied.

"Now, let's get this figured out. If I am to train you, then you will be around me for most of the day. I'd get tired of hearing "honored rider" all day long, and I think you would get tired of saying it. So, why not settle for this: while we are alone, you can just call me Ruskya, but when we are in public or with someone other than Duskya, then you will address me as "honored rider." Does that sound reasonable?"

"Yes, honored—I mean—Ruskya. I'll do my best to learn from you."

"Good. The first thing I would like to do is for you to meet Wyeth. Go ahead and leave your pack here at the entrance to my abode. We will walk on down a ways. There is a place where I enjoy meeting and talking with my dragon before going to bed. If you wish to make a habit of doing the same, there is room for Wylen, also."

They walked down the canyon enjoying the star-filled sky. Ruskya felt the nip of winter frost in the air, but both riders had furs wrapped around them that kept them snug and warm. Soon they came to a small side canyon, which had a log off to the side. Ruskya motioned for Kyn to sit down and then joined the boy, noticing the moonlight glinting off his light hair.

"You told me about your family at supper, but is there anything else you wish to share tonight?" Ruskya asked as he took a breath and smelled the warm aroma of rosemary and pine needles. He glanced over in time to see the icy blue sparkles land on the young one.

The boy tried to catch a few sparkles in his hand. He gazed down at them in wonder. Then he said, "You probably should know that I'm not a true youngling. I know that Honored Rider Glendyn knows, but you need to also. If you don't want to train me, I'll understand."

Ruskya looked at the boy in wonder. "What do you mean, you aren't a true youngling?"

"The procession was different this year. No younglings of ten winters came forward for the procession. The dragon rider then called for those who had seen eleven winters, but there were none to be found. Finally, a call went out to any of twelve winters to come. I came. My friend and I were in the procession two winters ago, and we were both passed up. This time, Wylen chose me. I don't know if that makes me a true rider or not."

Ruskya paused before answering, "Kyn, you are a rider not because of your age, but because of your dragon. Your dragon chose you. I do not understand why there were no younglings of the appropriate age for the procession, but your dragon chose *you*. That makes you a respected rider. Come six winters, you will be an honored rider. Never doubt that."

"Yes, honored rider," Kyn responded. "I can tell you why there were no younglings the right age. With the dwindling of dragons, the villagers have started to talk. The first winter, they were reluctant and yet hopeful that no younglings would have to leave the village and their families. Then, last winter, a man with strange-colored eyes came to the village. He started to speak against the dragon riders of Three Spans Canyon. He said that there are dragons throughout the world, and the riders were just keeping the dragons for themselves. He claimed to have proof, but I didn't see it or hear what it was. The villagers decided that they would sit back and wait. There were mixed emotions when the procession was mentioned this winter. Some, like my parents, said that it was a good thing. They thought that dragons were peace-keepers who make us better people. Others thought it was just the way of the dragon riders to steal our children. Since riders don't really come back to the village that often, there are rumors of what happens to the younglings."

Kyn fell silent, and Ruskya weighed the youngling's words. They felt true. He realized that as the only son of the merchant, Kyn would have had the opportunity to sit and listen to the village gossip. Ruskya was impressed with the youngling's ability to distill the information gleaned over a winter and put it in such a concise way.

Ruskya patted the youngling's knee. "Well, it's been a long day. It's time to head to bed. Why don't you call Wylen and tell him good eve."

"Wylen," Kyn called in a voice loud enough to wake the dead.

Ruskya cringed at the sound. It was a good thing his abode was away from the other riders, who were most likely still celebrating the new rider. Ruskya grinned; would they celebrate so much if they saw this?

As Kyn opened his mouth to call again, Ruskya stopped him with a hand on his shoulder. "Not like that. Like this."

Ruskya mentally called Wyeth. Wyeth landed agilely in front of the two riders. The youngling's mouth dropped open.

"How did you do that?"

"Just picture your dragon. Then mentally call to him. You will get the hang of it. Try and see what you can do."

Ruskya watched the young one's face as he tried to call his dragon. Shortly there after, a grayish blue dragon appeared at their feet. He was small, but no smaller than a dragon of two winters generally was. Ruskya had seen Wylen before, but now he weighed him with his dragon senses.

The dragon called to him, "Honored rider, may your dragon fly true."

"Respected dragon," Ruskya said out loud for the youngling's benefit, "may you fly true. I have asked your rider to call you so that he can start practicing communication skills with you. You also need to learn to hear his voice among all others. Be attuned to him. In time, it will be second nature. Until then, work on it daily."

Turning to Kyn he added, "Youngling, practice talking to Wylen. Tell him about things around you. Learn to share your thoughts with him. In time, you will have dragon sense. Now, I must bid you all good eve. Kyn, let me show you to your bed."

Mentally he bade Wyeth good night and thought toward Kyn, "You will do just fine, youngling."

Kyn paused in hugging Wylen and looked over at Ruskya, "Did you say something, rider?"

Ruskya paused and looked at the boy before answering, "No, I didn't, but come, it's time for bed."

* * *

Not more than a quarter of a glass later, Ruskya stood outside Glendyn's abode. He wondered what would happen if he tried again to see what the older rider was seeing. He envisioned Glendyn sitting in his favorite chair, the firelight glinting off his hair making it look the color of roasted nuts. Almost immediately, he saw instead his old abode where he had grown up. His mother was busy in front of the fire preparing tea. She looked the same as the day he had left her. When she had fixed a cup, she came and sat down at the table.

Glendyn's voice broke the silence, "Meredyth, I will fully understand if you decline the honor."

Ruskya's mother cut in telling Glendyn that she fully accepted the honor. She mentioned his father and how he had dreamed that the twins would be riders. The image seemed to swim for a moment and then steadied. Glendyn's voice came again.

"I will take responsibility for them as if they were my own," he pledged.

Ruskya gasped as he heard the vow that Glendyn had made to train the twins to be the best dragon riders they could be and to act as a father to them. The image faded from Ruskya's mind. He stood there dazed. That explained Glendyn's ardent faithfulness in both training and in being there for the twins. Ruskya remembered how he and his sister often wished they didn't have the rider's favor, for with the favor came responsibilities. Now, it made sense, and yet it didn't. How did Glendyn know his mother, and what did Ardyn have to do with his family? If no one in the family had been a rider, why had his father smelled of dragon fire? It didn't make sense. Ruskya shivered in the cold. The nights in the canyon were getting below freezing. If Ruskya didn't go inside soon, he would be freezing also. He decided to try one last thing.

Mentally, he called, "Glendyn, I am here." After a pause, he tried again. After the third call, he was ready to knock when Glendyn opened the door to Ruskya's upraised hand.

"Ah, Ruskya. I see I was able to foretell when you came." Ruskya hid a smile and let Glendyn think as he might.

"I got the youngling settled. He has potential, as you thought. He told me some interesting things about the villagers. He also said that he isn't a proper youngling."

"Yes, that is so. It was quite strange today. I wasn't able to inquire after the procession. I saw your mother beforehand, though. She sends you greetings."

Ruskya nodded. How should he ask Glendyn about what he saw? He was at a loss.

"What is troubling you, young one?" Glendyn asked using the affectionate term he had so often used with the twins.

Ruskya took a breath and began, "I did as you asked and probed you like I have probed Duskya."

When he didn't continue, Glendyn asked, "And what happened?"

"Glendyn, did you know my father?" Ruskya blurted out.

"Of course, I did," Glendyn answered confused. "I thought you knew that. We have talked of your father often." At Ruskya's blank stare, Glendyn continued, "We have talked of Ardyn many times and his strange thoughts for dragon riders. I have tried to follow his ideas as best I could."

Ruskya stumbled over the name, "Ardyn. Ardyn was my *father*?"

Glendyn stared at the young rider. "Yes, didn't you know that?"

"I never knew my father's name. I know what he looked like and smelled like. I never thought it important to know his name."

The older rider stepped toward the younger and placed his arm around Ruskya's shoulders. "Yes, your father was Ardyn, the man in charge of breeding the dragons. There was none like him. He couldn't ride dragons, but he could breed them. Wyeth and Wryn are among the last that he hatched."

"Ardyn," Ruskya tried the name out. "I should have known that we had a special father. I have very few memories of him, since he left when I had barely seen three winters, but those I do have are of a gentle man who smelled of rosemary and pine needles."

Glendyn smiled, "That is a very apt description of Ardyn. He had a gentle way, and he thought that manner should be present both in riders and in those working with any animal."

"Kyn seems to have that way about him," Ruskya stated.

"It wouldn't surprise me. He seems different, and not just because he has seen twelve winters. He has a different quality to him like you and Duskya have. Now back to what you were going to tell me. What happened when you probed me?"

"I saw my father sitting around a fire with you. You and he discussed what would happen if the dragon population disappeared."

Ruskya felt and saw the surprise on Glendyn's face. "When did you see this?" he demanded.

"At supper. That is why I didn't hear you ask me to train Kyn."

Glendyn stared at Ruskya. Ruskya felt the rider weigh him. He was adept enough now to know that Glendyn was using his dragon senses. Ruskya let himself be explored. He had nothing to hide. After a while, the probe disappeared, and Glendyn nodded.

"That's not all, Glendyn. I tried again before coming in tonight. I saw my mother fixing tea, and you," he faltered, "you pledged to protect my sister and I as your own, and train us to be the best riders we could become." The last was said only in a whisper, but Ruskya had added the mental thought also.

Glendyn stared at him. "I do not know how this could be, but you have seen my thoughts tonight. I have been thinking of your father's words about the lack of dragons. Then since you asked to return tonight, I was remembering the day of your procession."

Glendyn fell silent. Ruskya didn't have the heart to ask out loud, but thought, "Did you really make a dragon's vow to treat me as your own son?"

Glendyn looked up at Ruskya with surprise, and then tentatively a mental voice answered, "Yes, son, I did."

Ruskya locked eyes with Glendyn's royal blue ones and nodded. Finally he said, "I don't know what happened to break the barrier, but I can communicate with you as I do Duskya. I have never seen her thoughts, though, I guess, I have never tried that."

Glendyn asked, "So, communicating is no different than talking with your dragon? You use no words, only images."

Ruskya nodded. "I am trying it with Kyn. I do not know if it is working or not. I do know that he didn't stumble over some of the traditional greetings as much when I tried to mentally give him the answers."

Glendyn nodded thoughtfully. "Ruskya, if you can see my thoughts, that means that others can see them also. We must train so that we can learn to control our thoughts. You and I should meet each evening to explore this. I will also ask Duskya to work with me. I want you to teach Kyn whatever you can, but do not tell any other rider. Do you understand me?"

"Yes, honored rider," Ruskya answered his teacher. "Can I share your memories with Duskya? She'd want to know that our father was Ardyn. She'll also see through any lie I tell her in how I figured it out."

Glendyn laughed. "That she would. Yes, these two you may share. Others, you must first get permission. It is a bit odd to think that a youngling like yourself can just go through my memories and eavesdrop."

"Glendyn," Ruskya said solemnly, "I swear I will not use it against you. I will vow it if I must."

"That is not necessary, son. I trust you, as you trusted your father."

"There is a bit more about the procession that I think you must know." Ruskya changed topics, and then proceeded to share what Kyn had shared with him about the villagers.

"That makes sense. It also fits with your father's viewpoint of the villagers."

"Yes," Ruskya agreed, "but this man concerns me. Who is he, and why would he want to slander the riders? What could he gain from it?"

"I don't know. We may need to take some more trips into Woolpren this winter. It might not be a bad idea anyway for the villagers to see that we are normal people and our dragons are not to be feared."

They were silent for a while. Ruskya caught a feeling of tiredness from Glendyn.

"Are you okay, Glendyn?" he asked.

"I'm a bit tired. Why do you ask?"

"I just had a feeling that you were tired. It was almost overwhelming."

Glendyn smiled. "This communicating as we do with the dragons could be useful," he commented. "I just acted like I would with Wyden to communicate my feelings. I am curious why it didn't work before."

"I guess I didn't really try this way before," Ruskya admitted. "I just assumed with Duskya it would work, but no one ever said if they heard me before. Come to think of it, I may have been able to get my way a little easier with some of the other riders when I wished for things. Maybe they did feel a compulsion."

"Now that sounds like a youngling!" Glendyn's laughter filled the air. "Off to bed with you. You are going to have your hands full with training a youngling yourself."

"Glendyn," Ruskya asked running his hand through his short blond hair, "do you honestly think I can handle it?"

"I wouldn't have asked you to if I thought differently. Besides, I don't think so, I know so. There is something different about you and your sister and your dragons. You have learned beyond what I can teach you, and that should be impossible. You have proven theory wrong, but you've proven your father right. He thought it would be possible. I always thought it was just pride in his children. I don't know how he knew that Wryn and Wyeth would choose you both, but he had confidence in the pairing and in the outcome of that pairing."

Ruskya stood and headed for the door. "Good eve, honored rider."

"Good eve."

Outside the door, Ruskya thought a last greeting toward Glendyn, "Good eve, Glendyn, may fortune shine on you and your dragon."

A laugh sounded in Ruskya's head followed by the words. "And on you, my son."

CHAPTER 2: SEEING WITH NEW EYES

THE NEXT MORNING, Ruskya woke up to Wyeth calling his name before daylight.

"Wyeth, go back to bed!" Ruskya complained as he rolled over and pulled the blanket up over his blond head.

"No, Ruskya, you are now a dragon rider trainer. You need to be up before your youngling."

"Oh, all right," Ruskya groaned. "Does that mean I need to fix breakfast for both of us?"

"Probably. Would you like to go for a hunt first? Then you could have fresh meat for both breakfast and the evening meal."

Ruskya grinned. "You know how to cheer a rider up! I'll be out in a bit."

Ruskya shivered as he got dressed. Winter was definitely upon them. He took the time to start a fire in the hearth before he left. He knew the youngling would appreciate it, and besides, he would need a fire to cook the meat. If he had a pile of coals already warmed, the meat would be able to cook better. As he rushed out to greet Wyeth, he decided to see if Duskya was up. If she was, he could share the news from Glendyn with her and Wyeth at the same time.

As he reached Wyeth, in the little side canyon, Duskya answered him groggily. "Why are you so chipper this morning?"

Ruskya chuckled. He could just imagine his sister stretching and running her fingers through her dark hair trying to straighten it but only succeeding in making it messier.

"My dragon suggested a hunting trip before I start teaching the youngling," he explained. "That got me out of bed quickly."

He mounted Wyeth and soon they were airborne. Ruskya always

thrilled at the feeling of flying with Wyeth. At times, it was almost as if they were one. He felt this now, as he shared with his sister and Wyeth the conversation he'd had with Glendyn. He barely had to guide Wyeth, and the dragon seemed to see what he saw. Ruskya wondered if all riders experienced this type of oneness with their dragon.

As Ruskya described what had happened the previous night, his sister was surprised that he had seen Glendyn's thoughts, and what those thoughts had revealed, but she didn't think they should be surprised over the information about their father. She had always thought there was information that their mother had not told them about their father's disappearance. She agreed with their mentor that they should take more frequent trips into the village. Duskya said she would visit their mother this morning. The twins decided to try covertly reading each other's thoughts; afterward, they would let each other know and try to measure their success. Ruskya bid his sister good day and they broke their mental contact.

The hunting expedition was a success. Ruskya came back with several pheasants and a buck. He took the time to field dress them and packed them into a special pouch he had made. He knew the other riders would appreciate some fresh meat.

When he reached the side canyon and dismounted, he started to call out to Kyn mentally. He allowed time between the callings. He wasn't sure if Kyn heard, until he sensed the youngling wake up with a start.

"Kyn, don't be afraid. It's me, Ruskya. You're okay. Go ahead and greet Wylen. I'll be back to fix breakfast shortly."

The youngling seemed to relax. Ruskya decided he didn't need to hurry too much, but he didn't take his time, either, in delivering the meat to Marysa, another rider, who received it gratefully. He told her he needed to return to the youngling in his care. She was impressed with the honor that had been laid on him and urged him to return.

Ruskya had barely made it to his door when he felt a wave of fear emanate from Kyn, then heard a screech that made the hair on the back of his head rise. Pushing the door open he ran toward the little room that he had given Kyn, calling as he went, "Kyn, what is wrong?"

The boy couldn't make any intelligible sounds come out of his mouth. Ruskya tried to pierce the youngling's thoughts, but they were as jumbled as his emotions. He decided to wait until he reached the room. In the meantime, he sent soothing thoughts to the youngling. When Ruskya reached the room, he saw Kyn huddled on the floor with his face in his hands, his straw-colored hair slipping through cracks between his fingers. He seemed to be mumbling something.

Ruskya ran over to him and cradled the youngling in his arms. He remembered his own father doing something similar when he was wee little. Finally, Ruskya could distinguish the words, "my eyes."

He waited a while longer until the boy seemed calmer, then asked, "What is wrong, Kyn?"

The youngling took a shivery breath, then said, "Look at my eyes. Please tell me I am not going crazy. I-I could have sworn they were a different color. What do you see?"

Ruskya saw dark eyes the color of the night sky, full of fear and trepidation. Then it dawned on Ruskya what had shocked the boy so.

"Youngling," he said gently, "what color were your eyes last night when you went to bed?"

"What do you mean?" Kyn demanded. "They have always been green. My eyes were always different from my family. It was the one thing that I had that I could claim as special."

Ruskya smiled to himself, then decided to explain, "Well, young one, you have more than one thing to distinguish you from your family. You are a dragon rider. From now on, everyone will know that you are a rider. They will also be able to tell who your dragon is."

"What do you mean?" Kyn asked, calmer now. He was at least thinking straight.

"Kyn, I would have warned you about this, but I didn't expect it to happen overnight the first night," he paused. "Take a look at my eyes. What color are they?"

The boy looked and then replied, "They are a strange icy blue."

"That's right, but they were brown when I came to Three Spans Canyon. Each rider's eyes change to match the color of their dragon."

Kyn looked quizzical, "But Wyden is a grayish blue."

"Correct," Ruskya said with approval, "but when he matures, around his twelfth winter, he will darken and be exactly the color of your eyes. You will have a very handsome dragon."

Kyn stood up and looked back into the mirror, accustoming himself to the new look. Ruskya thought it looked nice on the youngling, and mentally conveyed that to the boy.

Kyn looked at Ruskya through the mirror, "You said that Wylen will mature around his twelfth winter. Could it be that my eyes changed because this is *my* twelfth winter?"

Ruskya was surprised at the boy's insight. He thought through the options before answering, "I think you may be right. Most younglings' eyes change about two winters after they come to the canyon. Come to think of it, my eyes changed just before my twelfth winter. Wyeth says it was his birthing day. That rarely happens, because most dragons have only had two winters when their riders have seen ten."

Kyn nodded, took one last look in the mirror, and turned to Ruskya. "I think I am ready for the day."

Ruskya nodded. "Each morning you will be responsible for cleaning your room. We'll eventually set up some household chores, but until then, just see what needs to be done. Can you handle that?"

"Sure, honored rider," the youngling replied. "I am used to doing chores around my home and in the general store. With five younglings, Ma always had work to do, and since I was the youngest, I often had the chores assigned to me, especially since my older siblings had left for abodes of their own."

"Then I'll leave you to take care of your room, while I fix breakfast," Ruskya said.

As he cooked the meat Wyeth had gotten earlier, Ruskya thought about what it would be like to have a youngling. What would the next few days bring? And, what would the new information about his father do to his relationship with Glendyn and the other riders?

CHAPTER 3: DISTURBING NEWS

BY THE NEXT MOON, Ruskya had settled into a basic routine. His mornings were filled with training Kyn in the art of becoming a dragon rider. The youngling was quick to catch on. Ruskya also worked with Kyn on communicating mentally not just to Wylen, but also to the twins and Glendyn. Afternoons were interspersed with trips to Woolpren or hunting excursions, and he spent the evenings mind training with Glendyn, who had found some interesting things in his research that helped further their training. By the start of the following moon, Ruskya could tell when Glendyn was trying to read his thoughts, and could repulse the tries ninety percent of the time. Duskya was less adept than Ruskya in reading Glendyn's thoughts, but she could communicate easily with anyone. Glendyn was learning to be tricky, but Ruskya was still able to sense the older rider's presence in his mind. Kyn participated in the mental training, too. He was doing quite well for a youngling. He couldn't yet repel any attempt to read his thoughts, but he could confound someone by not focusing on what was important. He could also communicate mentally with any of the other three riders without difficulty, as long as he was not carrying on another conversation at the same time.

The trips to Woolpren had become a priority. One of the three older riders went into the village nearly every day. When Ruskya went, Kyn generally went also. He was able to help his father in the general store and sometimes visit with his mother in the family abode. Duskya and Ruskya had used their time to reconnect with their own mother. Meredyth seemed surprised the first time one of her children walked over the threshold of her home. After that, she cherished each moment she could spend with them. The twins, at first, didn't share much of their lives as riders, but soon they opened up more and more. Glendyn had encouraged them to share with her anything they wished. He even suggested asking her if they could try reading her thoughts, but Ruskya hadn't had the courage to ask that yet. Thoughts were personal, and it had been hard enough to invade Glendyn, Duskya and Kyn's. He couldn't think of invading his mother's personal life.

* * *

On one such day, Ruskya visited with Meredyth while Kyn was at the general store. Ruskya was enjoying his mother's tea. He complimented her on the tea and thought of asking her where she found the leaves, but decided to wait.

"Mmm, there is nothing like your tea to comfort and relax, except, perhaps, for the smell of rosemary and pine needles."

Meredyth looked up at him. "Rosemary and pine needles?"

"Yeah, I remember Da smelling that way." Ruskya was quiet for a moment, then continued. "On the day of the procession, I smelled that same blend again for the first time since Da left. It gave me the courage to go on. Do you know what made him smell of rosemary and pine needles?"

His mother smiled. "The dragons," she whispered. "Did your dragon breathe on you that day of the procession?"

Ruskya hid his surprise. "Yes, he did. Have you seen it before, dragon's breath?"

A faraway look came to his mother's eyes. "Yes. It has been twenty-two winters since I felt it last. Your father had let me come to Philippi Canyon to see the dragons. There were seven: three hatchlings; two first-winters; two procession-ready dragons; and two who had seen three winters. The hatchlings were so adorable. Your father was tender and gentle with them. The first-winter dragons were trying to fly. They couldn't blow fire yet. The procession-ready dragons were distancing themselves from your father. They didn't even bother greeting me, but the ones who had seen three winters were different. These dragons stayed close to your father; he seemed to be able to communicate with them without speaking. The little baby blue one—although he wasn't little compared to the others—came up behind me and breathed on me. I looked up and saw amazement in your father's eyes, and when I looked down, I saw the icy blue sparkles. The smell of rosemary and pine needles engulfed me. Ever since, I have tried to recreate that smell, to feel the comfort and to know all will be well."

Meredyth's voice faded into silence as she remembered. Ruskya used the time to think and to talk with Wyeth.

"Wyeth, have you met my mother before?"

"The mate of Ardyn? Of course. It has been many winters since, though."

Ruskya nodded, and then called. "You breathed on her. Why?"

"She was discouraged and afraid. That is what dragon's courage is for." Wyeth explained as if it was obvious.

A smile crossed Ruskya's face. "Would you be willing to do so again?"

"Gladly, honored rider."

Their conversation was interrupted by a surge of shock from Kyn at the general store. It didn't have the feeling of danger, just surprise and trouble ahead.

"Kyn, whenever you can explain to me what is going on, I am here to listen," Ruskya called to the youngling. "I will head your way. It is almost time to leave anyway."

He felt Kyn's relief at once, and could only imagine the look in the youngling's dark eyes.

"Mother, I think it is time for me to go check on my youngling. Would you like to see that baby blue dragon again?"

Meredyth's eyes grew large, and Ruskya didn't wait for a verbal answer.

"If I can, I'll come by again this afternoon. I will take you to that dragon. He's seen more than three winters now."

Meredyth nodded, her pale eyes taking on a faraway look. "He has seen the same amount of winters as you, twenty-five."

"His name is Wyeth," he added as he bowed and left the abode.

Ruskya let his senses linger on his mother as he walked toward the general store. She was sad, yet expectant. He couldn't let his mind dwell on her; he needed to move on to Kyn and whatever was the problem there. He focused his thoughts on the youngling to see what he could glean from the boy; he saw the general store and a man he didn't recognize.

"I tell you, I saw him," the tall man with ebony hair was saying. "He was looking for the dragon riders. He wasn't from their colony. He said that his colony has a surplus of dragons in need of riders, and it doesn't matter the age, they'll take adults."

Ruskya broke the connection and hurried down the path. Soon he opened the door of the general store and felt the heat from the stove. The aroma of spices and cleaning liniment accosted his nose. He heard the man's voice grow strident as he protested.

"I don't care if no one believes me, I saw him! He said I could meet him tomorrow, and he would see if I was dragon rider material. If I am, I can go and be a rider."

Ruskya walked up to the tall, lanky man. He definitely looked like a rider, but Ruskya didn't know if a dragon would choose the other man. He had mahogany eyes that were almost lost in a sun-tanned face. He had at least five winters on Ruskya.

"Excuse me, honored sir," Ruskya entered the conversation. He heard the intake of breath as people realized a rider was in their midst. The man didn't seem to notice the others' reactions.

"Yes?" he answered.

"I just arrived, but I overheard you say that you are meeting someone tomorrow who will tell you if you can become a dragon rider. Is that right?"

"Yeah, what's it to you?" the man said, looking Ruskya up and down with contempt.

"Nothing, sir," Ruskya replied, sending signals and words of calm and innocence toward the man. "I thought it sounded intriguing, is all. Is anyone welcome to come?"

Seeing that Ruskya was taking him seriously, the man became friendlier, although the kindness did not reach his dark eyes.

"Sure. I don't know how many riders he'll accept, but anyone can come. He said to bring as many friends as I could who were strong, brave, and agile. He'll then see if we are worthy to be riders. Do you want to be a rider?"

Ruskya nodded. "Yes. Where do I meet him?"

"Does anyone else here want to be a rider?" the man called out. While the crowd mulled this over, Ruskya tried to do something he had never done before: he tried to mentally reach the whole group of people to impress upon them not to reveal that he was already a dragon rider. He figured the easiest way to achieve this would be to get others interested in what the man had to say. He contacted Kyn and asked for his help.

A woman about Ruskya's age stepped forward, "I would like to be a rider. Where do I join?"

"Anyone else?" The man waited for a beat before continuing. "You can meet me at Caravan Canyon just after the sun is straight overhead. The rider will meet us there. Go, spread the word." He walked out the door not waiting for any response.

The woman looked Ruskya over. "You look like you could fit the description of a rider. I'll see you there tomorrow." Ruskya nodded to her as she left. The few others that were there seemed to finish up their purchases in short order and leave. Soon Kyn, Ruskya, and the merchant were all who were left. Kyn let out a sigh.

"Honored rider," he said, "how did you think to do that? Did I help?"

Ruskya walked over and ruffled the boy's hair. "That you did, youngling. I don't think I could have distracted them all. Honored merchant," Ruskya addressed Kyn's father, "what do you know about this man?"

"That is Kyle. He has been unhappy since childhood when he was not chosen as a rider. That was when there were three or four dragons a winter," he added as an afterthought. "I don't know about his claims of a rider from another colony."

"That's why I was shocked," Kyn explained. "I didn't know there were other dragons. Where could this colony be, honored rider?"

"I don't know, Kyn, but I plan to find out."

"It doesn't bode well for the riders at Three Span Canyon," the merchant said, draping a hand around his son's shoulder. "With the current feelings of betrayal here in the village, I am surprised Kyle found anyone willing to go with him. Most people want to avoid the dragons. They want to keep their children. I don't hold to that, but that is what I'm hearing around the stove. I try my best to show them that they don't lose their children, but my voice is only one."

Ruskya nodded, "I thank you, honored merchant, for what you do.

Every voice is important."

"What will you do, rider?"

"I will go talk with my elder and then meet Kyle after the sun reaches its zenith. Kyn, bid your parents good day. We need to be leaving."

Kyn nodded and sent a mental, "Yes, honored rider," as he headed to the connecting door to their abode.

"You have done well with him, rider," the merchant commented, watching his son disappear through the entryway. "I never was able to figure him out. I think it would have been different if his twin had survived, but he didn't."

Ruskya's interest was piqued. "Kyn had a twin?"

"Yes, he passed on when Kyn was just a babe. We never figured out what caused it. We just woke up one morning to find only one living child in the bed."

"I am so terribly sorry, sir. I cannot imagine the grief that would have caused."

The sound of the fire in the stove filled the air.

"Kyn tells me you have a twin sister."

"Yes, I don't know what I would have done without her. She was my champion growing up. Once I became a rider, I gained some independence, but I was timid before that."

The merchant nodded. Before he could say more, the door opened, and Kyn and his mother entered.

"Ma packed us a supper, honored rider!" Kyn said exuberantly.

"You would think I don't cook well," Ruskya said with a laugh.

"No, no it's not that—" His face colored slightly.

Ruskya cut him off. "There's nothing like your ma's meals. I have enjoyed reacquainting myself with my own ma's meals. Thank you, honored woman. We will enjoy it."

Kyn's mother blushed as the merchant placed his arm around her. "Thank you for bringing Kyn to visit," he said. "It means a lot to us. I bid you good day, honored riders."

"Good day, sir."

Kyn gave them both a hug before turning and leaving.

Ruskya next headed to his own abode, telling Kyn that there was some unfinished business ahead. Meredyth answered the door with her cloak wrapped around her. She stepped outside and followed as Ruskya led the way down the canyon floor. He took them to a secluded spot where he and Duskya had played as children. Looking around to make sure no one else was there, he called out to Wyeth.

He watched his mother's face as Wyeth came into view and gently and gracefully landed on the canyon floor. Amazement and wonder were in her eyes, along with memories. She wiped away her tears with the cloak and stepped forward.

"Greetings, dragon. I am told your name is Wyeth." She paused as if expecting a reply, but none came. Wyeth bent his head to her and she reached out to touch his neck. "You have changed," she continued, "I like the icy blue. It fits you, but so did the baby blue when you were younger."

Wyeth nodded his head. Meredyth's laugh was a tinkling bell-like sound. Ruskya had never heard that before.

"So, you understand me, you just can't speak to me. So be it. Ardyn claimed you could talk his leg off. Maybe it's a blessing I cannot hear you."

The dragon pushed his head against her almost knocking her down.

"Now, none of that," she scolded, as she gave him a hug. "I am almost like your mother. I can talk that way to you."

She turned to Ruskya. "Is this the dragon that chose you?" At the nod she received from him, she continued, "And Duskya's was sky blue; his twin." It was a statement not a question. "Your father's wishes came true."

She turned back to Wyeth. "So, Wyeth, was it anything Ardyn said, or did you decide that day twenty-two winters ago before Ardyn left? What made you choose them? Whatever your reasons, thank you." These last words were said so quietly that only the dragon should have heard them. Ruskya, though, was listening in on Wyeth's thoughts; he was perplexed as to what it could mean.

Wyeth allowed Meredyth to hug him for a while longer, then moved away and lowered his head. He looked her right in the eye and spoke with emotion in what sounded to Ruskya like an unnaturally loud voice so that she could hear him.

"Honored lady, for your husband and your children, I give you something in return." He opened his mouth and gently let icy blue sparkles fall on Meredyth. Her tears mixed with the sparkles and left blue trails down her cheeks. She inhaled. Ruskya saw her back straighten and the determination enter her face.

Wyeth again spoke to Meredyth looking her in the eyes, "I need a pouch, now." In a quieter voice, he called to Ruskya, "Do you have one?"

Ruskya nodded and fumbled at his side. He pulled out a small pouch.

"Now empty it please."

Ruskya turned to Kyn and motioned for the youngling to hold out his hands. He poured the contents of the pouch into them, then handed the empty bag to his mother. Meredyth took it and held it out to the dragon.

Wyeth called, "Open it please, honored lady."

Meredyth opened the pouch and Wyeth brought his head down. The others watched with amazement as he blew sparkling icy blue dust into the pouch. When the pouch was full, Wyeth stopped breathing but did not move back. He looked directly at Meredyth and in a soft voice said, "Honored lady, can you hear me now?"

Meredyth nodded, her gray eyes full of wonder.

"What you hold," the dragon continued, "is a pouch of dragon courage. Use it only in times of dire need. It will stay active as long as the pouch is closed. When you open the pouch and take it out, the effects will wear off just as if I had breathed on you. Do you understand?"

"Oh, yes, honored dragon," Meredyth answered, her pale eyes brimming with tears. "I will treasure it. Only in desperate need will I use it. Thank you. Please, take care of my boy."

"That I will, honored lady."

Wyeth stepped away. Meredyth tucked the pouch inside her cloak, attached it to her belt, and turned to Ruskya and Kyn. She hugged them both and then walked away.

"May dragon's fortune shine on you, honored mother," Ruskya mentally called after her.

CHAPTER 4: A MEETING WITH GLENDYN

RUSKYA KNEW that if Kyn went with him to the evening training, he would give away all the information they had gleaned that day. He wanted to make Glendyn work to find the information. He also wanted to tell Glendyn privately about Meredyth and Wyeth. So, even though Wylen would not be big enough for Kyn to fly until the summer, Ruskya decided to have the youngling practice knots and braiding for a saddle. He provided Kyn with leather and taught him four different styles of braiding. The night promised to be quite cold, and the boy was set for an evening of work by the warm fire.

Before he arrived at Glendyn's abode, Ruskya felt his mentor trying to decipher why Kyn was not with him. He smiled as he pulled the cloak tighter around him and mentally pulled a cloak around his mind.

The evening was just Glendyn and Ruskya. Duskya had been invited to dinner by one of the other riders.

"So, you left Kyn to work with leather?" Glendyn greeted him.

Ruskya nodded, "I thought it would be good for him to get started on a saddle."

"I can see that. It looks like he is handling it, but barely," Glendyn chuckled. "I, at least, waited until you had seen," he paused to consider, "oh, twelve winters!"

"I also had to use a borrowed saddle to start with since Wyeth could fly when I arrived."

The thought of Wyeth was almost his undoing. He quickly thought of something else.

Listening to Glendyn's thoughts, Ruskya realized that his mentor was listening in on Kyn at the same time. Ruskya found that he could get the youngling's thoughts from Glendyn. It made him think of an idea; he contacted Duskya and asked if she could catch the youngling's thoughts by listening in on Ruskya's. He was relieved to find that it didn't work that way. The idea of an infinite chain of mental eavesdropping sent spiders walking up and down his back.

Ruskya was proud of Kyn. He was concentrating hard on the leatherwork to the point where he wasn't thinking of their afternoon at all. However, as the work became easier, thoughts of the conversation at the general store began to float through the youngling's head. Amid much grumbling of errors in the leatherwork and calling his trainer a few uncomplimentary names, Glendyn was finally able to extract that there had been a conversation with a man, and something about other dragon riders.

Glendyn turned to Ruskya. "So, that is it. Which are you right now, Ruskya, the trainer or the trainee? You gave me a great workout. Do not apologize," he interrupted before Ruskya could say anything, raising his hand as if to emphasize what he said. "I needed it. It also proves that I was right in assigning the youngling to you. You have a natural talent for teaching."

Ruskya bowed his head in thanks, allowing the firelight to make his blond hair golden.

"Do you wish to now clarify what I found out?" the older rider asked.

Ruskya nodded, "Kyn was in the general store when a man by the name of Kyle came in. He told a story about meeting a rider who was looking for other riders. He had heard of our colony, but didn't know where to find us. Kyle asked anyone who wanted to be a rider to step forward. He recruited two others to go with him tomorrow after the midday meal to meet this rider. The rider will tell them if they are rider quality."

"Two others? That is all he could muster? I would have thought he could find more."

"Others didn't believe him. The two others were a woman about my age and me."

Ruskya felt the shock but did not see it on Glendyn's face. The older rider just nodded. "So, where do you wish me to be for this?"

"If you could be somewhere close with Kyn, I think it may be a good idea. I don't want the boy where he could get hurt, but I want him to try to identify the woman, and he hasn't mastered long-distance mental contact yet."

Glendyn looked questioningly at him.

"Tonight I was able to eavesdrop on Kyn's thoughts through you. Duskya, though, was not able to read his thoughts by reading me."

"You are full of wonders tonight."

"The night isn't finished yet, honored rider. I have one more thing to discuss with you. I don't know if it was a wise thing, but it felt like the right thing."

Glendyn waited for Ruskya to continue. When he didn't, he mentally encouraged him.

"Glendyn, what do you know of dragon courage?"

"Dragon courage," the rider paused and steepled his fingers together while he collected his thoughts as if they were books scattered throughout a library, "is the ability of a dragon to breathe out fire without burning. It manifests itself as sparks that land on the person to whom the courage is being given. The fire then imbues the person with courage of a dragon."

After a slight pause, Glendyn continued, "The courage is only temporary. It may last from as little as few moments up to a full glass. In rare cases, it has been known to linger on for as much as half a day. People operating under dragon courage have won battles, proposed marriage, and done necessary everyday deeds that they previously lacked the courage for. Does that cover what you needed to know?"

Ruskya nodded. "I visited my ma today. I made an offhand comment about her tea, and found out more than I had ever known."

When the young rider did not continue, Glendyn inquired, "What was your comment?"

"I said that the only thing that brought more comfort than Ma's tea was the scent of rosemary and pine needles. My ma reacted strongly to that comment. I knew my da had carried that scent, but she related it to dragon's breath. I asked her how she had known that and she told me a tale of a baby blue dragon that had seen three winters. Ma had met this hatchling when she was with my da. This dragon breathed dragon courage on her."

Ruskya exhaled and then continued. "I took her to see Wyeth after the encounter at the general store. She couldn't hear him, but she could talk to him. I told her that he was baby blue when he met me. When she talked to him, she mentioned that Wyeth had met me before. I don't know when. I guess I could ask Wyeth, but if he hasn't mentioned it, I'm leery of asking."

Ruskya explained how Wyeth had not only breathed dragon courage on Meredyth, but had also given her a pouch of the sparkling dust. When he was done, he fell silent, almost exhausted from the telling. He realized there was a lot about his younger seasons that he did not know. Normally, a mother or a father would tell those tales to their children as the little ones grew older, but Ruskya had been taken away from his mother when he had barely seen ten winters and from his father when he only had three. What had he missed? Why was there this mystery surrounding his father?

"Don't chide yourself for what you cannot undo, Ruskya," Glendyn advised, having read his thoughts. "You must accept who you are and grow from there. Your parents were honored by the dragons. Your da was chosen to breed and raise their young; your ma was accepted, though she could not hear them. I do not know what Wyeth has in mind for your ma now, but it appears to me that she has a part to play in the dragon's history. As for whether you did right in bringing your ma to visit Wyeth, your dragon has answered that question. He would not have tried to speak to her, nor would he have filled a pouch with precious dragon courage if you had done wrong. I have never heard of dragon courage being distilled that way. You must keep it a secret, for there are some who would try to sell it as a commodity."

"Thank you, Glendyn. I do not know if you realize it or not, but you have fulfilled your vow to my ma. I think of my da often, but I have only vague memories. When I think of things that a boy should do with his da, you are the one who has done them with me. You have been the one to teach me. If it were not for you and Wyeth, I would not be the rider I am today."

Glendyn was speechless. Ruskya could feel the compliment affecting the older rider. He tuned out, deciding to let Glendyn have his privacy. He did not want to know what had caused Glendyn to make his vow; he just wanted the rider to know it was appreciated.

* * *

Soon after, Ruskya drew his cloak about himself and went out into the frigid air. A heavy fog had settled over the canyon. He was alone with his thoughts, or as alone as a dragon rider ever was, for Wyeth was constantly listening in.

"I meant what I said, Wyeth. Without you, I would not be me. Thank you for being here."

"Where else would I be? I promised myself to you when we both had just seen two winters. I could not do otherwise."

"*When*?" Ruskya almost vocalized the word, his amazement was so great.

"You must realize things were dangerous for your da then. I did not understand the ways of men, for I was too little; you will have to ask Glendyn for more details. Suffice it to say, your da feared for his life and for his family's. He had your ma bring you and your sister to the only safe place that he knew—the hatching cave. It was winter, but the procession had not yet happened. Wryn and I were going to be part of the procession that year. Little did your da know what his actions would set in motion.

"Your ma brought the two of you to the cave. You were just a little toddling child. Your sister was definitely braver. You stayed close to your ma's skirts, or to your sister. After a while, your sister decided to explore the cave and you tagged along. It was then that Duskya saw Wryn and waddled over to her. It took a while for you to follow once you saw us. Duskya went right up to Wryn and gave her a hug. You saw me and slowly decided to come to me.

"It was when you took the first step toward me that I chose you. I saw the determination and the bravery beneath the surface and realized that it wasn't fear but natural caution. I wanted that in a rider; someone who wouldn't go diving into danger right away, but would evaluate the situation and make an informed decision. You followed your sister's lead and gave me a hug.

"That night, your da let you both sleep curled up with us. He knew it was the safest place for you. No one in his right mind would disturb a sleeping dragon, even just a hatchling. The next morning your ma returned with you and your sister to your abode, but Wryn and I knew from that moment that you both were destined to be our riders. We waited until you were old enough for the procession to choose you."

There was silence after this revelation. Ruskya stood, staring at nothing until the chill crept under his cloak and he registered how cold it really was. He walked the next few steps to his door. He hadn't realized when he had stopped walking, but it was time to head inside. He had a busy day tomorrow.

CHAPTER 5: ANOTHER RIDER

WHEN RUSKYA AND KYN exited the abode the next morning, a heavy fog hung in the air so that the top of the canyon could not be seen. A thick layer of frost crunched under their feet. Each blade of grass seemed to be enlarged three times or more with tiny hairlike particles; it was as if each flake of ice built on the next to create miniature castles.

The riders went about their normal morning chores and training, but over it all hung an air of anticipation for the time when Ruskya would go to Caravan Canyon to meet with Kyle and the woman who wanted to be a dragon rider. Duskya had a bad feeling about the whole thing and tried to talk her brother out of going, but Ruskya was adamant. She opted to follow him with their mental link. Glendyn had decided that he and Kyn would wait at Meredyth's abode. Her place was the closest to Caravan Canyon they could get without freezing or drawing unnecessary attention. They arrived just before the midday meal.

Meredyth greeted them with hugs. When she heard that Ruskya couldn't stay but needed to go to Caravan Canyon to meet up with Kyle, she quickly set about making a snack and fixing tea that she poured into a container wrapped with skins to keep it warm. Ruskya thanked her and headed back out into the cold.

The fog had lifted, but still hung from the sky as low clouds. The frost clung to the sagebrush and grass, but the slightest wind would create a small blizzard. The cold sucked the breath away from the young rider, and he drew his furs tighter. He was glad his ma had fixed him some of her tea. He had tucked it and the snack she had given him away under his cloak where they would stay out of the cold.

Ruskya made it to Caravan Canyon in good time. He looked around for the others, but didn't see them. He wasn't sure if he was early or not.

He waited a few minutes and then heard some voices coming up the canyon toward him. He walked toward them and found Kyle and the woman just arriving from Woolpren.

"You made it here. Good," Kyle remarked. "I wasn't sure if you would when I didn't see you in Woolpren."

"You said to meet here at the canyon," Ruskya replied, "so that is what I did. I haven't been here long."

"So, where is this dragon rider of yours?" the woman inquired.

"I don't know," Kyle said, pulling the hood of his cloak closer around his face, while looking around as if the rider would materialize out of thin air. "He said to be here. He should be here."

"Unless, there never was a rider," she commented, looking up at Kyle with distrust.

"Oh, there was. You can take my word for it."

Before an argument could break out, Ruskya asked, "What does this rider look like?"

"He's built like an upside down pear: skinny in the legs and waist, but his upper body is big with muscles. He's got dark hair, and the strangest eyes."

Ruskya smiled inwardly at the description of the pear. That was exactly what many riders looked like. Their upper body was strong from maneuvering dragons while their lower body was often slender and lithe. Yet at the mention of the eyes, he got concerned.

"What was wrong with his eyes?"

"I didn't say there was anything wrong, just strange. They were turquoise."

The woman had been listening intently, but now she commented, "No one's eyes can be turquoise. That's impossible."

Kyle defended himself. "That's why I noticed them. They bore right into my skull. I *had* to notice them."

For once in his fifteen winters as a rider, Ruskya was glad for his unobtrusive icy blue eyes. He knew if his eyes looked differently, it would give him away. To deflect the attention, he said, "It could be something to do with dragons. No one knows what being around dragons can do to a person."

"I've heard that riders and dragons start to think alike," the woman commented, readjusting the earflaps on her hat and pushing red hair back from her face.

Ruskya noticed that her green eyes were constantly moving, almost like a caged animal looking for a way out. Even while she made the comment, her eyes searched out the corners of the canyon. Ruskya decided that might not be a bad idea. He let his dragon senses roam beyond his two companions. He was almost able to reach the village, but not quite. He could feel Duskya watching him.

While the other two continued to speculate about this rider, he called to Glendyn, "Can you hear what is going on?"

"Yes, Ruskya," Glendyn responded. "Kyn says that he recognizes the woman. He thinks her name is Carryl. He says she is a healer of sorts and only comes into Woolpren to sell her herbs."

"That makes sense," Ruskya agreed. "She keeps moving her eyes about looking for a way of escape, almost. I think she would be a good person to have on our side." At that moment, he felt something at the edge of his dragon senses coming from the opposite direction from the village. He couldn't quite make it out. It felt almost like a dragon.

"It is!" Wyeth's excited voice called. "Ruskya, there's another dragon coming toward you. I cannot sense its intention at this time; I cannot feel him, except through you."

"Glendyn, Wyeth says it is a dragon," Ruskya said in awe.

"Then believe your dragon. Be careful, Ruskya."

Ruskya decided to watch his companions for signs of anything amiss. Neither of them seemed to have picked up on the presence further out of the canyon. He figured that if he watched Carryl and took his cues from her, he would appear normal. A few minutes later, he noticed a sparkling frost fall upon the edge of the canyon behind them. Ruskya repositioned himself so that he could watch that side of the canyon without appearing to do so. Carryl noticed the shift and looked around. Her sharp eyes picked out the frost shift, also.

"Is someone coming?" she asked.

"Where?" Kyle asked, looking back the way he had come into the canyon.

"I don't know," Ruskya answered truthfully. He didn't know if there was someone with the dragon.

An uneasy silence hung over the group as they watched around the canyon. Ruskya's dragon senses saw the person first and flared away immediately; this was someone who would recognize dragon senses being used on him. Ruskya knew it was a man and that he was strong. He seemed different from Glendyn or any other rider Ruskya had met or felt. He immediately moved to guard his thoughts and his dragon senses.

"What was that?" Glendyn asked.

"It's the rider," Ruskya carefully called. "Do you think he can hear this?"

"No, Ruskya," Wyeth answered. "No matter how strong, another rider cannot hear a dragon's communications with his rider. Talk only to me. Glendyn can still watch through your thoughts."

"Okay," Ruskya answered shakily.

"Courage, young one," Wyeth called. With his dragon's words, Ruskya felt strength return to him as if he had just received dragon courage breathed on him.

"There," Carryl whispered, "there's a person coming down the ridge."

"Where?" Kyle demanded, sounding loud compared to Carryl's whisper.

Ruskya noticed the look of offense that Carryl sent toward the other man. She almost held him in contempt.

Before she could say anything, Ruskya replied, "She's right. He blends in with his brown and white outfit, but there is a man coming down."

The look Carryl sent Ruskya was the exact opposite of what she had thought of Kyle, her green eyes searched him, looking for what he was made of.

"How can you tell it is a male?" she questioned.

Ruskya thought quickly; he had known it from the first contact he had. "I thought I saw his figure as he came around that small bend," he said truthfully. The glimpse had been enough to confirm what he had known all along. Carryl nodded, satisfied, her hair bouncing like little springs.

They waited in anticipation for the next couple of minutes as the rider made his way down the canyon wall toward them. When he arrived, the rider paused before greeting his perspective riders. Even Kyle had the presence of mind to wait until he was addressed before talking.

Ruskya took this time to observe the rider. He was a tall man, imposing in height and build. Kyle's description of an upside-down pear came to mind. As Kyle had mentioned, the rider's eyes drew a person's attention. The rider seemed to be aware of the effect his eyes had on people, and he used it to his advantage. As soon as someone noticed them, the rider locked gazes with the person and proceeded to use dragon senses and something else, it seemed to Ruskya, to weigh the person. Ruskya had to fight the urge to block the intrusion. Instead, he let other thoughts filter through his mind that would mask what he really was thinking. It was similar to what he had done in training with Kyn and Glendyn.

Ruskya tried to figure out how the rider was intruding into his mind. The rider wasn't exactly trying to read his thoughts, but he was using more than dragon senses to see what each person was made of. As the rider moved on to Carryl, Ruskya mentally let out a sigh of relief.

"Wylen says that Glendyn wants to know what that was," Wyeth informed Ruskya.

"I wish I knew," the young rider replied. "It was more than just dragon senses, and yet it wasn't quite what we do with reading thoughts."

"I think it was more like he was compelling you to open up and let him in," Wyeth suggested. "Dragons do it often to get what they want from people. If the other lets you, then you can get past his defenses. With a human, it might be possible to actually control what the other person does."

"That goes against our code as riders," Ruskya said thoughtfully.

"You're right, but watch out. He's coming back," Wyeth warned just in time.

The rider had turned to all of them, but addressed Kyle. "Is this all you could find? I thought there would be more eager dragon riders from your village."

"I tried, sir," Kyle replied, nervousness causing his voice to crack. "These two were the only ones brave enough to challenge traditions."

"So, you were brave enough to challenge traditions, huh?" The rider practically sneered the word 'traditions.' "Well, I have several trials for you. Then we will see if you are rider quality."

"But, sir," Kyle protested, "I thought by coming out here we would become riders."

The man snorted a laugh. "Hardly! You must first prove your worth. Then we will see if you can become a rider."

Kyle quelled any further questions.

* * *

The next several hours were filled with trials. There were mental feats, physical endurance tests, and hunting chores. At times, Ruskya thought the rider wanted one of them to fail. He continually assigned more difficult tasks, some nigh unto impossible to complete. He kept trying to work with the others, but found the tests seemed designed for them to have to work against each other. He found this quite unnerving, since dragons work best when they work together. The riders at Three Spans Canyon had all been trained to work as a team to get their goals accomplished. The few chances he had to work with Carryl during the trials amazed him. He had never found a woman with whom he worked as well, other than his sister. He realized he was watching her more than Kyle and was hoping she wouldn't fail the tests.

When the fog had moved back into the canyon and all light was almost gone from the sky, Kyle whispered to Ruskya, "When is he going to decide? If he waits much longer, we won't be able to see to make it back to Woolpren."

Carryl heard the remark, for even though Kyle whispered, he was panting and his voice carried although the fog dampened all noises around them. "Maybe that is one of the final tests, to see if we can make it back home in inclement weather and low visibility," she suggested in her quiet way.

"But no one can see after dark," Kyle protested. "The rider has his dragon, but what about us?"

A bright light split the dusk and the smell of sulfur filled the air. The three turned to see the rider standing behind a newly lit torch. His stance bode no disputing. He seemed to be challenging them to come.

When they had all turned to look at him and come closer to the blazing torch, he said, "You wonder how to get home. Frankly, I am surprised any of you made it this far. You and your loud mouth should have died out a long time ago," he said, gesturing to Kyle. He turned to Carryl, "And you're a sorry excuse for a hunter; it's only by sheer luck that you were able to track anything at all." Lastly, he turned to Ruskya, "And you are so puny, you should have quit at the beginning."

Kyle started to make a comeback, but Ruskya nudged him in the ribs and stepped forward.

"You are right, sir, we shouldn't have made it this far, but we stuck it out. We encouraged each other. We are ready for your last trial."

"You think this is the end?" the rider scoffed. "You're more pathetic than

I thought."

The rider waited for other replies. Carryl stepped forward. "You are right, I did not track my best today; I should have done better. Nevertheless, I am what I am."

Kyle took the cue and said, "Even my big mouth can learn to be quiet."

The rider waited again. This time no one moved. The fog seemed to creep into their bones. Ruskya felt the touch on his mind again. His mind felt unclean after the rider moved on to the others. He wondered what the rider was searching for.

"I admit, there is only one more test," the rider said, as the sound of large wings beat in the air.

"You did bring dragons with you," Carryl said with awe in her voice. No sooner were the words out of her mouth, then an enormous turquoise dragon landed at the rider's right side.

The dragon's wings were larger than any Ruskya had ever seen, and the light of the torch made them glow in their iridescence. The dragon folded his wings, and Ruskya noticed the dark veins of blue streaking through the dragon. It reminded him of a large turquoise gemstone set into a cloak clasp or on a belt hook. There was something unnerving about this dragon. The dragon landed and Ruskya had barely taken in all of him, when Ruskya felt Wyeth's scream of agony.

"Wyeth, are you okay?" he called urgently.

Before Wyeth could respond, Duskya called to him, "Ruskya, is everything okay?"

Ruskya had no time to reply to his twin, for the rider had stepped up to Kyle and with a roar, brought his hand back and slapped Kyle across the face.

"What were you thinking, you imbecile?"

Kyle went down onto his knees at the force and unexpectedness of it.

The rider drew back his hand and smote again. "How dare you bring a rider here!"

Ruskya felt Carryl's shock run through her body. He didn't look back at her as he stepped forward and commanded the rider to stop the blow in mid-stride. "He knew nothing of it, sir. Do not take your fury out on him."

The strength and awe in Ruskya made the rider pause and turn away from Kyle.

"I met him in the general store yesterday. He didn't know that I was a rider. I asked for information, and he gave it to me. She," —he motioned to Carryl—"was there and that was the first I had met her as well." Seeing what the rider was going to say, Ruskya cut him off. "No, I didn't use any dragon abilities in your testing. I stayed away from it the moment I realized you were a real rider. At first, I thought the story Kyle had spun was a bunch of rubbish, at best, someone claiming to be a rider who was going to rob us."

He continued, catching Carryl's eye behind him. "I knew I had to prove to you that I could do it all without any extra help." He turned back to the rider, but kept his dragon senses focused toward Carryl. "I do not know about the other two, but I know that I am walking out of here tonight. I will not force anyone beyond their desires, but I know that your methods are contrary to dragons' nature. They work together as a team, and do not force others to work alone. I also know that if striking your new trainees is par for the course, I would not want to be a trainee. I would rather be alone in our village than with someone who would wantonly beat me. I will offer to these two trainees another choice: Go with this rider wherever he would have you go with no real hope of dragons—for dragons choose their riders, despite what he says, it isn't up to men; or come with me, back to the village and then on to our colony. I will offer safe passage and do all that is in my power to let you come help with our dragons. This I swear by my dragon."

Ruskya paused and glanced at Kyle, but Kyle avoided looking up. His eyes moved to Carryl. She was gazing intently at him, weighing his words for truth. He tried to shield himself from the rider's prying senses, and yet open himself up to Carryl's. She nodded imperceptibly.

The rider stopped them both. "Fine, come if you will, but I will tell you one thing rider," he spat the word out as if it was distasteful. "I will return. I have yet to find what I came for."

Ruskya cut him off. "And when you do, we will be waiting. If you harm one hair on the head of any of our villagers or damage the ground that they farm, you will find yourself up against dragons and riders. We will defend our village and its people."

The rider turned to Kyle. "If you are coming, get yourself up to the top of the canyon. A horse waits for you." As the rider mounted his dragon,

Ruskya thought he heard him mutter, "I will find Calamadyn." He flew off into the fog.

Ruskya removed his rucksack from under his arm and took out a piece of wicking, a small bottle of oil, and tack. He bent down and broke off a branch from some sagebrush and then wrapped the wicking around it and secured it with tack. Next, he poured some of the oil onto the wicking. He walked over to the torch and lit his own newly made one. He then turned to Kyle who was watching in amazement. "You have a choice," he said softly, "you can come with me if you wish."

Kyle's only reply was to walk over, yank the torch out of the ground, and head toward the canyon track that the rider had come down earlier that afternoon.

Ruskya turned to Carryl. He was unsure if he should say anything. She gazed at him and then broke the silence. "Is it true that you didn't do anything...dragony the whole time?"

He smiled at her wording and shook his head. "Not a bit, once I felt him here. I didn't want him knowing I was a rider. If I did anything 'dragony' he would have felt it. So, does that mean you'll come back with me?"

She paused and looked at him. "You can really let me help with the dragons?"

He nodded, sensing her need for the truth. "I cannot guarantee that the dragons will accept you, but I can let you come to them. I have sway with some dragon riders. I cannot speak for the whole colony, though. I did say I would do what is in my power, and I will hold to that."

She searched his eyes and nodded. She seemed to expect something more from him. When he didn't live up to her expectations, she shook her head and began walking.

Ruskya shrugged and wondered what he had done as he took off after her. He knew she couldn't get far without the light, but he still didn't want her to get too far into the fog.

As he went to catch up with Carryl, he called to his dragon, "Are you willing to talk to me yet?"

"Yes, and no, young one," Wyeth answered. "I will not talk about what happened with that dragon until we are face-to-face, but I will talk with you otherwise."

"Well, will you tell Glendyn to have some supper ready? Ma's tea is long gone, and we will be starving by the time we return."

"Why don't you talk to him yourself? I think you need the practice," was the surprising reply.

Ruskya sighed heavily and was about to call to Glendyn when Carryl turned to him and asked, "Aren't you even going to ask my name?" Without waiting for an answer she continued, "It's Carryl." Ruskya had already learned the woman's name from Wyeth, of course, but decided to keep this to himself.

"I'm Ruskya," he responded, finally catching up.

"Are you okay?"

Ruskya grimaced; leave it to a woman to notice. "Oh, just frustrated with dragons."

"Is it possible not to get frustrated with any living creature?"

"I suppose so. I guess, sometimes, when you receive attitude from all around it gets tiring."

She paused in her stride. "Sometimes it is more frustrating when it comes from animals than when it comes from people. You expect it from people, but not from animals."

He grinned. "You're right about that. Although, I think frustration arises most often when we don't understand each other. So, maybe there is something I'm not understanding." He wondered what it could be.

"Yes, most often when I'm frustrated with a situation, it is when I do not understand it." Carryl replied.

From there, their conversation flowed smoothly, and Ruskya learned that Carryl had grown up on a farm outside of Woolpren. From an early age, she had a knack for healing animals and finding the right herbs to make someone heal quicker. During a lull in the conversation, Ruskya was able to send a message to Glendyn to let him know they were coming. He felt unusually exhausted, but marked it up to being out in the extreme cold all day. He couldn't wait to sit down with a cup of Ma's tea.

Later, Carryl asked about the dragons. "You really think that I can do something with them?"

"I can only speak for the four dragons I know best. You can have as much time with mine as he will allow you to have; then, there's the dragon of the newest youngling I am training."

"Kyn is a good boy. He has always been kind to me at the general store."

"Besides Kyn, there is my trainer, Glendyn," Ruskya continued. "He will allow you access if I explain things to him. Lastly, there is my sister's dragon."

"You have a sister?"

"Yes, Duskya." He paused. "All of my life I have been defined by being a twin; I don't know where I would be without her."

Carryl stopped abruptly and turned to face Ruskya. "*You* are the twins? No, it can't be!" It was almost a whispered moan of protest.

Ruskya put a hand on her arm.

"What is wrong, Carryl?" he asked, voicing her name for the first time.

She looked up and her eyes were full of memories, looking like drawings of the inland sea Ruskya had seen.

"I waited for that day as if it would change my life forever. I was first in the procession line, but the dragons passed me by as if they didn't even see me. Then there were the two sitting off to the side, waiting. It was as if they knew someone was coming, but hadn't arrived yet. After what seemed like an eternity, a boy and a girl stepped out of line and walked over to the dragons. I couldn't believe their boldness. That was you and your sister! I never thought I would ever meet those confident younglings…" She trailed off into silence.

Ruskya again placed his hand on her arm, this time to move them along. He could see the breath rising from their faces and knew they should get inside soon.

"I am sorry that the dragons didn't see who you are. I do want you to know something. Kyn was in the procession two years ago. He was just chosen this year. I don't know if another dragon may do the same with you, or if the dragons will accept you as their healer. My da was like that; he couldn't ride, but he was able to breed the dragons and take care of the hatchlings."

Ruskya saw the hope in her eyes. He wondered what pains lay hidden behind her rough exterior of independence. He was seeing beyond it into a kind, loving-hearted woman. They walked the rest of the way in companionable silence. Ruskya felt drained; a normal day of training had never felt this exhausting. He wondered why. He also knew he needed to talk with Wyeth about what had bothered the dragon enough to make him scream.

CHAPTER 6: A HEALER JOINS THE RIDERS

RUSKYA OPENED THE DOOR and let Carryl into his ma's abode. Carryl saw that the room was an open living, dining and cooking area. At the center was the open hearth, and beside it stood a combination brick oven and stove. The room smelled of fresh bread and a meat stew, and the aroma of herbs permeated the air. Carryl recognized rosemary, thyme, sage, marjoram, and several others, besides a couple that she couldn't name. She stared as she saw a familiar woman hug Ruskya and force him to sit in a chair next to the fire, and then place a steaming cup into his hands. Carryl couldn't believe that Ruskya's mother was the herbalist!

Ruskya was talking then. "Ma, I want you to meet—"

"Lady Carryl," Meredyth finished for him. She enveloped Carryl in a warm hug and led her to another chair by the fire. Carryl found a cup of tea being placed into her hands as Meredyth continued, "You have grown since I last saw you. You had but fifteen winters when I went out to your farm to ask your da if you could apprentice with me."

Carryl found her voice. "You did? I would have been honored to accept, Lady Meredyth."

"Well, unfortunately, your da felt he needed you at the farm more than he could let you leave. I lost track of where you were after that."

"I stayed on the farm for another three winters. After that, I found a place of my own out in one of the canyons. I tend animals and try to find and dry herbs. I have sold several to Kyn's father," she nodded to the youngling.

"So you are my competition." Meredyth laughed.

"I did not mean to cause offense," Carryl quickly said.

"No, not at all. In fact, I have been glad that you were selling your herbs. You are able to find some that I cannot find. Now, before we starve this poor young one, let's eat." She ushered everyone to the table while Glendyn served the hot stew and bread.

*   *   *

During the meal, Ruskya tried to talk with Glendyn about the day, but the older rider kept shutting down the conversation. Finally, Ruskya understood that Glendyn would only speak of dragon business with fellow dragon riders. So, Ruskya decided to announce his decision.

"Glendyn, I made a promise to Carryl that she could come to Three Spans Canyon."

Ruskya saw that Carryl was watching the rider's face; she had probably caught the brief bit of shock and disapproval that crossed it.

"What did you have in mind?" Glendyn inquired, not letting any of his disapproval come through in his tone.

"Glendyn, how often have we needed a healer, either for a rider or for a dragon? I think Carryl will make a good healer. We can let Wyeth, Wryn, Wylen, and Wyden decide if they will let her come, and then they will spread the word to the others," Ruskya explained with enthusiasm.

"I will agree that we have often needed a healer, but why now and why her?"

"Glendyn, my own da was part of the dragon colony and yet not a rider. I would think that you of all people would understand the need. Why not?"

Meredyth set her wrinkled hand over Glendyn's smooth one. "Glendyn." Her soft voice was barely audible over the crackle of the fire. "Ruskya's right. You say that you want the villagers to know the riders are their friends and that they are approachable. Why not use a healer who is known among the villagers as a go-between? I would have had her as an apprentice ten winters ago, if her da had allowed it. She has learned a great deal on her own, but there are many things we can learn from each other, and from the dragons. Please, let us ask the dragons if they will let the two of us come."

*   *   *

Carryl held her breath, waiting for the rider's reply. She noticed the effect Meredyth's words had on the rider. It was as if the wall that had been up had cracked and then crumbled. Carryl hadn't realized that she wanted this so badly. It was a desire that had been buried for the past fifteen winters, but now that it had come to the surface, it would not be quieted.

Glendyn shook his head. "I am not sure if it is right, but I have done nontraditional things since Ardyn started raising the hatchlings. It seems that anything that touches this family is highly irregular and nontraditional. What is it about you?" He laughed wryly.

Carryl saw the sparkle that lit his royal blue eyes. She wondered at their strange color. They were quite nice when he laughed. She also observed the way that he looked at Meredyth, the tender glances of concern. She had seen that in very few men, and it made her respect the rider. She knew she would be safe with this group.

* * *

"Ma," Ruskya stated, "I know it is crowded, but would you mind if we stayed here tonight? I don't think I could walk another dragon span, let alone all the way back to Three Spans Canyon."

Glendyn looked closely at Ruskya. "Son, what is wrong? You have been very talkative, and now you aren't able to walk home."

"I cannot explain it, but today's trials were more exhausting than anything I have ever done. I don't know if it was trying to do things without dragon senses, or trying to keep the rider out of my mind. I just know that I am ready to collapse, and I still have to go out and talk with Wyeth."

"Ruskya," Meredyth interrupted, "you cannot go back out in the bitter cold. Can't this talk wait until tomorrow?"

"I don't know, Ma. I just know something went wrong."

"Wrong?" Glendyn repeated. "What do you mean?"

"When the turquoise dragon landed, Wyeth let out a painful scream. I don't know why. He won't talk about it until we are face-to-face."

"That *is* very strange. I know I would want to find out right away what was going on, but see if he is in danger right now, or if this talk can wait until tomorrow. You should let him know about Carryl, too, if you haven't already."

"I have done that, and no, he isn't in danger. I've been thinking about the turquoise dragon, and whether the dragon used some power or…" he faltered, "…I don't know. As soon as the dragon landed, Wyeth screamed, and the rider knew immediately that I was a rider, too. I had no time to communicate further with Wyeth. Has Wyden ever done anything like that before?"

Glendyn paused and thought. "Once before, Wyden would not tell me something except in person. It was about the death of a friend." Glendyn paused as if debating and finally ended. "Your da. It was as if he knew I couldn't handle the information on my own. He has not done anything like it since. Why would Wyeth respond that way to seeing another dragon?"

"I don't know, but I would like to wait until morning to find out. Ma, what do you say? Can we sleep here tonight?"

"Of course, son. Carryl can stay in my room, and you can take the loft upstairs."

As Glendyn rose to leave, Meredyth stopped him. "No, Glendyn, you stay, too. I want you around if something happens to my boy's dragon. I have a healer to help him with the physical exhaustion, but I need a rider to help him with this dragon problem."

Glendyn nodded and sat back down. "Thank you, honored lady. I accept the offer of hospitality."

Meredyth blushed. "Oh, Glendyn, you know better than to be so formal with me. Come, Kyn, let's find some blankets. Glendyn, help Ruskya get to bed."

Ruskya tried to wave Glendyn's attention away, but it was only halfhearted because he was already almost asleep in his stew bowl. Glendyn walked him up the ladder to his old bed. The loft seemed smaller to Ruskya than it had back when he had seen ten winters, but he didn't have a lot of time to think about it before he drifted off to sleep. He thought he heard Duskya calling his name, but it was indistinct. He did hear Wyeth's voice.

"Sleep well, little one. Courage for the journey I give you. I will need it, too. I will fight the turquoise dragon and his rider with you. This I vow."

* * *

Glendyn watched until Ruskya's breathing evened out and then went down to find Kyn. He thought it would be best for the boy to be near Ruskya, so he sent Kyn up the ladder to the second bed with orders that if Ruskya woke or talked, Kyn should get Glendyn right away. Glendyn half-wanted to stay up there himself, but knew that was not wise. He thought about reading Ruskya's thoughts, but wasn't sure if that would be best. He finally decided to wait. He sat down by the fire with another cup of Meredyth's tea in his hands and stared into the mug, letting the warmth and the aroma wash away the stress. Although he didn't look old, it was days like today that he felt ancient.

Meredyth's soft voice brought him out of the mental wanderings. "What is troubling you, friend?"

He looked up and saw her kind gray eyes looking into his. He nodded and tried to formulate into words what was wrong. She waited quietly. He liked that about her. She would wait for an answer and not prod. He needed to make sure that he came by more often. Meredyth was a good woman who had stayed true to the dragons, the riders, and himself despite very difficult circumstances.

What was it that was so important that Wyeth would only talk face-to-face? He remembered with great clarity the day that Wyden had done that with him. Glendyn had been in Woolpren gathering some supplies when his trip was cut short by a cry of grief from his dragon. He tried to ask the creature what was wrong, but Wyden had insisted on telling him in person. He rushed back to the canyon to find the whole colony in an uproar. No one knew what had happened, but it seemed as if someone had attacked the hatchlings. Their cave had been burned with dragon fire, and the young ones couldn't say what had happened. Wyeth and Wryn were too shocked to be able to communicate exactly what had transpired, and without having riders with whom they could directly relay memories, it was hopeless. All Wyden could say to him was that Ardyn had to be dead. There was no way a human could have survived the attack.

"Meredyth," he broke the silence of his thoughts, "why is it the twins have never said that Ardyn died? They always say their da left."

Meredyth nodded. "That's my fault. I never could accept that Ardyn died without seeing his body or finding anything that could tell us what happened."

This made sense to Glendyn. It would be easier to say that a father had left than had died a mysterious death. It would be hard enough for a mother to explain to twins who had barely seen three winters why their da would not be coming home.

"I don't understand how anything else could have happened, though," Glendyn said, gently.

The fire popped, sending sparks up the chimney. Steam from their mugs drifted toward the ceiling. Meredyth inhaled the aroma of the brew before saying anything.

"Do you think that Wyeth and Wryn saw something the day the hatchlings were attacked, and that now maybe Wyeth remembered something?"

"I don't know. It's possible, but I don't know why seeing another dragon would bring it up, when he had no problems with the rider. I guess we will just have to wait until morning."

* * *

Meredyth wished she could comfort Glendyn, but nothing she could say would help. She didn't want to relive that time any more than he did. The upheaval in Three Spans Canyon and Philippi Canyon was more than any rider wanted to remember. It was a good thing that Calamadyn had disappeared with Ardyn. Had others found it? Had it been wise to give the merchant's wife a small dose of it? Only a rider or two even remembered it. Those who did would not want it returned; she was certain of that. These thoughts filled her mind as she crawled into her bed. No, she was sure the herb would stay hidden along with the old nesting cave in Philippi Canyon.

CHAPTER 7: THE CAPTURE OF ARDYN

THE NEXT MORNING, Meredyth served a quick breakfast so that the riders and Carryl could return to Three Spans Canyon. Ruskya noticed the longing in his mother's eyes as he gave her a hug. He drew away and decided to see what his mother was thinking; he saw her desire to go with them.

He turned to Glendyn. "Can Ma come with us for the morning?"

"Please, Glendyn," Ruskya thought.

"You must be feeling better to start mental games this early," Glendyn said quietly. At Ruskya's confused look, he added, "You just begged me to let her come."

"I didn't! I was thinking it, but I didn't call to you."

Noticing that the others were waiting for his reply, Glendyn said to everyone, "Meredyth, do you wish to accompany us today?"

The light in her eyes answered the question. Glendyn shook his head and said, "Go gather whatever you need. Is there anyone who will need to know that you are gone?"

"No," she replied as she gathered a small bag and put it into a larger one. "I often go out looking for herbs. No one will notice me being gone or wonder about it."

"Then let's go."

They made it to the canyon without any trouble. Ruskya had called to Wyeth to meet him at their small canyon offshoot. Glendyn had decided to take Meredyth and Carryl to meet Wyden and Wylen. They had just arrived in the colony when Duskya came storming up to them.

"Ruskya," she called through the bond they shared, "how dare you go off and not communicate with me all day! If it hadn't been for Wyeth and Wryn, I would not have known how you were. Then you disappear from the face of the earth for the whole night! I should have you whipped!" She then enveloped him in a huge bear hug.

"What can I say, sister?" he whispered into her ear as she clung to him. "I couldn't communicate while the rider was there, and then I was too exhausted to do anything last night. I thought I had told Wyeth to have Wryn let you know I was fine."

"You did, but," she pushed him away and looked at him, speaking in a normal voice, "hearing from a dragon is not the same as hearing from your brother. Don't ever do that again. Do you hear me?"

Ruskya nodded. A lump formed in his throat. He realized that Duskya was truly upset. He wondered what he would feel if she had deserted him for that amount of time.

"I promise I will not do that again. If it is within my power, I will always communicate with you, sister. I so promise by Wyeth."

Tears came to Duskya's silver eyes, making them look like molten metal, and she nodded. Ruskya turned to see Carryl behind them.

"Duskya, I would like you to meet Lady Carryl. She is an herbalist and healer. Lady Carryl, I present to you Honored Rider Duskya."

The two women stared at each other for a while and then both simultaneously bowed to each other. Ruskya hid a small smile. They were too much alike to submit to each other, but he knew they would get along.

"Now, I have a dragon to talk to. If you all will excuse me, I'll meet up with you later. I'll stay in communication with at least one of you. Kyn, why don't you go with the others? It should be good for you. Besides, you can introduce Lady Carryl to Wylen."

Ruskya was anxious to see Wyeth. He wanted to see for himself that the dragon was fine. There was something strange about the wail he had heard, and it had been cut off so abruptly. He found his dragon sitting calmly, preening the underside of his wings. Ruskya ran to the dragon and fiercely hugged him. He sent messages and mental images of reassurance and love.

"Now, what is this thing that has disturbed you so?"

"I do not know how to answer you best," Wyeth responded. "Here, let me share what I saw when I saw the turquoise dragon."

Ruskya saw a cave with hatchlings in it. The feeling of peace and contentment permeated the area. The smell of pine needles and rosemary lingered in the air. The hatchlings were resting, almost asleep, when suddenly turquoise flames leaped down at them from above. Panic ensued. Cries of pain and fear filled the air. Ruskya heard Wyeth's voice call for Ardyn. It was a sad, plaintive cry. Again, the dragon fire spilled down onto the hatchlings. The turquoise flames covered the walls, and licked down them to try to reach the baby dragons. Wyeth called to Ardyn a second time. Now, Ruskya saw his father run toward the hatchlings, ignoring the flames and calling out to Wyeth.

"Wyeth, I need your help. Get the hatchlings out! Move them toward the exit. They will be able to get out if they go now. Hurry!"

Wyeth's confusion seemed to diminish. Ruskya saw Wryn come alongside them and the two of them started to work together with Ardyn to move the young dragons toward the entrance through the flames to freedom. At the last minute, a young hatchling veered away from the entrance as fresh fire fell.

"Wyeth," Ardyn called, "you get the rest of them out. I'll go get Wyn."

"Ardyn, no," Wyeth protested.

"Yes, you go take care of these hatchlings and your rider. Now! I will get Wyn out."

With an emotional pain so great that Ruskya almost could not bear to continue the memory, the young dragon moved the rest of the hatchlings toward the entrance. They had just broken through the entrance, when the sound of huge dragon wings came from behind them. Wyeth turned to see Wyn running for her life. Behind her, Ardyn was running as a turquoise dragon descended on them from above. It was the same dragon Ruskya had seen last night. Ruskya barely had time for this to sink in when the dragon swooped down, spewing more flames at the hatchlings. The pain was great, but not as great as the shock of seeing the dragon reach out with his talons and pick up Ardyn.

"Ardyn!" The cry was wrenched from Wyeth's being. A small stream of baby blue fire appeared, but nothing that could counter the turquoise dragon's fire.

"Go, Wyeth," Ardyn commanded. "Go! I will be okay."

It was clear that the turquoise dragon did something terrible, then, for Ardyn went limp. Wyeth stood helpless to do anything as the dragon flew away, a rider on his back, and Ardyn hanging limply from his talons.

The memory faded and left Ruskya drained. He found he had fallen to the ground on his knees. His head lay against Wyeth's leg. Wyeth's head was resting on his shoulder.

"You mean to tell me that the dragon that came yesterday was the one who was responsible for my father's leaving us?"

Wyeth sent a nod of agreement toward Ruskya.

"But, why? Why would a dragon attack other dragons?"

"I don't know, little one."

"Last night, Glendyn told us about Wyden's reaction the day my father disappeared. Why would Wyden say that my father died if in fact he hadn't?"

"That is because I was so young. I was the only dragon to see what happened to Ardyn. Besides that, I had never communicated with any human other than your father. You saw the memory. That is after twenty-two winters. I have had time to piece it together and reconstruct it, but I could not in a lifetime put it into words. At the same time, trying to get another human to see a dragon's memory is too difficult, unless that human is his rider. Glendyn could possibly see it now, but we both have grown in learning the ways of communication. No one knew exactly what happened to Ardyn. They assumed he died in the fire and that the dragon fire consumed his remains. I tried to tell them otherwise, but I was never able to communicate it. Later, it seemed like it was not important. Besides, no one ever mentioned that day again."

"Why don't they talk about it?" Ruskya asked.

"It is too painful, for one. Another reason is that they don't know what happened. It remains a mystery. Why discuss something you don't understand?"

"I guess so, but I would want to figure out why it happened."

"Yes, you would. That is because you are your father's son."

Ruskya paused at that. No one had ever compared him to his father.

"What about that other rider?" Ruskya asked.

"What about him?"

"Who is he? Why would he train riders to go against the ways of dragons?"

"I've been thinking about that," the dragon replied. "I think part of your exhaustion last night was from going against everything you are. When you go against the grain of your being, it is tiring."

There was silence for a while, then Ruskya heard his sister call. "Ruskya, are you ready for company?"

Ruskya looked up at Wyeth and then sent a mental nod to his sister.
"Are you okay?" Duskya called back. "You sound sad."
"I'll be fine."
"Carryl and I are coming. We are almost to the corner."
Ruskya stood up and wiped his face on a cloth in his bag. He
assumed he would be presentable to the two women.

He caught sight of them and watched. It was nice to see Duskya
befriending another woman. Carryl was pretty. Her red hair was pulled
away from her face with a green cloth that matched her eyes. It was rare
to see green eyes around the dragon colony. Every rider had eyes some
shade of blue. She walked with confidence and grace.

"Really, Ruskya," Duskya's voice cut into his thoughts, "I thought you
were beyond womanly charms."

Ruskya felt the heat rise to his face. "If you say so much as one word,
sister, I will…"

"What will you do?" The two women took several steps before
Duskya continued. "Don't worry; your secret is safe."

Then they were there before him. Ruskya felt Carryl's eyes on him and
again was sure the blood was rushing to his face. He felt Duskya's mirth at
his expense.

"Ruskya, are you all right?" Carryl asked. "You look almost as white
as you did last night."

Ruskya breathed a sigh of relief. He could explain that to her.

"My dragon just shared some shocking news with me. I will be fine
once I let it sink in."

He felt Duskya trying to inquire, but told her to wait.

"Honored lady, may I present to you, my dragon, Wyeth."

"I am honored," Carryl replied. "May you fly straight and true,"
Duskya laughed aloud at Ruskya's shock.

"She has caught on quite well to the greetings around here," Duskya
added for Carryl to hear also. "I almost thought she had been around
dragons before."

Carryl laughed. "I wish I would have had the honor of knowing
dragons before this, because this is wonderful."

The glow that covered her face had not been there yesterday or in the
general store the day before. Ruskya realized how much dragons could
change a person's life. "Even for the worse sometimes." He thought.

"Why do you say that?" Duskya inquired into his thoughts.

He shook his head. "Later, I promise. When it is you, Glendyn, Mother, oh bother, I suppose we will have to have Kyn and Carryl in on it too. Perhaps I'll send Kyn with Carryl for a lesson in healing; it would be good for a rider to be a healer also. Then it could just be immediate family."

"Family," Duskya replied back into his thoughts. "I like that thought. Glendyn is like a father."

Ruskya's mood shifted. Duskya caught it.

"It's about father, isn't it? I'll be quiet, now." Out loud she said, "I'm sure Glendyn and Ma have the noon meal about ready."

CHAPTER 8: A FAMILY CONFERENCE

UPON REACHING GLENDYN'S DOOR, Ruskya was met by Meredyth who exclaimed, "Ruskya, I heard the dragons! Wryn talked with me." As she hugged him, though, she caught his sadness. She held him a little longer, looking into his eyes, and then nodded.

"The meal is almost ready. Come, wash and sit."

Glendyn came in from out back where he had washed his hands and face at a basin. "If you hurry, you won't have to break the ice off the water," he called. Kyn went scurrying to obey as the others laughed. They all knew what it was like to wash in icy cold water.

Soon everything was ready and they were all seated around Glendyn's table. It was a little crowded, but that just made things a little bit cozier. After a short blessing, they dug into the warm stew and leftover bread Meredyth had brought with her.

Conversation flowed around the table. Ruskya found himself seated between his sister and Carryl. Carryl was glowing with the experiences of the day. Meredyth also was extra happy. Ruskya was sad that he had to bring up news that would change that. He almost understood why the dragons and riders didn't talk about it anymore.

"Is it always this loud?" Carryl inquired, interrupting his thoughts.

"This loud?" She must mean the table talk, he thought to himself. "No," he shook his head, "Glendyn usually eats alone. I often just eat with Kyn. That is a fairly quiet meal, also."

"No," she shook her head, "the dragons. Do they ever stop talking?"

Ruskya paused and looked at her. "What do you mean?"

"Just that. They all are talking at once."

Ruskya called mentally to Duskya to listen in on the conversation.

"Who can you hear talking?" he asked Carryl.

"Well, Wryn and Wyeth are quietly talking among themselves. Then there is Wylen and another dragon, having a game of chase. They are laughing and making all kinds of noise, just like children."

Ruskya called to Wyeth, "Wyeth, do you hear this? Carryl can hear the dragons."

"She is like your father, then. He often complained of the noise around here. That is partly why he moved the hatchling cave away from the colony."

"If she can hear dragons, I wonder..." He then said aloud, "Carryl, what is Wyeth discussing?"

"Well, he was talking with Wryn about someone named Ardyn. They were both very quiet, almost sad. Right now, he is there, but not really. I can't explain it."

At that moment, Wyeth was talking to Ruskya. Ruskya nodded, relieved. "He was talking to me."

"Oh, but why can't I hear that?"

"I don't know, but to be honest I am glad that you can't hear it. Often we discuss personal matters, but other times, we talk about things we would like to keep secret. I would hate to know that someone else could eavesdrop on our conversation."

"That would be bad," she agreed. "As it is, I will get worn down if I am constantly listening to dragon talk."

Ruskya smiled. "Wyeth suggests that you learn how to block it out. Then you can hear it only when you want to and not be worn out by it."

"That sounds like a good idea. He could have just talked directly to me, though."

"He tried, but you didn't seem to hear."

"Maybe if he uses my name, I will be able to hear who is trying to talk to me and what is just background noise." She paused. "Oh, that is better. Tell him thank you."

Ruskya smiled. "You just did. He hears you also."

She sat amazed, gazing into the air. Ruskya let her bask in the feeling for a while before he broached the subject of an herb lesson. She loved the idea, and soon after the meal, she and Kyn headed out for the afternoon.

The remaining four settled into comfortable chairs with mugs of Meredyth's tea. Ruskya took his first sip of tea and sighed. This was what he wanted: to relax with family, to see his mother happy, and to have his sister and Glendyn close by. The peaceful moment was interrupted by Duskya.

"Now, Ruskya, what is this all about?" She demanded, impatiently pushing her dark hair out of her face.

"Patience, Duskya," Glendyn intoned.

"Patience!" she blurted, her silver eyes blazing, "I have been patient—all day yesterday, and now today. When I arrived with Carryl, I found my brother in a teary-eyed mood. He wouldn't tell me a thing until we were all together. We're all together now, and I want to know what is going on."

Ruskya laughed wryly. "I don't know how much you really want to know, sister," he said. "I will try to put it into words."

He paused, and Duskya let him think. When he was ready, he began.

"Glendyn, you were correct about the subject that upset my dragon."

Glendyn looked at him with questions in his eyes. When Ruskya did not continue, he asked, "Someone died?"

"No," Ruskya was quick to assure everyone. He sighed again. "It's about the day the hatchlings were attacked."

Meredyth turned white as a sheet, and Glendyn's small movements stopped. He gazed fixedly at Ruskya. Duskya was the only one left with anything to say or do. She rose and started to pace.

"Would someone please make sense?" she asked quietly.

"Duskya," her brother called mentally, "sit down. It was the day father…" he paused then decided to use the words, anyway, "left us."

Duskya almost fell back into the chair; a helpless sound escaped her lips.

Ruskya let them all regain their composure before continuing. He put into words the pictures he had seen. He explained about the turquoise-blue dragon fire. Then he told them about Wyn: how she had bolted back toward danger, and how Ardyn had gone after her while Wryn and Wyeth helped the others. When he came to the part about the turquoise dragon flying off with Ardyn's limp body in its talons, he paused. How could he tell them that? Glendyn and Duskya could see his memory, but his mother couldn't, and she deserved to know. He took a deep breath and continued. The only sound after he finished was that of Duskya sipping her tea. Finally, Glendyn broke the silence.

"I don't understand why he's telling you this now. I understand that I wasn't able to comprehend Wyeth's thoughts, but why now?"

Before Ruskya could reply, his sister started to speak slowly. "The turquoise dragon. You saw a turquoise dragon yesterday, and it was when Wyeth saw the dragon that he screamed. When he screamed, Wryn went nuts, too. She reacted as if she was hurt. She wouldn't talk, almost *couldn't* talk. The dragon in Wyeth's memory and the one you saw yesterday are the same one, aren't they?"

Ruskya nodded. Glendyn stared, and Meredyth exclaimed, hurt and anger in her pale eyes. "But how? Why did you tell me he was dead? I couldn't believe it without evidence of his body, but why say he was dead when you didn't know?" The pain in her eyes almost drove Ruskya to take back the words. He wished he could, now, but he knew he would not have been able to live with himself if he had kept this from her.

"Ruskya, you did the right thing," Duskya's voice cut through his mind.

"I know, but it doesn't make it any easier."

"No, it doesn't. I'll be here like always, though."

Ruskya nodded to her his thanks.

"Meredyth," Glendyn began as he took her hand, "I told you what Wyden told me, and what I was able to glean from a baby dragon who had never talked before."

"Glendyn," she replied, "he had talked to Ardyn."

Glendyn showed surprise. "Really? Then why was it so garbled when he talked with me? I couldn't make head or tails out of what he said, other than the fact that Ardyn was gone and a dragon was responsible."

"But, Glendyn," Ruskya exclaimed, "that is exactly what happened!"

Glendyn paused thinking, a far-off look clouding his blue eyes. "I guess you are right. It made no sense to me at the time. If you hadn't shared the memory with me, then I would believe it still. It was easier to assume that he had died in the fire. Dragon fire burns hot enough to consume everything."

Meredyth nodded. Ruskya noticed how frail she appeared. Her graying hair was a stark contrast with Glendyn's brown hair with only a few gray strands. Ruskya wondered for the hundredth time how old Glendyn really was. With riders, unless you knew when they were chosen, you could not tell their age. They stopped aging when their dragon reached thirty-six winters, or when the rider reached thirty-six whichever came first. His mother, on the other hand, had almost seen sixty winters.

"What I don't understand," Duskya broke the spell of Ruskya's ponderings to voice a question to all, "is why they attacked in the first place?"

"Right," Ruskya agreed, "and what is Calamadyn?"

Meredyth caught her breath, and Ruskya felt Glendyn's shock as if he had received a physical blow to the stomach.

"Where did you hear that, Ruskya?" Glendyn asked in a tight controlled voice that betrayed none of the underlying turmoil Ruskya could feel emanating from him.

"The dragon rider said that he would get it the next time he came back."

Meredyth put her hand in her face and let out a soft moan. Ruskya thought he heard her murmur, "No!"

"What is this thing that has both of you so upset?" Duskya demanded.

Ruskya inwardly thanked her. She was able to get right to the point when he was more timid.

Meredyth looked up at Glendyn with an almost pleading look. "They need to know."

Glendyn nodded, resigned. "Calamadyn is an herb that your father stumbled upon. He tried to help the hatchlings grow and become strong. He found that if he rubbed it on a nestling, then the egg would become twins. The egg would mold and grow to make room for two hatchlings to come from a single egg. As he worked with it, he soon found that he could inject the oil from the herb directly into the egg, and the egg would grow with two humps. These humps were two dragons. These dragons were better attuned to each other and their riders. They seemed to have different abilities, even for dragons.

"When you two had seen a winter and several seasons, one of these dragons that had been bred with Calamadyn was hurt by a stray arrow. Its twin just about went crazy. The twin's rider was able to keep the dragon from hurting himself, but not before he hurt another rider who was trying to help calm him. Your father vowed then and there to stop using the herb. Unfortunately, it was not that easy. The riders had gotten used to the idea of having extra dragons for processions and the villagers had found more of their children being sent off when they reached ten winters. To up and stop that would dry up half of the dragon reproduction; it was impossible. Your father started to wean away from using it, but there was rebellion and dissension in the colony.

"Several riders went looking for other dragons and tried to start their own colony. Looking back now, I think they must have found other dragons and riders, for where else could the turquoise dragon have come from? Unfortunately, the dissension led to your father being beaten for his views, and threats on the lives of your entire family. We thought the worst was behind us when the attack came one day without warning. No one could understand how a dragon could attack other dragons—let alone hatchlings. At that point, we decided to mourn our loss and move on. Since your father was the one who knew how to use Calamadyn, the knowledge died with him. We figured it was better to forget."

Glendyn fell into silence, but Meredyth picked up the conversation.

"When your father saw the way the dragon twins reacted when one was hurt, he became concerned for his own children."

At the look of question from both of the twins, Meredyth continued. "I could not bear children. Yet both your father and I wanted children badly, so badly that I asked him to see if the herb would work on humans. I used it in my tea for several months. Finally, I became pregnant. Your father believed that because of Calamadyn you would be closer, just as the dragons were. He wanted to see what would happen if Calamadyn dragon twins chose Calamadyn human twins. He didn't have that thought in mind during the night we spent in the hatchling cave, but he often wondered if Wyeth and Wryn had chosen their riders that night."

Ruskya felt Glendyn tense up. This was news to him, Ruskya realized.

Meredyth continued. "When they didn't choose at the procession, Ardyn had mixed emotions. He was afraid he had disturbed the order of things, yet at the same time he was excited thinking that maybe his twins had been chosen. At that time, he was also considering a change to the order of the processions. He thought younglings of any age should be allowed to come to a procession, and that a dragon should not be limited by who is around, but should be able to choose freely from the villagers."

"You mean to tell me," Glendyn said with more emotion than

Ruskya had ever heard in his voice before, "that these two were at the hatchling cave before the procession of Wyeth and Wryn?"

Ruskya knew his mother could feel the accusation from Glendyn, but she didn't back down. "Yes, it was when the threats had come. Ardyn was afraid to let us stay in the abode alone overnight, and he had to be there for the nestlings that were ready to hatch. Wyeth and Wryn would be ready for the procession that winter. I brought the twins with me. Duskya eventually meandered over to Wryn, and Ruskya went toward Wyeth. They slept together that night." She paused as she controlled her emotions. "Ardyn was wrong, though. He thought they were safest sleeping with a dragon. It was a dragon that took him."

This last statement seemed to diffuse some of Glendyn's anger. Ruskya decided to help more.

"Glendyn, we went through the procession properly. No one else needs to know about the earlier choosing, if you don't want them to."

Glendyn thought it over. Ruskya controlled any thoughts of pleading. He didn't want Glendyn to be influenced by his thoughts.

"You are right. Your dragons were wise to wait. This could cause problems though, now that the last three dragons have chosen riders in an unconventional way."

"How would it cause problems?" Duskya asked. "It may go against tradition, but aren't the dragons the ones to choose, anyway? Why shouldn't they be given the chance to choose whom they desire?"

"You are so much like your father, it is going to be the undoing of me." Glendyn groaned, rubbing his hand across his face. "We cannot change tradition just like that! It takes time, and requires the changing of people's opinions."

"People's opinions are already starting to change," Ruskya quietly pointed out. "The procession this year was not just younglings of ten winters. For the next procession, why not invite all of the children who want to come—they can be any age their parents think is acceptable. Riders should not force others to come for a choosing. I don't think a dragon would want to choose someone who is unwilling."

Glendyn thought about it. "We have another winter before we must decide what to do. Until then, let's deal with what we have. We have one set of Calamadyn twin dragons with Calamadyn riders. Let's work together and prepare for the turquoise rider."

"I hate to disturb your nice neat box, Glendyn," Meredyth interrupted, "but you have another Calamadyn rider."

"Who?" Glendyn asked. "I thought the knowledge died with Ardyn."

Meredyth looked at him and shook her head. "You should know better than that, Glendyn. Ardyn wasn't the herbalist; I am."

He stared at her. "Knowing all you know about the herb, who would you give it to?"

"Someone with four daughters who wanted to have a son more than anything."

Glendyn still just stared uncomprehending. Ruskya decided to help a bit; he thought toward Glendyn, "Kyn."

Slowly, confusion took the place of incomprehension. "But Kyn isn't a twin."

Meredyth smiled, "He is; his twin is not living anymore."

"When Kyn was young, his twin died suddenly in the night," Ruskya added. "His father mentioned it when we were last there."

"That would explain why he could speak to you, Ruskya. I wonder what other things he will be capable of."

They fell into a thoughtful silence, which was broken for Ruskya by a mental call from Kyn, "Honored rider, we're back. Is it okay to return to Glendyn's abode?"

"We are done," Ruskya answered him. "Come warm up."

He decided to try something different and called to both Duskya and Glendyn, "Kyn is back. He'll be here shortly."

Both of them replied, almost simultaneously, it was almost difficult to keep the meanings straight. He pieced together an acceptance in their replies. Ruskya decided that next time he would let them know there were two conversations going on. That was too difficult to do more than once.

Next, Ruskya decided to talk with Meredyth; after all, she had heard the dragon's voices today.

"Ma," he called. He didn't have to wait long for a reply.

Meredyth immediately looked up at him and replied, "Yes, Ruskya?"

"I-I," he stumbled surprised at the immediateness of the reply, "I was just wondering if you could hear me."

Meredyth's shocked expression told volumes. At her audible answer to an inaudible question, both Glendyn and Duskya had glanced up. They smiled realizing what was going on.

"Don't worry, Meredyth," Glendyn called to her.

Duskya added her own voice, "Ma, this is how Ruskya and I communicate all the time. It is how the dragons communicate."

"Oh," Meredyth replied somewhat amazed.

"See if you can call back to us," Ruskya suggested. "Just think what you want to say in your mind."

The three riders saw the concentration on her face as she tried to communicate, but none of them heard anything.

"Couldn't you hear me?" Meredyth asked in exasperation.

The others shook their heads, but Ruskya added mentally, "Don't worry, Ma. Remember, just two days ago, you couldn't hear dragons either. Now you have heard two."

Meredyth's face lifted. "You are right. I can now hear my children's dragons, and I can hear my children."

Glendyn looked up at that comment. "Meredyth, didn't you hear me?"

Her gaze met his and she saw the disappointment there, but slowly had to shake her head. "I'm sorry, Glendyn, I didn't."

Glendyn let the disappointment slide for now. He reached out to Kyn and called, "See if you can tell Meredyth that you are coming."

"Yes, honored rider," Kyn replied; then he turned to Meredyth, "Honored lady, we are back."

Meredyth's eyes got big. "Kyn is back?"

Duskya laughed, "Yes, he's coming."

"Honored lady, it was wonderful!" the youthful voice went on, "The things you can do with plants to help people and animals is amazing!"

Meredyth laughed. She forgot Kyn was not right there. "Yes, it is amazing."

The others looked at her; then Glendyn said, "Maybe long-distance communication should be kept to simple matters of conveying information, not conversations."

Meredyth looked at him and then realized what she had done. "Oh, yes, maybe that would be better."

At that moment Kyn opened the door. Carryl's voice trailed him from behind. "Young one, aren't you supposed to knock on the door or something? This is an honored rider's house, not your own."

Glendyn got up and went to the door. He ruffled Kyn's hair as he passed the youngling, "You should have explained that you already did," he mentally reprimanded the boy, but it didn't phase Kyn; he continued with his exuberant conversation with Meredyth.

Glendyn called to Carryl. "Come on in, honored healer. We were expecting you. Kyn sent a dragon rider call out to let us know you were here."

Ruskya was surprised at Glendyn's bending of the truth. Yes, certain riders—namely four—seemed capable of communicating this way, but not all riders. What was Glendyn up to?

"How was your day, Kyn?" Duskya asked.

"It was wonderful!" Kyn, in his eagerness and excitement, forgot to add 'honored rider.' Ruskya decided to ignore it this time. "The things you can find to help animals and humans right at your feet!" Kyn continued. "It is amazing! I never realized the things I was stepping on."

The others laughed.

"He is a quick learner," Carryl added. "You have a good pupil, Ruskya."

"I don't know if he realizes how blessed he is," Glendyn commented. "Having a student who is able to learn is half of the work of a teacher."

Ruskya noticed Kyn's face and smiled. He remembered when he would blush at the slightest compliment. He was glad he was past that stage. He decided to rescue his youngling.

"It's probably time for my youngling to head home and get the fire going for supper."

"Yes, honored rider," Kyn said. Mentally, he added, "I already did, but they don't need to know that do they?" Ruskya sent a smile to him.

"No they don't. That would just add to their razzing you about being such a wonderful student."

Kyn bid everyone good eve and headed out the door. Meanwhile, Duskya had agreed to have Carryl stay with her until the healer could find something more suitable.

"I wish I had a youngling who could get my abode warm," Duskya commented.

Ruskya mentally called to Kyn, "No more slothfulness. Head over to Duskya's and start her fire." He then switched to his sister, "Wish granted, honored sister."

"What?" Duskya started to ask him, then understood. She sent a silent thank you to Kyn.

"Ruskya and Duskya," Meredyth said, "Glendyn has agreed to take me home. I have enjoyed my time here today more than you could ever know." As she gave them each a hug, she added, "I will cherish the memory of this day."

"I would love to see you come back, Ma," Ruskya informed her.

"Me, too," Duskya added.

"Well, we'll have to wait and see," Meredyth said. "I'll talk with Glendyn on the way home. I always was able to get him to do things for me, even when I was a child."

Ruskya and Duskya exchanged mental glances. Ma knew Glendyn when she was a child? They decided to ask Glendyn about it later.

With Glendyn leaving, the others decided to leave his abode also. It was, after all, the polite thing to do. Ruskya walked the girls over to their abode and then headed home.

CHAPTER 9: A TRIP TO PHILIPPI CANYON

THE NEXT MORNING, Duskya and Carryl awoke to a winter storm. The cold had crept into the small abode. Duskya stoked the fire to prepare some porridge.

"The dragons are talkative this morning," Carryl commented. "It appears that a couple of the early risers tried to fly from their crags and almost got blown into the rim of the canyon."

"No one was hurt, were they?"

"No, but they all decided they weren't going to leave their crags this morning."

Duskya chuckled. "Sounds like a good idea. I've never liked being out in the snow and wind, either."

"I would hate to have to try to get up to the crags to help a wounded dragon," Carryl added. "I'm fairly nimble of foot, but those crags are extremely high."

"That they are. I have only been up in the crags when Wryn has taken me up. I wouldn't want to try to climb it at all."

"That makes sense. I'll have to see if one of the dragons will take me up there, just so I can familiarize myself with the layout. I don't want to have to do that during an emergency."

"I hadn't thought of that," Duskya mused. "I might be able to have Wryn take you up."

"Or Wyeth," Carryl added. "He was a big help yesterday afternoon."

"What do you mean? What did Wyeth help with?"

"Kyn and I went to Philippi Canyon on our herb exploration. When I got there, I wondered if having some dragon eyes would be better than my regular old eyes. So, I asked Kyn to call Wylen and I called Wyeth. Both of them came. To be perfectly honest, I don't think Wyeth has a future in herbology, though Wylen, on the other hand, could. He was able to pick out the right herb from above the canyon rim. Wyeth seemed skittish near the south end of the canyon."

Duskya's disbelief spread across her face. "You called Wyeth when you were in Philippi Canyon, and he came?"

Carryl's face was the exact opposite; calm as if she had done nothing out of the ordinary. "Yes."

Duskya just stared at her. Finally, she asked, "Does Ruskya know?"

"I don't know. I didn't think it was important at the time. Obviously, I was wrong. Did I misjudge some protocol?"

"Well, usually, no one can call another's dragon that way. Secondly, even if we could talk with the other dragons, the riders consider it impolite to talk to another dragon if you are not standing with the rider."

"Oh, I didn't know. I thought, since you were all conferencing in Glendyn's abode, that it wouldn't be a problem."

"I doubt it was a problem. I am just surprised, is all."

Duskya set about preparing the porridge. While she did this, she decided to wake up her brother. "Hey, sleepyhead," she called. "It's time to be up and awake."

"Who are you calling sleepyhead, sister? I'll have you know that I have been up and out at personal peril. This storm is not the average storm. I almost got lost going out for firewood."

"Well, are you okay?"

"Yes, but I think today is going to be a day to stay inside."

"Carryl says the dragons decided to stay in their crags also since a couple were almost hurled into the Canyon rim."

"Are they okay?"

"She says they are. She also says that Wyeth went with her to Philippi Canyon yesterday."

"I heard," Ruskya said dryly. "I also heard that she called him from Philippi Canyon, and he went."

"Yes. She also said that Wyeth ignored the southern end of the canyon."

"I'll ask him about that. In the meantime, I had a talk with Wyeth about just traipsing off with any old person. You know what he told me? He said, 'Carryl isn't just any old person. She's one of us, and one of you.' He wouldn't tell me what he meant."

"He said that?"

"That he did. He seemed to think it was the same as answering a call from you."

"That's an interesting thought. Well, our breakfast is about ready. Have a good day!"

"See you later, maybe."

* * *

They didn't see each other for three days. The snow and wind continued to blow as they entertained themselves with various training techniques: Carryl tried to communicate with other dragons and introduce herself to them; Kyn worked on communicating mentally, and on blocking others from reading his thoughts; Duskya and Ruskya experimented with what they could do. Glendyn was involved in much of this activity, but seemed a little quiet. Ruskya wondered what had happened between Glendyn and Meredyth on the trip back to Woolpren, but thought asking in person would be better. In the meantime, he filled Kyn in on the turquoise dragon and Calamadyn twins.

On the third day, Kyn woke up and announced, "I want out of this dwelling!"

Ruskya agreed. "Let's ask the dragons if they can make it out of their crags. If they can, then we can head out and at least visit others in the colony."

"Wylen says the others are flying around the canyon. They aren't going far from home, but they are out," Kyn replied.

"That's good enough for me. Let's eat first."

After a quick bite, they headed out into the white world. The wind had pushed the snow into piles that stacked up in odd places. Some spots were completely bare of snow, while other spots were three feet deep. Kyn proved that he was still a youngling by collecting snow into a ball and throwing it at Ruskya when he wasn't looking.

Ruskya laughed. "You don't know what you have started, young one. I am the master at snowball launching. Just ask the dragons, they will tell you."

There followed an intense snowball fight. The snow wasn't wet enough to really stick and hold together, but the two managed to at least throw handfuls of the stuff at each other effectively. When Kyn finally admitted defeat, they both were almost drenched and the air around their faces looked like a dragon breathing, as they puffed out of their noses and mouths.

"Now, look what you did," Ruskya reprimanded in play. "We'll have to go change clothes or we will freeze to death out here."

Kyn looked sheepish, and Ruskya caught the intent of his look.

"Oh, no you don't. You just surrendered. You don't want to end up in the snow bank headfirst this time, do you?"

Kyn eyed him, but must have decided that Ruskya could follow through with the threat. "No, I guess you're right. I don't want to go back in yet."

"We will come back out, but first we need to get dry clothes on. That's part of being a rider. You must realize how to take care of yourself so that you can take care of your dragon. If you don't take care of yourself, your dragon will be left to watch out for both of you. That's not Wylen's job. His job is to be a part of you and defend you, but not from yourself."

"From whom?" Kyn wanted to know.

"Good question, youngling. I think I can answer that: I think Wylen will defend you against the turquoise dragon."

Without another complaint, the youngling headed back to the abode.

"I'll change faster than you, rider," Kyn called over his back.

Ruskya laughed, remembering times like this with Glendyn. He needed to pay the older rider a visit and find out what was going on. He wondered if he should ask to see the memories, or if there was a better way to address it. He didn't think Duskya would have any helpful ideas, but sometimes she got more information out of people then he did.

He changed quickly so Kyn wouldn't beat him back outside by too much, then mentally contacted his sister and told her about their morning. He learned that Carryl wanted to go back out to Philippi Canyon. Ruskya warned against it, unless Duskya and two dragons went with her. He was afraid of the snowdrifts. Duskya agreed to keep him informed of their plans.

By the time Ruskya finished changing and talking to Duskya, Kyn was back outside. The look on the youngling's face said, "I told you so."

Ruskya decided to ignore it for now. He wondered how many of those looks Glendyn had ignored. It was a way of life for younglings to want to challenge their teacher and prove themselves better in something.

They wandered over to the small off canyon and called Wylen and Wyeth down. The dragons seemed as eager to be free as the riders were. Ruskya wondered if Wylen's attitude had rubbed off on Kyn. If Kyn had been younger, or Wylen just a little older, he would have let the two try a first flight, but Kyn's weight was still too much for Wylen to handle.

"Kyn, go have fun with Wylen. Enjoy the outdoors. Get your energy out. Find other riders and enjoy their company. I'm going to go find Glendyn."

"Yes, honored rider," Kyn mentally replied, back to being serious.

Ruskya just shook his head and thought, "What am I going to do with him?"

"You'll keep me and teach me everything you know. You'll guard my back when Wylen is guarding my front," Kyn replied.

Ruskya looked back, "You heard that?"

"Yeah," Kyn answered out loud. "I thought you meant for me to hear."

It was Ruskya's turn to look sheepish. "Not really, I must not have held my thoughts close enough to myself. Duskya can sometimes hear my thoughts even when I am not planning on her hearing them."

"I'll be careful," Kyn replied. "I don't want to hurt you, honored rider."

Ruskya nodded. "I understand. Go have fun, and yes, I will guard your back."

Ruskya went to find Glendyn. The older rider was probably flying with his dragon. Ruskya called Wyeth back and climbed aboard. The cold air rushing through his lungs felt good. He laughed into the wind.

"Wyeth, I love this! I wish I didn't have to go down to earth sometimes."

"I know. Unfortunately, then you wouldn't have your friendships with the others."

"True, but isn't a rider's relationship with his dragon enough?"

"No, a rider needs other people. A rider really needs a mate, just as dragons need mates. I have noticed the lack of mates in our colony. It does not sit well with me. I remember in my hatchling years there were always dragon pairs around. Now, they are just the few old dragons from before. The new dragons don't seem interested in mating."

Ruskya thought about it. Wyeth was right. That was the reason for the lack of hatchlings. There were a few older dragons who were still mating and producing eggs, but they were almost beyond the egg-bearing years. Why weren't the younger dragons mating?

"I don't know," Wyeth answered his unspoken question. "They seem more interested in their riders or in their nest mates to worry about mating."

"What about you, Wyeth?"

"I am coming up on that time. I will be old enough to mate in five winters, but I have not found a dragon that I would want to mate. I would want to mate for life."

Ruskya hadn't thought about it. Why didn't the riders marry? Was it the same reason? Had Glendyn never found someone he could love? And what about himself? His relationship with his twin seemed to take all the time he ever had. He never really looked at any other woman.

"What about Carryl?" Wyeth asked.

"What about her?"

"You like her, don't you?"

Ruskya felt the heat fill his cheeks. "Do you have to get that personal?"

"We were asking about mates. She is new to the colony."

"Yes, but she isn't a rider. I don't think I could watch my wife die before my eyes and know I had possibly several hundred more winters left."

"True. But, I think Carryl is going to find a dragon, or a dragon is going to find her."

"If you say so," Ruskya replied. "You have interesting ideas about that woman anyway. You say she is family, and you let her call you."

"I can't explain it, Ruskya, but she fits in here. I would do all in my power to protect her. It is as if she is my rider also."

Ruskya was shocked. "Do other dragons feel that way about her?"

Wyeth paused, "Wryn says she does, but she is family. I would have to ask the others, and I don't know if that is wise with Carryl listening in."

"Do the other dragons realize she can hear their conversations?"

"I don't know. She has introduced herself to almost all the dragons in the colony. When she talks with us, it is different from talking with you. It is more like talking with a dragon." Wyeth paused and thought. "It is like talking to your da. I talked with him the way I talk with the other dragons."

"Maybe that is why you feel so protective of her. Maybe she reminds you of Ardyn, and you don't want the same thing happening to her."

"That could be," Wyeth agreed. "There is one thing, though, that I won't do for her, but I might do for you."

When the dragon didn't continue, Ruskya urged. "What?"

"I won't go to the hatchling cave for her, but if you want to go, I will take you there."

Ruskya felt the air leave his lungs. The hatchling cave where his da disappeared? Did he really want to go there? After a moment's pause, he realized what his heart's desire was.

"Wyeth, I think I would like to go there. You let me know if the memories are too painful, and we will leave. Okay?"

Without a word, the dragon changed direction. A short flight brought them to Philippi Canyon. Wyeth headed toward the southern end, and Ruskya noticed that it became a bottlenecked canyon there. From the air, it almost looked like a person could step across at its narrowest section. Wyeth flew down to the canyon floor at an archway. Ruskya recognized it from the memory his dragon had shared.

The rider dismounted and gazed up at the rock. He could still see the turquoise dragon with his head ducked out of the archway and the rest of his body covering the entrance to the cave-like canyon. In the talons of the dragon lay his da. Ruskya put a hand on Wyeth.

"How are you doing?"

Wyeth gave him a small nudge with his head. Ruskya shook the image of the turquoise dragon from his mind and started to walk with Wyeth. They entered the opening, which was barely large enough for the two to walk through abreast. Sagebrush grew on either side. The snow had piled into the corners, but left a clear path in the middle. After the archway, the narrow canyon led for about three spans further in. After those three spans, the canyon became a cave. It widened out and had a large amphitheater-style look to it. There was a hole up at the top of the cave large enough for a dragon to fit through at a dive. Ruskya assumed it would let smoke out of the cavern from a fire pit. He walked toward the center, while Wyeth split off and meandered toward the side. There didn't seem to be anything left from twenty-two winters ago. Ruskya found the remains of a fire. It looked like someone had recently stayed here. He noticed Wyeth sniffing at a place that almost resembled a nest. The dragon started to paw at something there.

"What did you find, old one?"

"I don't know."

"Do you want some help?"

"Not yet. I'll let you know."

Ruskya tried to envision his da in this cave surrounded by nestlings and hatchlings. It was hard to imagine, since he had only seen five nestlings in his fifteen winters as a rider. He wondered if Wyeth was right about the dragons not mating. Out of the blue, the picture of Carryl's red head and green eyes seemed to fill the area. It was as if she could make things right here. Ruskya shook his head. It was the dragon messing with his mind. He wandered over to the edge of the cave. It looked like whoever had camped out here had used this side as a bedding down place. Ruskya bent down to look and a presence seemed to come at him. It was the turquoise dragon rider!

Ruskya spun around expecting to see the rider, but there was no one there.

"Wyeth," Ruskya called with a slight quiver to his voice, "Are we alone?"

Wyeth reached out with his dragon sense, then replied. "There is no one here, but there is a feeling that someone has been here. I do not know who, but I do not like the presence that has lingered, even after the storm."

Ruskya thought for a moment and then replied. "Is it possible that someone stayed here through the storm and just left this morning?"

"Possibly."

Ruskya went back over to the fire. He tried to tell how old it was, but he had never been very good at that. Next, he decided to look for tracks other than his and Wyeth's. He found a boot print and a dragon print. The dragon print was too large for Wyeth.

"Wyeth, you may want to see this. I think a dragon was here."

"I know he was here," Wyeth's voice carried an ominous threat as he called from where he had been scratching in the dirt. "I found a scale. Do you want to guess at the color?"

Ruskya looked over and then blended his sight with Wyeth's. "It's the turquoise dragon! Why would he return here?"

"He was looking for Calamadyn, right? Why not start where he knew it had been last used."

"That makes sense. But why stay on after the trials?"

"I don't know. He may have decided to work with Kyle for a while and holed up here. The storm hit and they had to wait it out."

"True." Ruskya nodded his blond head. "And I did find boot prints. I don't think the rider wore boots with heals, but Kyle did. I'll keep looking."

No matter how hard they searched, they didn't find anything else. Numerous plants grew inside the cave. It seemed the place sheltered them from the severe weather outside. They were about to go when Ruskya felt another dragon approach.

"We're not alone, Wyeth."

"I know, but it is okay. It is Glendyn and Wyden."

Ruskya looked at Wyeth. There was no way out without meeting the other rider. Ruskya seemed to know that Glendyn didn't want to have company, but there was no helping it. Ruskya decided to let his trainer know they were here.

He first tried to get an idea of where Glendyn was: he was outside at the archway. It was almost as if he was debating coming in or not.

Ruskya called to him. "Glendyn, go ahead and come in."

"Ruskya," the call came back holding surprise, "what are you doing here?"

"Wyeth brought me out. I didn't want to scare you, so I thought you should know we were here."

Ruskya felt the nod that Glendyn gave and sensed the rider moving forward. He let the older rider privately hold his own thoughts close throughout the passageway and when he first stepped into the cave. Ruskya could tell that Glendyn was struggling with memories as he walked to the center fire pit and knelt down.

"How often did we talk right here? It was like when he was a child and we would go camping, only I was the one with the wife, then."

Glendyn fell silent. Ruskya didn't think the older rider knew he had spoken aloud. He let the rider gather his thoughts. Glendyn stood and walked over to a side nest that Ruskya hadn't noticed.

"The only nest to stay intact. It's not much to look at after twenty-two winters, but it once held the hope of the colony—Calamadyn twin dragons. What went wrong? Why do the dragons not mate? It has been too many seasons for me to continue as if all is well. Too many generations have gone by."

Ruskya pondered this. How old was Glendyn? He'd had a wife at one time—what had happened to her? The older rider was voicing the thought-provoking questions that Ruskya and Wyeth had been discussing earlier.

Finally, Glendyn turned and crossed the cave. "Ruskya, my son, you are the hope of this generation of riders. If you cannot figure out how to change things, then the riders will die here."

Ruskya was shocked. What did Glendyn mean?

"I mean that the dragons are dying out. Our dragons are not mating like they should be. If there are no new dragons, then Kyn will be the last of the riders. I will not take another youngling for a single dragon and deny him the companionship he needs. Kyn is doing okay because he is a Calamadyn twin. In being a twin, he can communicate with all of us. It seems that Calamadyn twins don't need the other companions the way other younglings do."

Ruskya understood then what Wyeth had said earlier. "Maybe that is true of Calamadyn dragons also, honored rider."

Glendyn thought it over, "You mean that the dragons have their companion in their twin and don't need a mate? I hadn't thought of that."

"Neither had I," Ruskya admitted. "It was Wyeth who saw that."

"We need to find a way to change things. I think Carryl will help. Will you work with her?"

Ruskya swallowed then nodded. "Sure. She wanted to come out to Philippi Canyon, but I told Duskya they should come together and with another dragon."

"I felt someone up at the other end of the canyon."

Ruskya watched Wyeth preen in the sun that shone through the center hole of the cave creating dust rays. Turning back he decided to ask Glendyn about some of the things that had bothered him.

"Glendyn, do you mind if I ask you some personal questions?"

Glendyn shook his head. "Go ahead, son." Ruskya smiled. He noticed the older rider used the title son more and more often, and he liked hearing it.

"I was wondering about the relationship between you and my parents."

"What about it?" Glendyn encouraged him.

"Ma said she could always get you to do as she wished when you all were children, much to Da's dismay. I just heard you say that the times around the campfire pit were like when Da was little; you also mentioned a wife."

Glendyn silently nodded his head and took a deep breath. "Ruskya, you deserve to know this. Your parents were my niece and nephew."

Ruskya stared at him in disbelief, "But they said no one in my family had been a rider!"

Glendyn shook his head, "My brother was your great-grandfather. When I was chosen as a rider, and he wasn't, he didn't want anything to do with riders. He forbade me to come around his family, and I accepted it, like a fool. I was too interested in dragons and the colony. I didn't need family."

"Many winters passed. My brother was killed in an accident. I decided to go into Woolpren for the burial. I met a girl there, Caralyn. She was pretty, kind, and understood as much as a non-rider could about the ways of a rider. After a winter, I married her. We never had any children. It was a pain for Caralyn; she loved children. She was a healer, like Carryl. She helped at many births. One such birth was your ma's. Unfortunately, after the birth, your ma's ma died. Caralyn wanted to adopt your ma, but your grandfather would not hear of it, though he did let us help around the abode. Yes, your ma could have just about anything she wanted from Caralyn and me. The world revolved around her. As your ma grew, she met Ardyn, and brought me back into contact with my great-nephew. At first I didn't tell Ardyn that he was my nephew. Even from the beginning, though, he seemed to like the idea of dragons. When he found out I was a rider, he wanted to meet Wyden. I was a little leery about that, but finally he cajoled me into it. Actually, it was Meredyth asking that broke my resolve."

He paused in the telling for a while allowing his blue eyes to sweep the cavern, then continued. "Looking back, maybe it would have been better if I hadn't introduced him to Wyden, but then you wouldn't be here either." He smiled and put his hand on Ruskya's shoulder.

"Well, he immediately won Wyden's heart, and soon all the dragons were clamoring for him to stay. It was shortly after he joined the colony as nestkeeper that my Caralyn died. I mourned her, as did your ma and da. Some of the other riders criticized me for marrying a non-rider and said behind my back that it was only just. I shut my heart away that day and vowed not to let anyone else get that close to me again. Your parents had a way about them that broke down that barrier. Yet, when your da died, I withdrew from the world around me. I hurt your ma in the process, something I had vowed I would never do. I ignored her for the next eight winters. I often wanted to go see her when I was in the village, but I let my responsibilities as rider and trainer get in the way.

"I didn't see her until the day Duskya opened the door of your abode. It was a shock, to say the least. That was when I promised her to take care of you both. After all, you were family. If Caralyn had her way, you would have been my grandson and my great-great-nephew at the same time. Talk about a confused child." A chuckle escaped him, and he continued.

"You didn't need that confusion to begin with. I think you can handle it now. Your ma asked that I share this with you also. I came out here to try to think. So, do you think badly of me?"

"Badly, why? You did what you thought best. I-I just, I never thought that you were that old. I always thought of you the same age as Da."

Glendyn laughed a full-hearted laugh. "No son, I am not the same age as your da, although my body is the same age as he was when he died. Remember: to tell a rider's age, you have to judge their dragon's age. The larger the dragon, the older the rider."

"Glendyn," Ruskya said almost in awe, "then the turquoise dragon is another generation past Wyden."

Glendyn nodded. "He has seen many winters. His rider is very cunning, from what I gathered from the trials he set out for you."

"Wyeth and I think he came here after the trials with Kyle and got stuck here in the storm."

"What makes you say that?"

"Wyeth found a scale. I found a boot print similar to Kyle's and the fire pit has been used."

Glendyn knelt down and looked at the pit. "You're right. It was used last night, but not this morning. Where is the scale that Wyeth found?"

Ruskya and Glendyn walked over to where Wyeth had found it. It was still on top of the ground in plain sight. Glendyn bent down, picked it up, and examined it.

"It is a normal scale. No strange markings or disease seem to be present. Nevertheless, I think I will keep it to be safe. I hear the others are coming this way. Should we go meet them, son?"

Ruskya swallowed a lump in his throat and nodded. He couldn't talk if he wanted to. Glendyn bent over and gave Ruskya a hug. Ruskya responded and hugged him back. Glendyn might not be the da Ruskya had lost, but he was still family.

"Thank you, Glendyn. You know, you will have to tell Duskya your story, or she will feel left out."

"That's the problem with Calamadyn twins." He laughed. "Let's go tell your sister that her family is growing."

Ruskya smiled. It was good to have family. He realized that talking to Glendyn about mates might not be such a bad idea after all. There were still questions roaming through his head, but for now they could wait. He resolved to enjoy each day as it came, and to find out who the turquoise dragon was and what he had done with his da.

CHAPTER 10: CALAMADYN

"**DUSKYA, LOOK** at this one," Carryl called to her new friend.

Three days locked in the same abode had cemented their friendship. It had been many winters since Carryl had a real friend. She had always been on the farm, never allowed to go into town unless it was to deliver milk or eggs—that didn't engender friendships.

"What did you find?" Duskya called. She was somewhat distracted by Ruskya's feelings. She wasn't sure where he was, but he had heard some disturbing news. She considered calling to him, but decided to let him contact her, if he needed her.

Carryl pointed to a small plant that had survived the storm. With care, she uprooted the plant and placed it into her bag. Duskya realized her home was soon going to be overrun by plants if something didn't change. Carryl had already picked up three others, and was now approaching yet another plant growing alongside the canyon wall.

"Duskya, have you ever seen this plant?"

Duskya came over to look. "What is it?"

"I don't know. It is dormant right now, but look at this leaf. It is similar to what your ma puts in her tea."

Duskya looked closer. "Not exactly, but I see what you mean. This one has another angle to it. Ma's are three-sided leaves. This one is four-sided," she paused, then added. "If it is dormant, how did you find the leaf?"

"It was still attached. It was as if it was hanging on for dear life," Carryl explained. "I've never seen anything like it, other than in your ma's tea."

She put the leaf in her pouch and pulled out some paper and a stub of charcoal with which to write. Duskya had been impressed with the healer's note taking. Each plant that they had disturbed in any way was noted and then placed on a hand-drawn map.

Carryl had just put the leaf away and turned to go on when she suddenly paused in her movements.

"What is it?" Duskya asked.

"Wyden and Wyeth are here in the canyon somewhere. They just found Wyn and Wryn."

"Well, before we leave, I'll call to Ruskya. How much more ground do you want to cover before we leave? It is almost midday."

"Let's just do this last corner here," Carryl said. "I am getting hungry."

Duskya agreed. She let her thoughts roam to Ruskya and Glendyn. She tried to read their conversation, but it was too well shielded. She had noticed that since the run-in with the turquoise dragon, Ruskya's thoughts could be harder or easier to read, depending on his mood. There were times when he was not saying a thing, but his thoughts flowed to her readily. When she tried to proactively read his thoughts, though, she almost couldn't anymore. She did sense that the current discussion was a conversation concerning her.

Carryl quietly worked for another quarter glass, before Duskya heard Ruskya's call.

"Sister, where are you?"

"We are at the north end of the canyon. Here." She looked around her and then looked toward the south of the canyon. She sent the mental image to her brother.

"We'll be there shortly," he called back.

Within moments, Duskya saw the dragons in the sky. They landed nearby; the riders dismounted, and walked over to the women. Ruskya gave his sister a hug.

"Don't ask," he replied to the question he knew was coming. "Glendyn will talk with you later. It's good news, though."

She nodded. "If you say so, brother."

"What have you found?" Glendyn asked Carryl. "Any interesting plants?"

"Oh, yes," she replied, "the typical herbs around here."

"Like what?" Glendyn asked. "Did you find any thyme, rosemary, or chamomile?"

"Yes," she looked puzzled. "You know your herbs?"

Glendyn laughed. "Don't look so shocked, healer. I was actually married to a healer. She was constantly making sure I had the right teas to keep me healthy. I tried to tell her that a rider stays healthy because of his dragon, but she wouldn't believe me." A wistful look came to his face with the memory.

Duskya shot her twin a questioning look, but Ruskya just grinned at her. "There's more where that came from," he mentally told her.

Carryl, seeing that Glendyn truly was interested, started to walk back over the land she had covered and shared what she had found. Ruskya found it intriguing that anyone could know so much about the land and the plants under his feet. He understood why Kyn was so impressed.

"Would you like to see my samples?" Carryl asked after they had covered the whole terrain.

"Why don't we eat our noon meal at my home," Glendyn replied. "Carryl, you can share your findings. Then I can chat with Duskya about a few things."

They all agreed. Ruskya and Glendyn had mounted their dragons before Ruskya realized that Wyn was there. He looked at his sister wonderingly. Duskya just shrugged.

"She got permission from Marysa," she called to him.

He watched as Carryl climbed up on the dragon with ease. Where had she learned that?

* * *

The flight home was uneventful. Ruskya checked in with Kyn and found he had a lunch invitation from another rider. Ruskya okayed it and told him to meet back up before dark.

Glendyn had set a pot of stew on his stove before he had left. The aroma filled the small abode, and they all enjoyed eating and talking together. After lunch, Carryl shared her findings.

"Carryl," Glendyn asked, "have you ever had a place for all your plants before?"

Carryl looked up at him with wonder. "There is such a thing?"

"My wife, Caralyn, had such a place. I could draw up some plans for you."

"I could help build it," Ruskya offered.

Carryl remembered the leaf she had thought was like the tea leaf Meredyth used, and found it at the bottom of her bag.

"Oh, Glendyn, do you know what this is? I found it on a dormant plant."

She handed the leaf to Glendyn. His reaction was profound. He almost dropped the leaf then exclaimed, "Where did you find this?"

"You know it, then? I had never seen it before."

"I know it. I thought I had eradicated every last plant from that canyon."

"What is it, Glendyn," Duskya asked.

"This, young rider, is Calamadyn," Glendyn answered.

Duskya and Ruskya just stared at it. Carryl was still in the dark.

"I've never heard of Calamadyn. What is it?"

Ruskya looked to Glendyn, but Glendyn seemed lost in thought.

"Carryl, you're about to learn some dragon history," Ruskya replied. "It was discovered that, when applied to dragon eggs, Calamadyn could produce twins. It also seems to have this effect in human women who are otherwise unable to have children. The drawback is that these twins have very strong bonds with each other. So much so, that they feel each other's pain. If the pain is bad enough, it can make the other twin insane. If that twin is a dragon…" he let the thought hang in mid-air.

"That wouldn't be good at all," she agreed.

"Therefore, about twenty-two winters ago, it was banned. Now, the turquoise dragon rider wants to find it."

"That's where I had heard the word before. He said it after the trials, before he left."

Ruskya nodded. "I think you also should know that Calamadyn twins can communicate like dragons between themselves and others. I don't completely understand how it works, because it didn't work for many winters, and now it does."

At her lost look, he realized he hadn't said things clearly. "Sorry, I didn't finish my thought. Duskya and I are Calamadyn twins. So is Kyn. His twin died when he was a baby. I don't know if he even knows he had a twin."

She nodded. "That's why there are these blank spaces between you two sometimes."

"Blank spaces?" Duskya asked.

"It's like when dragons talk with their riders. There is a gap in the conversations I hear. Glendyn had said there was a way of dragons and their riders to communicate, so I assumed that's what it was."

Duskya nodded.

Glendyn came back around. "Carryl, do you know exactly where you found this?"

"Sure," she said as she pulled the map from her pouch. "Here is Philippi Canyon. We were in this area here. This is where I found it." She pointed to the map.

"Who drew this?" Glendyn asked.

"I did."

"It is good," he complimented her. "I may ask you to do some maps for me, if you wouldn't mind."

"I would be glad to," she agreed, flushing with the compliment.

"How do you get rid of it, Glendyn?" Ruskya asked.

"Last time I just uprooted all of the plants, and then burned them."

"Aren't you afraid of ruining the other plant life in the area?" Carryl asked. "All plants depend on each other. If one goes missing from the ecosystem, then the others will change over time."

"I hadn't thought of that," Glendyn admitted. "I'll need you to take a look at the plants in the area and see how they work together."

"I could go this afternoon," she replied.

"How are you going to get there?" Ruskya inquired.

"Well, there is that. I suppose I could find a dragon who isn't busy."

"Speaking of that," Glendyn commented, "you can't just go borrowing rider's dragons. Even if the dragon gives you permission, you have to get the rider's permission as well. Is that understood?"

"Yes, honored rider," she agreed, subdued. "It's just that Ruskya said to take a dragon today, and I don't have one."

"I know. You also need someone to go with you. So, if you can find someone willing to make the trip." Glendyn paused and looked toward Ruskya.

Ruskya grinned. He knew he had just been set up, but he didn't mind. He turned to Carryl "I'll go with you, if you can find a dragon"

"You can use Wyden if he will allow you," Glendyn offered.

"Thank you, Glendyn," Carryl said, her green eyes expressing her full gratitude.

The older rider smiled at her. "It is my pleasure."

The two soon left, leaving Duskya and Glendyn to talk. Ruskya knew it would be a good thing. He felt that this trip might be a good thing, too.

CHAPTER 11: THE ATTACK

THE ATTACK WAS SUDDEN and swift. No one knew what had happened. Wyn and her rider were out flying one day, when a projectile hit Marysa. Wyn flew erratically to avoid any more pain. If Marysa hadn't been securely in her saddle, she would have fallen to her death. As Wyn tried to escape, a streak shot past her and pain caught her flank. She cried out, bellowing blue flames toward her attacker, but her opponent had already moved. The pain came again on her opposite side. Once more, she twisted her body and sent blue flames toward the enemy. Nothing seemed to work. Through the haze clouding her mind, she saw the ground coming up to meet her. She spun and raced back to the safety of Three Spans Canyon, calling for help as she went.

Carryl was the first to hear the cries of anguish and agony. She ran to get a rider. The first person she saw was Ruskya.

"Ruskya, help! Wyn and Marysa are hurt. I can't understand more than that."

"I'll go," he called on the run. "Go get supplies ready to help both of them. I'll call Duskya, Kyn, and Glendyn. Kyn can help you."

As he ran, he summoned his friends. He also called Wyeth, who landed in front of him. Ruskya bolted onto his dragon's back and took to the air. He reached out to find Wyn. If Carryl could feel her, then she was within reach of his dragon senses. He felt her cry more than he heard it, and guided Wyeth to it. He sensed the attacker and realized who it was—the turquoise dragon.

"Wyeth, prepare yourself. We are going to fight the turquoise dragon. Wyden will be here soon, but until then, we're on our own."

Wyeth responded by letting out a bellow and an icy blue stream of flames.

"All right, let's go!" Ruskya yelled.

"I'm right behind you," Duskya called to him. "What is it?"

Before Ruskya could get too far into his explanation, he saw Wyn fighting to stay aloft. He sent a mental image to Duskya of what he saw. She responded with a visual of something coming up on his left. Then Ruskya saw the turquoise dragon. His talons were extended and ready to rip into Wyn's left wing. The two dragons were slightly below Ruskya, and Wyn was rapidly losing altitude. With a roar, Wyeth descended slightly so that he was even with the turquoise dragon and let loose a stream of icy blue flames. This was not sparkly dragon courage but real dragon fire. The turquoise dragon broke away from Wyn to face this new and greater danger.

At the same time, Duskya arrived and Wryn sent silver blue flames at the turquoise dragon. If the dragon had been alone, he may have ended off the fight right there, but he had a rider. The rider pulled the dragon back and surveyed the scene. Ruskya again felt the touch of the rider's mind, but this time he was ready to block it.

"So, you come at me with a young and inexperienced dragon?" the rider taunted Ruskya, speaking to him mentally.

"Don't believe him," Duskya's voice broke through the fog that was starting to cloud Ruskya's mind. "He has some way of controlling you. Break it off."

Ruskya nodded and replied to the other rider, "You will not take anyone with you today when you leave. And, leave you will!"

With that, Ruskya sent a mental battle cry to the rider. He also decided to try to probe the rider's thoughts to confuse him. He found if he reached into the rider's mind the way he had with Glendyn's, he would be useless in a fight; so, he let the memories wash over him and continued to probe and confuse as he fought. Wyeth had taken a frontal attack to the turquoise dragon. Talons were out and slashing. Ruskya felt his dragon's pain, but continued to attack. He hoped Duskya was faring better, but there was no time to communicate with his twin.

A reply came, nevertheless. "We are fine. Keep at it. I'll hold Wryn in check from Wyeth's wounds."

Ruskya mentally nodded and urged Wyeth forward. The dragon needed no encouragement. He caught hold of the underbelly of the turquoise dragon. Ruskya clearly saw the veins of darker blue spreading along the scales of the dragon. He wondered if they were blood vessels. The surrealness of the situation caused a distant part of his mind to wonder how he could be attacking a dragon, but then the turquoise body spun and silvery flames licked at Wyeth and along Ruskya's back. Two screams and roars echoed and mixed together in his mind and in the air. Wyeth fell away, as did Wryn. The twin dragons were confused. Ruskya could barely think straight.

"So, you are Calamadyn twins," the rider's voice called. "Both riders and dragons. Interesting. We never were able to produce human Calamadyn twins. How did the scum do it?"

Without meaning to, the rider had broken through some of the confusion caused by the wounds when he mentioned Ardyn. The twins and their dragons rallied.

"My da was NOT scum!" Ruskya screamed.

Then he heard Duskya calling, "Ruskya, no! Don't lose control. He only wants to goad you to do something irrational."

Ruskya nodded, but the rider had heard the call.

"Da, huh? Well, you will be glad to know that he died painfully."

Ruskya breathed deeply. He didn't need to hear this. With great determination, he placed a shield around his mind. He constructed a mental brick wall that extended outward toward the rider. There was no way that the rider could get under, over, or around it. Immediately, Ruskya felt relief. He could no longer hear the rider's thoughts. He saw the rider and the dragon waiting for their next move.

"Wyeth, breathe fire."

Wyeth answered with his fire, as did Wryn. Ruskya quickly rebuilt the brick wall in his mind. He wasn't sure if it would work. When the turquoise flames came, they washed around the dragons, and Ruskya's mind began to burn. He wasn't sure how long he could hold the mental wall. He was about ready to drop the wall, when the fire stopped. The burning continued for a while after, but he then felt relief again.

Duskya interjected. "What are you trying to do, brother? Get yourself killed?"

"We have to give Wyn time to get home, and then we have to make it back without this dragon," Ruskya replied emphatically.

"But we need to do it in one piece."

"Do you have any better ideas?" he demanded.

At her silence, he continued the mental shield and tried to think of a way to get close to the turquoise dragon without getting hit with his flames. It was too painful to try to hold the wall against the flames for long. Suddenly, he flinched as he saw more dragon fire. It took a moment for it to register that it was royal blue and coming from the rider's right. It was not aimed at the twins. Glendyn had arrived!

The turquoise dragon roared and shot flames back at the twins. Wyeth and Wryn dove to avoid them, and only a few spilled onto Ruskya's mental shield. Even so, Ruskya cringed. Wyden continued to spray his dark blue fire as he charged to get a talon through the turquoise wing. Both dragons started to spin. Ruskya was sure they would lose control, but neither dragon did, nor did either manage to get a talon into the other. Ruskya felt Glendyn's indecision a moment before Wyden faltered.

"The rider," Ruskya thought. He broke the mental wall enough to send confusing thoughts to the rider again. This time it was easier. The rider was tiring. The threefold attack had done its job.

"Ruskya," Kyn's voice broke through the mental battle, sounding excited, scared, and small, "Wyn and her rider are back. They are not well."

"Kyn," Ruskya rebuilt his wall once again to take the time to call to his youngling, "take a deep breath. Remember the courage that Wyeth gave you? Use it now. You can help Carryl. Do as she asks. Save Wyn and her rider."

Ruskya mentally removed a few bricks to open a small hole to go after the rider, only to see that he was retreating.

"You have not seen the last of me," the rider called back. "I will get the Calamadyn for me and my dragon. We will have superior dragons!"

"Ruskya, Duskya, come," Glendyn called. "Let's get back home. You both need rest, and I need you to explain what happened. That is one experienced dragon. How did you manage to wear him down so much before I got here?"

Ruskya just shook his head, too exhausted to say anything.

Duskya answered. "I'm not sure exactly, but Ruskya created a shield in his mind and somehow he confused the rider. I was able to see some of how he did it and tried to do the same, but it didn't work as well. Glendyn, he knows we are Calamadyn twins. He said that Da died painfully." With that, Duskya, too, fell silent.

Glendyn could only send comforting thoughts to both of them as they headed home.

CHAPTER 12: THE AFTERMATH

UPON DISMOUNTING at Three Spans Canyon, Ruskya found he could not stand. He held to Wyeth's side as Kyn came running up.

"Hurry, please," the youngling called both mentally and verbally. "Carryl needs help. Please, someone get Meredyth, and the others come with me."

Ruskya stood rooted to the spot, unable to move. Wyeth bent down and nuzzled him. "Little one, climb aboard. I will take you to Carryl."

Ruskya nodded and slowly clambered back aboard Wyeth. Glendyn, who had not dismounted, flew off to get Meredyth. Duskya walked unsteadily after Kyn. Ruskya wasn't able to follow anything Kyn was telling Duskya, but he was able to spot the icy blue sparkles that fell on the boy and on his sister. He mentally thanked his dragon and let his head fall against Wyeth.

* * *

The next thing Ruskya knew he was lying on a bed. He opened his eyes and saw Carryl's green ones gazing at him intently.

"Are you here to stay?" she asked him.

Ruskya nodded. His throat was dry and his mind foggy. He couldn't remember much. He saw not only concern, but also pain in her green eyes.

"Can I leave you here with your sister, and you won't do anything to hurt her or yourself?"

Ruskya looked puzzled. What did she mean? Then he understood. As a Calamadyn twin, anything he did to hurt himself would hurt Duskya also. He nodded that she could go. She stared down at him with uncertainty, but something seemed to pull her away. Ruskya heard an inhuman cry of rage and pain from outside the room.

"I'll be back when I can, Ruskya," Carryl called running toward the sound.

"What is it?" Ruskya thought hoarsely.

"It's Wyn," Duskya replied coming into his field of vision. "Marysa didn't make it, Ruskya." Her eyes were red-rimmed from tears. "Carryl is trying to save Wyn. No one has ever tried that before. Usually, the dragon dies with his rider."

Duskya brought over a cooling tea. "Carryl said to have you drink all of this. It will help clear your thoughts." She paused. "Ruskya, what did you do to the turquoise dragon's rider?"

Ruskya shrugged. What could he say? Even he wasn't sure what he had done. He had done what felt right. He tried to sit up to take a drink, but immediately fell back into the pillow.

"Would you let me help you?" Duskya said, a little perturbed, her eyes flashing like fire reflected in a chrome grate. "There was a time when you couldn't do anything without my help. Now you go off and attack a dragon rider! What are you going to do next? You'll be the death of me."

Ruskya knew that she was just venting her emotions. Especially since all of this was said while she helped prop him up on some pillows and held the mug of tea to his lips.

After a couple of sips, Ruskya replied in a stronger thought, "Without me, you would have a boring life, and you know it, too."

Duskya smiled. "You're right, but it helps to keep you in line. You almost killed us both with that dragon fire shield. What gave you that idea?"

"It worked didn't it? We couldn't have stood up to his fire without it."

"Yes, but next time, let me help you, and we can make it through without the mental wear and tear."

Ruskya tried to sit up, but Duskya pushed him down. "Not yet, silly."

He nodded understanding. "How is Carryl?"

His sister looked at him funny, then replied, "I don't know."

"Well, can you see if you can feel her? I'm too exhausted or else I would do it myself."

Again Duskya gave him that look.

"What?" he asked. "I just want to know if she is okay."

* * *

Duskya stretched her mind to find her roommate. It was easier than she thought it would be, almost like finding Ruskya, but not quiet that effortless. She found Carryl and felt her exhaustion and her struggle to somehow control the wild dragon. Carryl had given the dragon half of an herb remedy and the creature was calming down. Carryl still didn't know if it was going to work or not. She was talking to the dragon in soothing tones, calming her.

Duskya turned back to Ruskya and saw that he was asleep. She sat down and thought about what Ruskya had just had her do. Why had she not taken the training with Glendyn seriously? She had only used it with Ruskya, Kyn, and Glendyn. She decided to try to stretch beyond that. She thought of another rider and immediately located her. The rider was with her dragon, feeling upset at the thought of Wyn and her rider. Duskya pulled away. She reached out to Glendyn and found him. He was with Meredyth. The two were holding each other in a hug. Glendyn seemed to be explaining about the attack. He led her back to Wyden and helped her up. Meredyth seemed to protest, but Glendyn insisted. He put his arms around her protectively.

Duskya pulled away. It was still difficult to think of Glendyn as a distant uncle. He was more like a da. Maybe he would always be that way.

Carryl entered the room.

"How's Wyn?" Duskya asked.

"She's doing better. She's resting, but I can't leave her for long. How is Ruskya?"

"He's sleeping. He was worried about you."

Carryl smiled. "That figures. Is he always like that?"

Duskya nodded. "How are you doing, really? You look exhausted and I'm not even using any extra senses to dig deeper."

Carryl chuckled. "I am tired, but that is the life of a healer. When a patient doesn't come through, it wears on you. Then, when there is another patient that is touch and go, a healer has no time to relax. I will be okay. I am taking breaks and drinking some restorative teas. Meredyth is on her way, I think she will be here shortly. I can't seem to tell distances, but I can feel Wyden's presence."

"Just you be sure to tell us when you need breaks. What you are doing with Wyn is unheard of. Dragons in grief tend to die. I don't know how you are actually getting through to her with your words."

"Well, I don't know if I *am* getting through. And I'm not using words, per se; it's more like images of hope and comfort."

"You're talking to her like a dragon talks to its rider," Duskya said in amazement. "It's a deeper communication than words. It is how Ruskya communicated with me when we were in the battle. He didn't have time for words, but he sent me images of what he was doing. I don't know if he was even aware of it after the first time. I think he just hit a point where things happened without him thinking." She shuddered. "I don't ever want to go through that again, but I have a feeling that until the turquoise dragon is defeated, we'll have to keep fighting."

"Then I will have to find a way to protect dragons and riders from the effects. It is too terrible to have to treat these wounds of the living dead."

Duskya watched Carryl leave the room to tend to Wyn, and sent comforting thoughts her way. She was rewarded with a mental 'thank you.'

"I'll have to try this more often," Duskya thought. "Maybe the reason Ruskya's mind is stronger is because he is willing to try things, when I don't even think of them."

She reached out to Meredyth. Was her ma close enough to find? At first, she had no results. She tried again, this time more determined. She pictured her mother and Wyden. She found Wyden first, and then her ma. Glendyn was helping Meredyth down from the dragon. She couldn't hear the conversation, but she could see that they had just landed at the colony. They moved along toward Duskya's abode where the wounded had been set up. Kyn came up beside them and hugged Meredyth. She returned the hug and seemed to say something to the youngling. He ran on ahead of them.

Duskya's concentration was broken when the door opened quietly. Kyn walked in, a bit out of breath from running.

"Your ma wants to see you," he said in a whisper. "I'll stay with Ruskya. Is he all right?" Fear tinged his voice. Whatever courage had possessed the youngling when they had first landed seemed to have evaporated. The boy was much like Ruskya had been—timid and easily afraid. She wondered what had become of that side of her brother. It wasn't there today in the battle.

"Honored rider?" Kyn prompted. "Is he okay?"

Duskya nodded. "He's just sleeping. He was fatigued beyond anything I have ever seen."

"Carryl says he was even more tired than after the trials of the other dragon rider. Anyway, go to your ma. I'll keep him company."

Duskya took one last glance at her brother and sent comfort to him. She had no reserves of her own to help heal him, but she could give comfort.

"Thank you, youngling," she added and left.

*   *   *

Kyn knew the others were going to stop to see the dragon first. He hated the thought of the dragon rider's death, and shrunk away from the dragon's grief. He didn't want Wyn to die, too, but everyone was saying that she would—that it was the way of life with dragons and their riders. He felt despair overwhelm him, until he remembered Ruskya's admonition to be strong and draw from the dragon courage. He called to Wylen.

"How are you doing, little one?"

Wylen didn't answer.

"Wylen," Kyn called softer and gentler, "can you hear me? Show me where you are. I need to know that you are okay."

The young dragon responded with an image. It was almost overwhelming for Kyn. The little dragon was curled up in a ball in his crag away from everyone. His head was hidden under his wing. A sense of despair and fear came to Kyn.

"Wylen, you are not alone. I am here. As soon as I can, I will come to you. You are safe. No one is going to hurt you. When your turn comes to fight, you *will* be strong, and you'll work with Wyeth and Wryn to defeat the turquoise dragon."

As he said the words, Kyn felt confident that they were right, and he let the words imbue him with confidence and courage. He felt Wylen's spirits perk up. The young dragon lifted his head and looked around, turned around in his crag, and settled down for a relaxing rest. Kyn nodded; it was a good sign.

Next, he reached out to his trainer. He felt awkward at first, but he pushed the feeling aside as he tried to read Ruskya's thoughts. The turmoil that was there almost made Kyn back down. He thought of Ruskya not recovering, and that gave him courage to continue. Thoughts of Wyn being attacked, of turquoise fire billowing around him, of pain and wounds, of Ardyn's death, and of Wyeth's health mingled together in Ruskya's mind. Kyn didn't try to sort through the thoughts; he just let them swirl through him as he helped ease the turmoil.

He took a washcloth and soaked it in the tea Carryl had made, then placed the damp cloth on the rider's forehead. He again reached out and touched Ruskya's thoughts. This time Kyn, dove deeper. He had a theory that the turquoise rider had sent some kind of dark thought deep into Ruskya. He wanted to try to find it and get rid of it. Probing deeply, he found the other rider's presence and the fear that was there.

Kyn jumped when he heard a voice he had never heard before intone, "I will kill you, just like I killed your da." The evil in the voice was chilling. Kyn withdrew for a moment to think. What could he do? He dampened the cloth again and placed it back on Ruskya's forehead.

"Ruskya," he quietly called into the sleeping rider's ear. "Ruskya, you must fight. The rider will not win. He must not kill you. Do you understand? You have bravery, friends, and a dragon that will help you overcome him. You must root out that evil thought and defeat him."

He paused and debated whether he should try again. He heard Meredyth's voice, "I'll check in on Ruskya, and then give you a break, Carryl. You need to get some sleep."

He backed his mind away from Ruskya, but sent some healing thoughts his way while he pressed the cloth on his forehead. He envisioned the tea seeping into Ruskya and dissipating those thoughts.

Kyn greeted Meredyth as she opened the door. "Good afternoon, honored healer."

"I am not the healer, little one; I am the one who just knows the herbs. I don't know how to make them heal like Carryl does. How is he doing?" she queried, resting a weathered hand on her son's forehead.

"I am not really sure." Kyn debated telling her what he had done and decided not to. Instead, he said, "He is sleeping. Duskya was able to get him to drink some tea, and to talk with him for a little bit. I thought of using the leftover tea to soak a compress."

"I hadn't thought of that," Meredyth admitted, "but it could work. I know when he came home the other night, something was affecting his mind, too." She paused. "I brought some of my tea. I'll try to have some ready when he wakes up."

"I'll see that he gets it," Kyn said.

Meredyth sat down beside Ruskya and held his hand. Kyn reached out to Wylen and saw the little dragon curled up, sleeping peacefully. That was good. It looked like everyone was resting. He closed his eyes for a moment. When he opened them, Meredyth was gone. Carryl came through the door and saw Kyn.

"How is he?" she asked in a soft whisper.

"I tried a few things like you showed me," he said, then added, "and a few things of my own."

"Nothing that could harm my patient, I assume?"

"No, more dragon-rider type things," he admitted.

"Riders or that twin bit he was telling me about?"

"What do you mean?"

"He said something about there being a special kind of twin. It has something to do with what the rider is after—that plant I found."

"I don't know about that, I just tried to help heal his thoughts. I also helped Wylen not be so terrified."

"Good. Then you are learning from what I have told you."

"Yes, and trying to combine it with what Ruskya and Glendyn have been teaching me."

"You're a good student," Carryl said, smiling.

"You are tired. Let me help you."

Carryl looked at him. "How deep do you mean to go, young one?"

"I will let you keep your privacy," he said.

She nodded, and Kyn reached out with refreshing thoughts. He thought of the herbs she had taught him and chose one that was good for reviving and energizing. Then he reached into her thoughts. He was careful to stay just on the surface. He found her worry over Wyn, her grief over the dead rider, and her concern for Ruskya—a concern that seemed deeper than Kyn had realized. He respected her privacy though, and left those feelings untouched. He imagined squeezing the healing herb over those troubling thoughts, then pulled back. Carryl's face had relaxed. Kyn waited for a while to see if she would say anything. When she didn't, he quietly backed out of the house and went to visit the injured dragon.

* * *

Carryl rested for almost a glass. She stayed by Ruskya's side, and for a time she was at peace with the world. She didn't know or understand what the youngling had done, but she knew it had worked. She was still aware of the dragon conversations around her, but they were not as intense, nor was the pain from Wyn. She looked down at Ruskya. What was it about this rider that drew her to him? It had been many winters since she had trusted a man, but she trusted him. She couldn't comprehend it. His icy blue eyes flickered as she watched him. They seemed to focus on her and then reach deeper.

"Was it you?" he asked, "Did you bring the peace?"

She shook her head. "No, that was your youngling. He has a way of mending thoughts."

"Kyn," he whispered. "How?"

"He said something about blending what he has learned from you and Glendyn with what he learned from me. Whatever he did, it is nice."

Ruskya looked at her. "Yes," he agreed. "I haven't felt so rested since before our trials at Caravan Canyon. The turquoise rider seemed to set me wrong."

"Well, you will still need to rest tonight. You also received burns. I want you to heal completely before you are up and around."

"Yes, honored healer," he said with a salute.

"Don't mock me, rider," she said, her green eyes flashing.

"I'm not," Ruskya said with dead seriousness. "I see you as an honored healer. I," he faltered, "I wish you were a rider also."

"So, do I, rider. So, do I."

They both fell quiet, and Ruskya drifted back to sleep. Carryl quietly got up and walked around back. She found both Meredyth and Kyn with the dragon. Wyn was calmly lying on the ground. Carryl couldn't tell whether she was distressed.

Meredyth saw her first and greeted her. Kyn looked up shyly. She nodded approval to him.

"How is Wyn doing?" she asked.

Meredyth shrugged. "I don't know. Kyn seems to think she is quieter."

"Have you tried your methods with Wyn, Kyn?"

"No. I didn't think it was right to mess with a dragon."

She nodded. "I understand. You two may go rest for the evening. If one of you could stay with Ruskya until Duskya returns, that would be best."

"I'll stay." Kyn jumped to his feet ready to go.

Meredyth thanked him and headed out.

Before Kyn left, Carryl held out a hand. "Thank you, Kyn. You have something special. Ruskya woke up and wondered if I had given him the peace. He said he hadn't felt that good since before meeting the turquoise rider in Caravan Canyon."

The youngling blushed, but Carryl continued. "Kyn, keep working with your dragon rider healing techniques. They may be needed more than you realize in the coming weeks."

CHAPTER 13: AN UNEXPECTED RIDER

CARRYL WAS ALONE with Wyn. She looked at the dragon, but couldn't hear anything from her. It seemed so strange. Earlier there had been conversation, even if it didn't make any sense; all Wyn could do was incomprehensible muttering and screaming. Now there was nothing. Wyn seemed to be resting peacefully now, but Carryl wasn't sure. She had seen grief before. There was a time in grief where the person would revert inside and not let anyone in. Was the dragon doing that now? She couldn't let Wyn die of grief.

Carryl sat down and called out to her. "Wyn, girl, please come back to me. I need you here. Can you hear me, girl?" She paused. What could she do to reach the dragon? She remembered an herb that sometimes brought energy and life back to a person who had been depressed. She wondered if she had any of it. She dug around in her pouch and found a very small bit left. Crushing it in her hand, she placed the little pieces into a pot. Getting up, she stoked the fire that had been burning nearby. Pouring a little water over the leaves, she placed the pot back near the fire to warm.

She sat back down and reached out to the dragon's mind, trying to find the places the animal would sink into. She blocked out the other dragon conversations buzzing around her and focused in on Wyn. When the water was warm, she made a compress and placed it on the dragon's head. The wing and external wounds were healed; it was Wyn's mind that Carryl was concerned about. Reaching out, she tried to talk to the dragon in ways the creature would understand. She sent pictures of peace, of calm, and of life with the other dragons. Then she decided to try something else. She sent a picture of the turquoise dragon to Wyn. Wyn responded with violence. She tossed and swung her tail around. Carryl had to duck to avoid being hit.

"Wyn, calm down. Take it easy. You have to be well before you can fight the turquoise dragon. We can work together, but only if you get well. Can you do that? Will you let me help you get well?" Carryl felt the nudge ; Wyn was looking at her with gentle questions in her eyes.

"Carryl? Can it be true? Is Marysa gone?"

Carryl sighed. "I am sorry to tell you that she is, but please, stay with me," she pleaded, afraid the dragon would regress back into her grief.

"I will stay, Carryl. I will not leave you." The sound of water dripping off the eaves lent a peace to the evening. "Will you leave me?"

"No," Carryl said with firm conviction. "I will be here as long as you need me."

"Then please, be my rider."

"What?" Carryl asked with disbelief.

"I want you to be my rider. Will you?"

"I would be honored. I never thought there would be a dragon that would want me."

"Since you worked this hard to save me, young one, you deserve to be my rider. No one else has ever done anything like that for me."

"I think you are forgetting a couple of the others who sat with you today."

"No, I am not. It was you who encouraged them to stick with it. I will stick with you."

"Thank you, Wyn," Carryl said from the bottom of her heart. She gave the dragon a hug. "Get well now, will you?"

Carryl felt the affirmative answer. She leaned up against the dragon's warm side. Wyn reached down and snuggled her new rider under her good wing. The two fell asleep like this, and it was how Glendyn found them the next morning.

"What is this?" he asked in awe. "Carryl, are you awake?"

"Hmm," she asked sleepily. She cuddled further under the warm wing. "Is it time to get up already?"

Glendyn laughed. "I don't know what is going on around here anymore, but I do know that we just may have a chance against this turquoise dragon. Carryl, how did you save this dragon?"

Carryl sat up and realized where she was and who was talking to her.

"Oh, honored rider." She floundered for the words as she struggled to stand up. "I-I…" The sun crested the canyon rim and shone in Carryl's eyes. "I don't know exactly. She," Carryl paused. How could she explain what Wyn had asked her last night? Would the dragon still hold to it this morning? "She let me sleep here," she finished lamely.

"Don't worry, Carryl. Whatever you did, it is okay. You pulled her out of her grief. I don't know what she will do from here on out, but she is alive because of you."

"Glendyn," Wyn called to him, "Honored rider, I chose Carryl as my rider."

Glendyn stared at the dragon. "Are you sure? Is this really what you want? If something happens to her..." He didn't finish.

"Then I will do my best to protect her. She is free to share my thoughts and my life."

Carryl was staring at both of them. She had heard dragon conversations before, but she had not heard human and dragon conversations before.

"Who will train her?" Glendyn inquired.

"I will," the dragon answered.

"Very well." Glendyn turned to Carryl and started to speak. Upon seeing her expression, he paused. "I see you heard that. Therefore, I welcome you, rider. Do all in your power to protect your dragon."

"Yes, honored rider, I will protect her."

"Now, let us go see about the other patient, healer-rider," Glendyn commented wryly.

"Duskya was with him during the night. She didn't call me, so I am thinking that he slept peacefully. His youngling has a way of healing the mind. I'm not sure exactly how it works, but I tried something like it with Wyn."

"Well, I can't tell if anything is wrong either," Glendyn admitted. "I was hoping he would be well enough to start training some riders in battle technique."

"He may need another day's rest before you give him too much work, Glendyn."

"He may not have it, Carryl. The turquoise dragon will be back. We don't know when."

"Let's see what Ruskya has to say," Carryl compromised.

At their quiet knock at the door, Duskya opened it and greeted them.

"Come on in. Have either of you had breakfast? You can join us if you wish."

Ruskya was sitting with her at the table. "Carryl and Glendyn, come on in," he welcomed.

"Ruskya," Carryl asked as she took a seat, "how are you?"

"Thanks to you and Kyn, I am doing wonderfully. And how is Wyn?"

Carryl paused with the spoon halfway to her mouth. "She is doing fine."

"Fine?" Glendyn replied. "I have seen two miracles today. The first was Wyn and the second, smaller one is you, Ruskya." He paused. "I take that back, it was three miracles. You, Ruskya, are the third. The second miracle was hearing Wyn take Carryl as her rider." Duskya and Ruskya stared at Glendyn as if they hadn't heard right. Carryl blushed.

"Glendyn," she tried to say but was interrupted by Wyn's voice. "He is right. No other person your age has ever been chosen by a dragon. No other dragon has ever had two riders, either."

"Carryl," Duskya called, "are you okay?"

Carryl shook her head. "Sorry, I am just getting used to the conversations including me. It's a little disturbing. Do you get used to it?"

"Conversations?" Duskya asked. "What are you talking about?"

Ruskya was quicker to catch on. "Yes, it gets easier. You just have to learn how to carry on two conversations at one time. Would you mind sharing with us what happened?"

Carryl smiled. "Gladly," she replied setting down her spoon. "I really don't know how to explain, though. I was pleading with her to come back to me. I was sharing pictures of life, but then I sent a picture of the turquoise dragon. She came to life. After I calmed her back down, she asked me if it was true about Marysa. When I told her it was, she asked me to stay with her and be her new rider."

"You had an actual conversation with her and she asked you to be her rider?" Glendyn was incredulous. "I guess I should not be surprised anymore by what happens around here."

"Welcome, rider," Duskya said. "You will be a refreshing addition."

"Thank you."

Ruskya looked at Carryl intently. "Welcome, respected rider," he said.

Again, Carryl blushed. To have Glendyn announce it as so was one thing, but to have Ruskya use the official title was another. She still couldn't believe it was true. She was so flustered that words would not come.

Instead, she heard them in her head as if she was trying to communicate with a dragon. "Thank you, honored rider."

Ruskya's voice answered although his lips did not move, "You are welcome. I am honored to have you as a fellow rider."

Her eyes got large as she looked at him. He smiled and nodded while the words came to her. "Do not be afraid. You may be able to talk with me, Duskya, and Kyn this way. I will explain more later."

As Glendyn cleared away the bowls, he asked Carryl to give Ruskya a clear bill of health to go out and talk with other riders. She would have rather it be anyone other than Ruskya right then, but she remembered to put on the healer mentality and went to look over his burns. They were healing nicely, almost too quickly. She was impressed. She gave Ruskya the okay to go out, but with a firm command that if he should get tired, he needed to come back and rest. Duskya assured Carryl that she would see to that. The three older riders were about to leave when there was a knock at the door. Duskya opened it to reveal her mother and Kyn.

After receiving a hug, Meredyth walked over to Ruskya. "What are you doing out of bed, young man?" she demanded, her pale gray eyes flashing.

"Honestly, Ma, I have the healer's permission. I am doing much better. I am told that physical healing is thanks to Carryl and the mental healing is thanks to Kyn. Am I correct, young one?"

Kyn looked up at him shyly. "I just tried to do what you and Rider Glendyn taught me. I blended it with what Healer Carryl taught me, and hoped it worked. I wouldn't have done anything that could hurt you, honored rider."

"I know, young one. I thank you. You did what a good brave student would do. You took initiative and because of it, I have had the best rest I have had in a long time. I am now ready to go help others learn how to fight this rider."

Meredyth came near and gazed into Ruskya's eyes. "Your eyes are clear, but I would like to see the physical wounds. Not that I don't trust the healer; it's a maternal thing. I have to see for myself."

Ruskya nodded and took off his tunic for a second time. His back was healing with no scars, just some red blotches where the turquoise fire had singed through his tunic. Meredyth was surprised.

"What did you use, Carryl?"

"Just the leaf you showed me for burns, lady Meredyth," was the reply.

"But that leaf should take three days to have these kinds of results!"

"That's what I thought you had told me," Carryl agreed. "But you can see for yourself that he has healed."

Meredyth looked at Kyn. "What exactly did you do?"

Kyn looked down. "I soaked a compress in the tea that Healer Carryl had given him, and placed it on his forehead. I envisioned it reaching its way into the nasty thoughts as I dug down into them." Here he paused and shuddered. "I told him he needed to live, and I sent some healing thoughts his ways."

"What nasty thoughts?" Ruskya quietly asked putting a hand on Kyn's shoulder.

"I heard a voice, Ruskya," Kyn answered almost in a whisper. "It was awful. He said he would kill you like he killed your da. You can't die. You can't!" Kyn flung his arms around the rider, weeping. Ruskya held him and soothed his back.

"I won't die, little one," Ruskya whispered into Kyn's mind. "I will fight him. He will not get away with the deaths of my da or Wyn's rider—first rider," he amended.

Kyn looked up at him, "Wyn is okay? She has a new rider?"

Ruskya smiled and nodded. "Respected rider Kyn, I present to you respected rider Carryl. Although she became a rider after you did, you should still treat her with greater respect because of her age. She will still be teaching you about healing, but I want you to try to teach her about speaking with us through our mental connection. I don't know how much she will be able to do, though. Do you understand, youngling?"

"Yes, honored rider." Turning to Carryl he said, "Respected rider, it is an honor to welcome you. I will gladly offer you any assistance you may need in learning about dragons and communicating with other riders. I will willingly learn from you the art of healing. I do ask, though, that I get to try some more of healing thoughts, please?" he pleaded.

Carryl laughed. "Of course, little one, or should I say, respected rider. I'll get used to the traditional greetings, but in some ways I like the regular names better."

The others laughed and agreed.

"Carryl, would you take Meredyth home? Maybe take Kyn with you and on the way back you can discuss his new healing methods,"

Glendyn said.

"Yes, honored rider," Carryl replied. "May I finish the dishes first?"

"Sure," Glendyn answered. "You may even have some helpers. Do make sure that you check in with your dragon before leaving. I know as a healer you would do so, but as a rider, you also need to make sure that you are communicating with her regularly."

"Yes, honored rider."

The others left, leaving Carryl with Meredyth and Kyn to clean up the little cooking area. The dishes were done in no time at all. Meredyth went to gather her things while Kyn called to Wylen. Carryl went out to Wyn. The dragon was not there.

In a panic, Carryl called, "Wyn, Wyn, where are you? Wyn!"

"Peace, little one," Wyn called to her. "Listen to the conversations and find me. I am fine."

Carryl calmed down, feeling embarrassed. She listened to Wyeth and Wryn talking about the wonder of Wyn choosing Carryl. She heard Wyden telling an older dragon about his part in the rescue of Wyn. The younger dragons were all talking about how the older ones were saying they were going to go to war. There was confusion and flurry of conversation. None of it, though, seemed to include Wyn herself. Where was she?

Carryl reached further. She pictured the dragon in her mind and found her out hunting. She wasn't quite flying, but she wasn't limping along, either. She was taking short flights and returning to walk where she could. Then Carryl saw her rise up in the air and swoop down in a dive that resulted in a squawk and some creature was in the dragon's talons. Carryl felt Wyn's joy that she had found food. When Wyn landed and started to eat, Carryl pulled away.

"Did you find me, little one?" Wyn asked.

"Yes, you went hunting. How is your wing?"

"It hurts a little, but seems to be healing fine."

"Would you like me to send Kyn to help it heal faster?"

The dragon was a little leery. "How?"

Carryl explained what she knew, and then told the dragon that they were going to Woolpren. It was decided that Wyn and Wylen would meet them halfway home, but Wyn was going to keep an ear out for Carryl. Carryl was to open her mind to Wyn the whole way. Carryl wasn't too sure about that, but agreed.

* * *

Kyn showed up to the abode first. Carryl asked him about letting her dragon into her thoughts. He explained that the work would be the dragon's responsibility. The dragon would follow and, basically, see what Carryl saw. Carryl nodded, understanding.

The trip into town was uneventful. Meredyth said that she would prefer going to the general store first to gather a few things she needed at home, and Kyn wanted to see his parents, so it was decided that all three would go.

Upon entering the general store, they noticed a large crowd had gathered. Several farmers with homesteads outside of the village canyon were there along with several villagers.

"I say, I saw dragon fire," one farmer was stating. "It was turquoise and icy blue. I also saw small spurts the color of the blue flowers in the canyons."

"Dragons don't fight each other," another stated. "Even if they did, they stay away from the village."

"I don't care what you want to believe," the first farmer answered, "but I saw what I saw."

Someone turned and saw Kyn. "Hey, let's ask a rider. Here's one. He'll tell us that dragons don't fight each other."

The whole crowd turned on the three newcomers. The man who had recognized Kyn as a rider, called out, "Kyn, welcome home. This farmer has a tale that sounds outrageous. Tell us, Kyn. Do dragons fight each other?"

Kyn paused. The moment he saw the conversation going this way, he had called to Ruskya but Ruskya was too far away. He called Wylen to see if he could help, but the little dragon didn't know the answer. Kyn took a deep breath and drew on the courage that Ruskya had shared during the battle.

"Byran, if you would have asked me that question a few days ago, I would have said of course not. Unfortunately, there is a dragon—a turquoise dragon—that is no good. He attacked one of ours yesterday. Several of our dragons came to her aid. That would be what this farmer saw."

The room erupted into an uproar, everyone trying to talk at once. Farmers afraid for their crops, villagers afraid more children would be taken to become riders in order to help fight. Kyn let the noise continue for a while, looked at Carryl and then decided to do some damage control.

"Quiet!" he called in a voice neither Carryl nor Meredyth would have believed was his. It was full of power and authority. They had heard it in older riders, but not in Kyn.

The pop of wood in the stove made someone jump; otherwise, it was silent.

Kyn held the silence for a heartbeat longer; then said, "This turquoise dragon is not one of ours. The riders of the colony are preparing to fight. I do not know if the turquoise dragon has more allies where he came from or not. I do know the rider is the same one that Kyle was in here talking about half a moon ago. Have any of you seen Kyle since?"

Negative murmurs filled the room. "We haven't seen him since that day," Byran said.

"He left with the rider," Kyn informed the group. "He thinks there is a dragon waiting for him, and that he's going to become a rider. If that's true, then there may be more dragons coming, but I do not know. I do know that the riders and dragons of Three Span Canyon will protect Woolpren. That is our sworn duty. Never before have we had to do so, but we will. This I swear upon my dragon."

Carryl stepped forward, "And I," she added.

Meredyth also put in her word, "I will speak for my children. My twins will protect the villagers. I would suggest that all farmers come into the village. It is winter and there are no crops. There are several box canyons that can be used as corrals. Bring your animals and your families. There are more rooms in the upper levels. Come and be safe here. I will send word to my twins and more dragon riders will come and talk with us about what we should do. Is that agreeable?"

Those standing around stunned seemed to regain speech capabilities. They all started to talk at once. The first farmer came up to Carryl.

"What about your da? Will he come into the village?"

Carryl hid a shudder. "I cannot speak for him as you well know, Davyd. If you ask him, he may, but he is stubborn. He would not allow me to leave for an apprenticeship; who knows if he will leave for his own safety."

Davyd looked at her. "It is still that way between you two?"

She nodded but said nothing.

"I had hoped you had been able to mend things. Your da is a hard man but not a bad man. I believe there is a good heart below what was crushed when your brother died."

Again, Carryl only nodded. The thought of Conyr was not what she needed right now.

"Would you go with me? Perhaps your voice will help him hear reason."

Carryl considered, "If I go, your chances of reason may be thrown out the door. He doesn't want to see me."

"There you are wrong, child. He has asked about you recently."

Carryl sighed. "Then yes, I will go, but I doubt it will do any good."

The farmer placed his hand on Carryl's shoulder. "You are a good daughter. I don't quite understand how you can vouch for the riders, but you are in the company of Kyn and Meredyth." He paused, then said "Didn't you go out with Meredyth's boy and Kyle to meet this rider?"

Again, a sigh escaped her. "Davyd, I did, but I did not join up with the turquoise rider. He was cruel like my da—no, worse than my da. Meredyth's boy as you call him, offered me a healer position with the riders. I have been there ever since. I am learning to heal the dragons when they need it." She paused, wondering how much to say, but decided it would be good to tell this farmer how badly Wyn was hurt. "I saw the dragon that was attacked by the turquoise dragon." A shiver ran up her spine at the memory. "The rider was dead before I could do anything. The dragon had burns and slashes all over her, but the worst part was her grief for her dead rider. They will need a healer in this fight. I do not know exactly what the trouble is but I do know the turquoise rider is looking for an herb I have never heard of before. He thinks he can find it around here."

"Then it must be rare indeed," Davyd said. "This rider must be terrible. You have changed, Carryl. You are no longer the shy little girl I once knew. Meet me at the mouth of Blalock Canyon at midday. We will go see your da."

"I will do what I can. I have responsibilities to Kyn."

"Leave him with his da for the afternoon," the stocky farmer suggested.

"I will see," was all the commitment that Carryl would give. She looked around the room and noticed most of the crowd had dispersed. Kyn was talking to the one called Byran.

Carryl walked over and overheard Kyn say, "If you help us fight, you don't have to worry about the riders. There are no extra dragons right now. Your grandchildren are safe."

"How can I be sure of that, Kyn?" The man wanted to know.

"Byran, have I ever lied to you before?" Kyn waited for the man to acknowledge the question with a shake of his head. "Then trust me now. There are no plans for a procession next winter—not for another two winters, at least. By then, the methods may be changed. There is talk among the riders to change things. I was not chosen by normal methods," Kyn noticed Carryl and added, "neither was she. Change comes slowly to dragons, but with this attack, some things will need to change quickly for the good. I believe the processions will be one of them."

"I hope you are right," the man said with a sigh. "Until then, we have our families to protect. Will the turquoise dragon come here?"

"I don't know," Kyn replied. "Kyle knows about the village and that riders were villagers at one time. He may try to come here. I don't see what advantages it would give him, though. I still agree with Lady Meredyth that everyone should come here. The dragon fire can't eat through the rock walls. The canyon itself is narrow and easily defended."

"Then I will do as you say, and get my family together. My older children have made families of their own and are out on farms. I will go warn them to come home. We still have room above the abode where they can all stay. Good day, rider."

"Good day, Byran."

CHAPTER 14: MAKING AMENDS

CARRYL HAD LEFT KYN with his da and saw Meredyth to her abode. She had talked with Wyn, who was a little apprehensive about Carryl going to her da's farm, but agreed to let her go. Carryl almost wished that Wyn had said no, but here she was waiting at the mouth of Blalock Canyon for Davyd to arrive.

Davyd was the nearest neighbor to Carryl's farm. Growing up, Carryl had played with Davyd's kids when there were barn raisings or harvesting festivals. Davyd had always been kind to Carryl, especially after Conyr's death. Her da had always blamed Carryl for the unfortunate farming accident. In theory, she understood her da's rage. Carryl had always been the small one, and Conyr always stood up for her. Her da saw Conyr's tenderness toward his sister as a weakness. Conyr was kind and compassionate, and her da's favorite. If anyone should have died, according to him, it should have been her. It was Conyr's death that had driven her to cultivate her knowledge of the herbs, and to find more uses for them. She experimented, promising to herself that no other patient would die if she could help it.

Another quiet voice entered her thoughts. "Little one, you do not count success by those who die or live, but by the lives you touch in the process."

Carryl jumped. "I forgot you were listening in, Wyn. I'm too far away to hear the dragon conversations at Three Spans Canyon. I forgot you were here with me."

"I will always be here, little one. You cannot go on blaming yourself for what happened so long ago. Live life not with regrets but with the present and the future in view."

"Thank you, Wyn. I will remember that. Oh, here comes Davyd. He has a wagon with him."

"You decided you could come," Davyd said as a statement not a question. "Good. Hop up. I wish I had the time to take you by the farm, Nataly would love to see you."

"I guess she'll just have to wait until you come into the village."

"That she will, but I don't know if she will believe me that you are the dragon riders' healer."

"Why wouldn't she? She knows how good I was with the herbs."

"True, but in her eyes you are still the little girl of six winters playing with her brother in the hay."

Carryl nodded and blocked the images, but a few came to her mind unbidden: her brother calling her name from up in the hayloft as he jumped into the hay below; Conyr tripping and missing the hay. She shut her eyes, but the images still came.

"Wyn, help! I can't do this."

"Yes you can, little one. You were strong enough to help me fight off the turquoise dragon's curse. You can fight this nightmare."

"That is the problem. It is not a nightmare, it is what happened. My da always said it was my fault, but I had cleaned up the hayloft. I don't know how Conyr tripped."

"Hush, little one," Wyn said.

At the same time, Davyd laid a hand on her shoulder. "I shouldn't have said that. I am sorry. I didn't realize it still hurt so much."

Carryl nodded. "At times the memories are as clear as the day they happened. No herb I have found can dissipate these memories."

"Would you really want them gone?"

"Well, not gone, but not so strong."

"He needed someone to blame, and you were there. He never could understand your relationship with your brother. He thought it was weakness on your brother's part to care so deeply for someone. He would rather blame you for Conyr's death than remember your brother with weakness."

The creak of the wagon wheels filled the winter air along with the crunch of the hard-packed snow. Too soon for Carryl's liking, the farm came into view. It was more rundown then she had remembered, but it was still the farm. The barn, corrals, fields, windmill, the abode and the lone tree all brought back bittersweet memories. She sighed.

"You can do it, little one," Wyn called. "It looks like a nice place to have grown up. Not enough crags for my taste, but it would have worked nicely as a hatchling."

Carryl smiled. "Yes, it was nice as a hatchling, for the most part."

"See," Davyd cut into the conversation, "you did need to come out here."

Carryl laughed. Having two conversations at once was complicated. She decided to agree with Davyd. "I may have needed it after all, but I don't know about seeing Da."

Davyd nodded. "I think he needs to see you, though. You have changed. You may have more sway than you believe."

They pulled up to the yard and Davyd disembarked. Carryl waited a second too long, for Davyd swung around to her side and offered her a hand down. She wondered what her da would think of that. Would it make her look as if she couldn't do things on her own? It was too late to do anything without looking rude. She took Davyd's hand and as gracefully as a lady, she descended from the wagon. Davyd stared up at her with surprise.

The door opened to the abode and a man stuck his balding head out. "Davyd is that you?" he demanded with a gravelly voice.

"Sure it is, Casey, and you know it, too. You're just jealous 'cause I got myself a pretty young lady with me, but you have no need to be. If anything, you have all the right in the world to be proud."

Carryl steeled her face and looked up at her da. The man seemed to have shriveled in the last few years into a husk of who he had been. She wondered what had happened to make him this way. Her mind went to the herbs that could help him gain back his strength.

"Whatchya mean?" Casey called confused. "Whadda I have ta be proud of?"

"Casey, man, don't ya even recognize your own kin?" Davyd said, motioning for Carryl to come closer.

She moved to his side. She was determined that this man would not see her cringe. She held her head high and heard Wyn's voice saying, "Make your family proud, little one, your whole family, this man and the ones back here waiting for you to come home." A smile played along Carryl's lips making her face younger and brighter.

"Carryl, baby?" her father whispered. "Is it you? Have ya come back home?"

Carryl nodded unable to speak. She couldn't ever remember her da using those soft tones with her before.

"Why, baby? Why did ya leave and not come back?" Something broke in Carryl's heart. She ran the next few steps to her da and engulfed him in a hug. Tears streamed down both of their faces.

"I am home now, Da," she answered. "Davyd convinced me you wanted to see me. I didn't believe him, but Da, he was right."

"'Course I wanted ta see my baby girl. Why wouldn't I?"

Carryl stepped back and surveyed her da. "It doesn't matter right now," she settled on saying. "I don't have long, but we need to talk. If you want, I can fix us some tea to share before we have to go back to the village."

His face fell. "Ya can't stay? A cuppa tea would be good, though. Go 'head an' make some."

They walked into the dwelling. It was similar to the dragon rider's abodes with one open large room for dining, cooking, and living. The door to the bedroom was open. At the back, a ladder led up to the loft where Carryl had spent many sleepless nights. What had changed her father so? She set the water to boil and found some cups. One look told her they needed washing. Finding a cloth to use for cleaning, she began the chore of cleaning up the cooking area. While the two men talked she busily worked. It was good to do something for her da of her own accord. She found some tea and some chamomile in her supplies and sprinkled the leaves into the mugs. She had found some stale bread and decided to make toast with the sweet jam her da always kept on hand. She placed it all on the table and called to the men.

"Da, Davyd, tea is ready."

As they sat down, Casey looked around amazed. "Is this my table?"

"Yes, Da, it is," Carryl said as she placed his mug in front of him. "Enjoy." She sat down with the two men. Casey looked up at her and stared.

"Davyd tells me that ya've become quite a healer."

Carryl nodded. "I never thought I would get to work with dragons, though."

Casey glanced at Davyd. "Ya didn't say nuthin' about dragons ta me. Whatcha mean?"

Carryl told her da of meeting up with Ruskya and being offered a chance to work with the dragons. She also told of the attack, and how hurt both Ruskya and Wyn were, and how she had helped bring them both back to health. Her da stared at her amazed.

"My girl did all that? I do have somethin' to be proud of, Davyd. I have a healer fer a daughter."

"That ya do," Davyd agreed. "The problem is though, that rider and dragon that attacked. I saw it. They started over my fields and passed south. I could see them for over two spans as they fought in the sky. It was horrid. I hated to think what dragon fire would do to my crops or my abode.

"I went to Woolpren to warn them, and that's when I met up with your daughter, a rider, and the herbalist Meredyth. They confirmed what I saw. Then the herbalist suggested that everyone come to Woolpren to be safe. All the farmers can bring their stock in and make a large corral outta those box canyons. I'm going to head over to my farm and collect Nataly and our things and head back. Do ya want to come with me?"

"Now Davyd," Casey began, "ya know I don't take to meetin' up with all those folks."

"Da, please. Listen to us. I can't guarantee that the dragon and his rider would come through here, but if he does, I couldn't live knowing that you were left here. I saw what that rider did to Ruskya, and I saw what his dragon did to Wyn and her rider. I don't want that to happen to you. Please come with us."

"Yer goin' daughter? Yer gonna be in the village?"

Carryl sighed, "I can't say how long I will be there, but I will be there for a while and will definitely be coming back at frequent intervals to check on you and the others."

"If yer gonna be there, then I guess I could come."

Carryl stood up and gave her da a hug. "Thank you, Da. Let's get your things together." Casey got up and slowly started to gather his things.

"Davyd, why don't you head home and swing back around for us. That will give Da more time to gather what he needs and to say good-bye to the place for awhile."

Davyd nodded and said good-bye. Carryl helped her da gather what he would need to be comfortable for an extended stay in the village. Then she went ahead and cleaned up the tea.

"When did ya grow up?" Casey asked, pausing in the doorway watching her. "Ya never used ta help around here."

Carryl sighed, looking straight into her da's gray eyes, so much like her brother's had been. "I guess when I had to clean up my own place. I realized it was easier to clean up small messes than to let it pile up."

"Thank ya," Casey said quietly.

"For what?"

"Fer comin' back and for cleanin' up aroun' here."

"You're welcome, Da."

* * *

The ride back to Woolpren was uneventful. Upon arrival, they found several other farmers had returned. Animals lowed as they were corralled. The village seemed to be in an uproar trying to gather everyone together before the winter sun set.

Carryl sighed. She had told Glendyn she would be back before dark with Kyn, having given him a healer lesson. She was supposed to also have learned from Kyn. There was no way that was going to happen. She decided to try to communicate with Glendyn through Wyn.

"Wyn, can you get a message to one of the other riders for me? Tell him what has happened and ask if I should try to come back tonight or wait until morning."

In the meanwhile, she needed to get her da settled with Davyd and Nataly. She found Kyn helping his ma clean rooms for farmers.

"Kyn, how are things going here?"

"Hectic. There have been at least ten farmers and their families who have come back to the village. I have been helping get everyone into abodes."

"Where would you suggest that I set up my da and Davyd and his daughter?"

"There is room over the general store. Why don't you bring them in and introduce them to my da. Ma will help them get settled."

Carryl helped to get the farmers and their families settled. Later, she heard from Wyn. It had been decided that they would stay the night at the general store.

CHAPTER 15: THE AQUA DRAGON ATTACKS

THE RIDERS spent the night quietly talking among themselves. Kyn and Carryl shared the various techniques they had used to help bring healing to those around them, while Casey and Davyd quietly chatted about the good old days. Every so often Wyn chimed in, and Carryl practiced keeping track of two conversations at once.

Finally, dawn came and with it time to prepare a meal. Carryl was tired, but not as badly as she had thought she would be. She met up with Kyn's father and helped fix breakfast for everyone.

The day turned out to be run-of-the-mill. Carryl and Kyn took their leave and headed back to the dragon colony in Three Spans Canyon. When they arrived, they found that Glendyn had decided someone who could get messages to the riders should stay at the village. That meant someone with a dragon. He liked the way that Carryl had thought to use Wyn to communicate with another rider via his or her dragon.

The riders had mobilized themselves into groups to try to learn battle technique from Ruskya. Things hadn't worked exactly as Glendyn had planned. They had discovered that Ruskya and Duskya were the only riders who could use mental imaging to block dragon fire, but several of the dragons had the ability to shield themselves and their riders. As the group's healer, Carryl realized that it was to her advantage to find armor that would protect both the rider and the dragon.

"Kyn," she called to the boy as he swooped past her, "do you know anyone in the village who is good with leather? I need someone who can fashion some kind of protection for our riders and dragons."

* * *

The next couple of days fell into a routine. Kyn had commissioned someone to do the leatherwork. Carryl kept busy with trips to the village and her new responsibilities with the dragons. Kyn tried to teach her what he had done with Ruskya, but for her, this healing method seemed to only work on dragons. Conversely, the youngling's technique worked with humans, but only his own dragon. It confused Carryl. Ruskya suggested that it might have something to do with Calamadyn.

Five days with no sign of the dragons brought dissent in the village. Although it was winter, the farmers did not like being cooped up in the canyon. They wanted to return to their homes. No matter how much Meredyth or Carryl tried to persuade them, several families headed back out to the outlaying farms. Carryl sighed, knowing her father would soon join them. She had been able to get to know him on a different level in the past days and they'd developed a mutual respect for one another. Yet, she knew he did not belong in the village. He was staying only because she was there.

Two days later, Carryl visited the village alone to check on her father. He was anxious to move back to the farm and told her so in no uncertain terms. She resigned herself to the inevitable and agreed to let him go back the next day. She met with Meredyth and found that others were also ready to leave. She knew it was time to let them go, but it would be harder to protect them all when they were all out on the farms.

As she walked back to the general store with some of Meredyth's tea in her pouch, she heard footsteps on the canyon floor behind her. Turning, she saw the last rays of light glinting off the blonde hair of a little girl of about five winters. A boy of about ten winters shielded the girl as best he could. Tears streamed down the little girl's face. The boy was trying to be brave, but there were dirt tracks on his cheeks where tears had been rubbed away and his brown hair was an unruly mop. They both were disheveled, dirty, and tired. She ran to them. The little girl, seeing her, hid behind her brother. Her brother put a protective hand on her and held out the other to stop Carryl. The act was so pitiful, that Carryl stopped mid-stride.

"It's okay," she called to them softly. "I won't hurt you. Come, I know where you can be safe."

"No, Da said to go to the general store. That's where we must go," the boy answered with his last remaining courage.

"That's this way. Let me walk with you."

"I guess that would be okay. Bryna, stay beside me and you'll be okay. I won't let them get you. I promise."

"Can you explain what happened?" Carryl asked.

"D-dragons," the little girl said with large fear-filled eyes.

Carryl gasped and asked no more; she silently contacted her dragon.

"Wyn, get here quick. Tell Glendyn and Ruskya that there was a dragon attack on one of the farms. I may need Kyn. If so, let him ride you if that would be faster. Please, I need you here."

Since it was about time for the evening meal, there were not many villagers out. Carryl hated to disturb anyone, but she was going to need Meredyth soon. She decided to wait until they reached the general store and send someone to get her.

The little girl seemed to be repeating the word "dragons" over and over. She was in shock, Carryl realized. The boy just stared down the canyon pathway, determined. Carryl wondered what they had seen and where their parents were. Why had the dragons attacked a farm?

"Patience, little one," Wyn called to her. "You cannot speed things up by stewing about them."

"You are right. What did you find out?"

"Ruskya is coming too, and Kyn."

"No, Ruskya should stay in case they attack the colony. Please, they need him more there."

"I don't know if he will listen. He wants to be near Kyn to find out what exactly is going on. He has to be closer than Three Spans Canyon to do that."

"True, but he doesn't have to come all the way into the village. I would love to have him here to help, but I think he is needed more there. See if he will compromise and stay closer to the colony."

"I'll try."

By then they had reached the general store. As they opened the door, the boy collapsed on the threshold. The little girl began to cry hysterically and shriek, "Dragons, dragons!" The merchant ran from behind his counter and picked up the boy. Carryl gathered the little girl into her arms.

"These are Terry's little ones," the merchant observed as he laid the boy down beside the warm stove. "Byran's grandchildren." Carryl felt the boy for a pulse and noticed how cold his skin was. She realized they had come the whole way without a cloak.

She sprung into action, asking the merchant for hot water and blankets. He quickly pulled two blankets off the shelf and brought them to her. She chafed the boy's small hands in her own to try to bring some blood circulation back. She looked up to see the merchant's wife holding a pot of hot water. Carryl directed her in getting some things from her pouch to brew some tea. She pulled out a small pouch and held it under the boy's nose.

A few seconds later and his eyes fluttered sparkling blue in the lamplight. "Wh-where am I?"

"You are at the general store. Can you tell me your name?"

"Calyb. Where is my sister?" Fear came into his eyes and he started to struggle.

"She is right here," Carryl moved so that Calyb could see his sister. "Can you tell me a bit more about what happened?"

He shuddered and then looked at the merchant. "Da said to tell you, sir, that the dragons are back. He told us to run. Ma was going to run, but the dragon got her in its claws." The boy paused, collecting his thoughts. "I pushed Bryna under some sagebrush. We watched the dragons land and then one rider climbed down off the dragon. He pulled Da up by his shirt collar and held him there. If it wasn't for Bryna, I would have run back.

"Then the other rider jumped down and went to get Ma from his dragon. It was that no good traitor, Kyle!" he shouted tearfully. "He picked up Ma and brought her in front of the rider I didn't recognize. That one laughed and said that Ma would be good co-collateral." The boy stumbled over the unfamiliar word. "Whatever that is. Then he asked Da about some plant, but Da didn't know. The rider got rough and beat Da, but Da wouldn't say, because he didn't know anything. Then Kyle held Ma up. The rider laughed." The boy shuddered again and paused in telling.

Carryl squeezed his hand. "It's okay, take a break if you must."

The boy shook his head. "They hurt Ma to make Da talk. I hid Bryna's face. Da still didn't know and couldn't tell them. He seemed to plead with them to stop, but they didn't. Kyle's dragon," The boy took a breath then continued, "killed Ma. The other rider killed Da. Then they got on their dragons and let the dragons breath fire all over the farm. There is nothing left. When the dragons had gone, we ran here." The boy lay back exhausted. Fresh tears came to his eyes and his small frame shook. Carryl took him in her arms and held him. She asked the merchant for the tea and gave the boy a sip. She offered some to the little girl who was rocking back and forth whispering, "dragons, dragons."

"Carryl," Ruskya's voice came to her, "are you okay?" Carryl looked around expecting to see that Ruskya had walked into the building, but he hadn't. She realized he was calling to her in her mind, as dragons do.

"I'm okay, but something terrible has happened. A farm was attacked by two dragons. Kyle was riding one and it killed the farmer's wife. The other rider killed the farmer. Their two children saw it and are here with me at the general store. I will need Kyn to help heal their thoughts. Ruskya, you must stay there to help the other riders fight these dragons."

"Carryl, hush. I will be where I am needed. Right now you need me to help calm you down."

She smiled. He was right, the story had upset her. "I am fine now. Thank you," she replied. "How close is Kyn?"

"He'll be there in a few more moments."

Carryl told the merchant to expect Kyn for the night, and then turned her attention to Ruskya. She related as best she could the boy's story and relayed the farm's location to him.

"That is close to Philippi Canyon," Ruskya realized. "The turquoise rider used it once before. He may use it again. It would be perfect for a small number of riders and dragons, too. I'll tell Glendyn and see if he can send a scouting party."

The boy was starting to rest when the door opened, and in walked Byran. He came to the stove and looked down at his grandchildren. A sob escaped his throat. "Is it true?" he asked in a whisper. "Are they really gone?"

Carryl nodded. "Kyn will be returning shortly. He has a way of healing that may help the children sleep and help to erase some of the horror that they experienced." She shuddered just imagining what the boy had seen. "It was not pretty, Byran. The dragons have obliterated the farm."

Byran nodded and knelt down to pick up Bryna. "I'll be back for Calyb in a bit."

"Don't hurry. I'll stay with him until you get back."

Carryl didn't see who had gotten the door for Byran. She looked up to see her father standing beside her, watching how she held Calyb.

"You have a way of healing, don't you? I always noticed it, but it irked me that it didn't show up until after Conyr's death. I blamed you for not being able to stop it. That was wrong."

Carryl looked up into his gray eyes full of sorrow. "I am sorry that there was nothing I could do. I have vowed to help anyone I can. I do it in his honor."

Her father nodded as tears glistened in his eyes. He stayed there until Byran returned, then helped Carryl up as Kyn came bursting through the door.

Kyn looked at Carryl and mentally called, "Are you okay?"

Carryl smiled. "I am fine." She called back. "I need you to help Byran's grandchildren." Kyn nodded and followed Byran out the door.

"Here, Carryl," the merchant's wife offered, "have some tea. It's Meredyth's brew. She gave me some for the times when Ruskya brings Kyn to visit and doesn't have time to swing past her place."

Carryl took the mug and inhaled the aroma. Just the smell was enough to help her relax. She wasn't sure if there would be another attack tonight, but she knew that she needed to be ready.

She had just finished her tea when Ruskya called to her. "Carryl, I have to go. Contact me through Wyn. The dragons are attacking Three Spans Canyon."

Carryl sighed, but sent encouraging thoughts to Ruskya. "I'll be fine. Go safely. If you need me, call me through Wyn. I'll come help any who need it. Be sure everyone wears their armor."

She heard his chuckle. "Always the bossy healer, aren't you?"

"I just don't want to have to patch anyone up or lose any of you."

"I hear you," he answered faintly. "Take care."

"And you," she called, not sure if he heard or not.

Kyn walked in then with a discouraged look on his face. Carryl handed him a mug and poured water over the tea leaves. "Drink."

He nodded and, as she had done, sniffed the healing aroma. After a few moments of quiet, he spoke. "I didn't know dragons could do such horrible things. How can they be so mean?"

Carryl just listened. She knew there wasn't much more she could do than that.

"They seemed to find pleasure in giving pain to that farmer and his wife."

When he didn't go on, Carryl was a bit worried. He looked defeated. She didn't know what she could do to help. She looked up to see Meredyth had entered the general store and was headed their way.

At Meredyth's puzzled look, Carryl explained, "He just came back from helping Byran's grandchildren. Their parents were killed by dragons and their farm was razed."

Meredyth nodded. She looked at Kyn and laid a hand on his shoulder. He looked up at her with distant eyes. "Please, Kyn, what do you need?"

Kyn just stared at her. Finally, he whispered, "I'm afraid."

Meredyth dug into a pouch at her side and pulled out a small leather bag. Gingerly, she opened it, placed two fingers in, and pulled out a pinch of icy blue sparkling dust. She sprinkled it over Kyn then carefully, almost reverently, closed the pouch. Carryl saw the change immediately in both Kyn and Meredyth. Meredyth's change was more subtle, but it was there nonetheless. Kyn's was radical. His head lifted, his back straightened and his dark eyes sparkled.

"What was that?" Carryl inquired.

Meredyth shook her head. "Not now. I'll tell you later."

"Thank you, Meredyth. Are you sure it was a wise use of your precious pouch?" Kyn asked.

Meredyth nodded. "You needed it more than I did. We need your help here."

"And maybe back at Three Spans Canyon, too," Carryl added.

Kyn nodded at Meredyth's shocked look. "Yes, they attacked there just before I arrived."

"We need to get the word out to any farm near Philippi Canyon," Carryl added. "Is there anyway we can do that?"

Meredyth thought. "We should ask your father, Kyn. He may know someone who would be willing to go. I could help." She motioned to her little bag. Kyn nodded and went to ask his father. Now that they were alone, Meredyth explained to Carryl what was in her pouch. Carryl stared in awe. She hadn't known that dragons could do that.

"Yes, little one, there is a lot that you do not know about dragons. We surprise ourselves sometimes with what we can do. I have never seen you in need of courage; otherwise, I would have given you some."

Kyn came back with his father who said he would go alert the farmers. Kyn protested, but his father was adamant. Meredyth sprinkled some dragon courage on him to help him along the way.

CHAPTER 16: BATTLE OVER THE VILLAGE

UNDER COVER OF DARKNESS, Carryl and Meredyth hiked to an unused side canyon where Wyn could land. Carryl was afraid that if Wyn came during the daylight hours, she would be mistaken for an enemy dragon and shot by the villagers. Kyn helped erect a stable that would house the dragon from prying eyes. When all was prepared, Carryl called Wyn to come.

While they waited for the dragon to arrive, Carryl felt a flicker of something, perhaps a presence of an unwanted visitor. She spun around quickly, but saw nothing.

"What is it?" Kyn inquired, looking around and reaching mentally to see if danger was near. He could not sense anything.

"I don't know," she said with a slight pause between words. "I sense a presence." After a pause her eyes lit up and her hand went to her mouth, "They're here!" was all that came from her lips.

Kyn glanced down the canyon and saw no one. He looked up into the slit of a sky that was visible to him, but all he saw were stars in a sky the color of his eyes.

"Who and where, Carryl?" he asked laying a hand on her shoulder.

Carryl didn't reply. She just held her hand up for him to be quiet. Kyn obliged and waited patiently. He wondered what this next threat was going to be. As he waited, he gazed up at the sky. He reflected on how the last moon cycle had affected his life. It was amazing how things could change so rapidly. He had gone from the merchant's son to a dragon rider and healer. The night sky reminded him of Wylen. He wished the little dragon was larger so that they could be in this fight together with the others.

Carryl interrupted his thoughts. "There are at least three dragons somewhere within my range of hearing. They want to attack now, but their riders have other plans. I think one of them is Kyle's dragon, because he was boasting of attacking more humans." She shuddered. "I won't repeat what he wants to do with them. How can a dragon be so cruel?"

"Maybe dragons are like humans, and there are both good and bad ones."

"Maybe. I need Wyn here to help protect the villagers. I don't know if we should bother Duskya, Ruskya or Glendyn with the news."

Kyn thought for a while and then replied. "They should be notified, but I don't know if they can do anything. They are busy with the battle at Three Spans Canyon. The last I checked, no one was seriously injured, but they are not doing well."

Carryl sighed. She couldn't be in two places at once, and she needed to be here for now to defend her father and friends.

"There is nothing we can do tonight, except get Wyn settled. Why don't you head to bed? I'll be there as soon as Wyn comes."

"I don't like leaving you to roam the canyon at night alone."

"Kyn, who is going to bother me? Those here in the village know I am a rider. Besides, everyone is in their bed, scared."

Kyn reluctantly agreed and left.

Carryl didn't have long to wait for Wyn. The dragon landed in the moonlit canyon gracefully, the moon making her wings an iridescent purplish-blue. "Have I told you that you're beautiful?" Carryl asked her, giving her a hug.

Wyn set her head down on Carryl's shoulder. "Thank you, little one."

"Are you ready for a fight again, ancient one?" Carryl jokingly called the dragon.

"Ancient, huh?" Wyn replied. "I don't feel ancient. I am not the baby around here anymore, but sometimes I still feel like it."

"I know." Carryl laughed, relieving some of the tension. "It's just strange that you keep calling me 'little one.'"

"'Little' is in reference to your size, not your age. If you have seen as many winters as Wyeth and Wryn, then you are older than me."

Carryl looked up at her dragon with new eyes. "Really? How many winters have they seen?"

"Twenty-five—the same as their riders. I am two winters younger than they are."

"I am the same age as Ruskya and Duskya. I was in their procession, but no dragon chose me."

"For which I am grateful." The dragon almost purred in Carryl's mind.

"All right, back to business. Are you ready to fight?"

"You bet I am."

"There are at least three dragons within my range of hearing. I will try to keep an ear out for them while I sleep tonight. You do the same and call me at the slightest hint of danger to the village."

"I will, little one. Go, peace be with you."

"And you, my friend."

*　*　*

The next morning, before the sun reached the top of the canyon wall, Carryl was awakened by Wyn's insistent call. Immediately, she was awake. She headed out to Wyn's canyon after quickly getting dressed, wishing that she had some of the leather armor, but figuring she would have to make do. She tried to call to Kyn to warn him, but wasn't sure that it would work.

She mentally called as she would to Wyn, "Kyn." When nothing happened, she called again louder. "Kyn, wake up!"

"You don't have to yell, Carryl."

"Sorry. Wyn says the dragons are on their way. They aren't communicating among themselves yet, but I believe her. I'm heading out."

"Be careful. I'll do what I can from down here."

"Let's go, Wyn," she said, as she mounted her dragon. With two wing beats, they were in the air. Two more and they cleared the canyon rim. Carryl looked out and shielded her eyes from the sun rising in all its brilliance. In that bright light, she saw three specks in the distance.

"It looks like we have our work cut out for us, Wyn," she commented. "Are you ready?"

"I am. No dragon should have to fight another, but no dragon should ever attack a human, either. Therefore, I must deliver justice to the one who has so offended."

Carryl nodded. They stationed themselves as a sentinel over the canyon. Carryl mentally stretched, trying to identify the dragons. She felt the dragon that had boasted of killing the farmer's wife; that would be Kyle's. Then there were the other two who had conversed the night before. She could feel them moving in closer, but so far, they were not talking. She wasn't sure if they could feel her, but since she was facing the sunlight, they could probably see her better than she could see them. She waited for their move. She knew she was outnumbered, but maybe she could keep them away from the canyon until others could come and help.

Then, seemingly in no time, they were upon her. The aqua dragon was in the lead, with blue-green and cyan dragons following in a V-formation behind them. The aqua dragon spat fire, and Wyn swerved to avoid it. Her dive led her into the fire range of the blue-green dragon. Again, Wyn veered off. By now, the aqua dragon was in range. He dove to bring his talons across her wings, but Wyn spun and was able to graze his wings instead. The aqua dragon let out a roar and fell a few feet. Carryl heard the dragons talking as they fell back to regroup.

Carryl held Wyn in check and listened. They wanted one dragon to draw Wyn out into a trap where the other two could take her down. Carryl and Wyn discussed a plan to make it look like they were falling for the trap, but to then reverse and attack. It was possible that Wyn would take some damage, but the dragon was willing to try. She decided to let them make the first move.

The aqua dragon came first. Wyn attacked, and he fell back, as the dragons had discussed. She allowed him to lead her seemingly blindly into the other dragons' line of fire. Just as she could feel the cyan dragon make the call to attack, she instructed Wyn to fall as if attacked. Then, as the other three dragons descended on her, Wyn spun around and sprayed her purplish-blue fire at them. All three roared in pain and tried to spew their bluish-green fire back, but Wyn had reversed direction and was coming from above them. Her talons raked their wings and her fire spewed. Carryl had never heard such noise before. The roar of pain from the three dragons was almost too much to bear. She blocked it from her mind, instead seeing the image of a farmer's wife being slain by the aqua dragon. She urged Wyn to keep fighting.

They tumbled downward as Wyn herded the dragons into an area where she could keep them under her control. She continued to spew forth fire and tried to attack with her talons, but soon the three broke away and ran.

"Not now, Wyn," Carryl said, holding her dragon back, "let me take care of your wounds." The dragon had been so intent on justice that she had not realized she had been hurt. "Let's stay here and watch them leave; then we will go back to the canyon." Wyn agreed, sucking in air.

Soon the three dragons had disappeared into the distance in the direction of Philippi Canyon. Carryl noticed a couple of spurts of fire that the dragons gave as a parting shot. She wondered which farms were being fired upon, and hoped there were no people there. Waiting a little longer to make sure the dragons would not return, Carryl descended into the canyon.

Kyn was waiting for her with Meredyth, her father, and a handful of villagers. She wearily dismounted, but gave Wyn's flank a steady hand of thanks. She ignored the onlookers and examined every inch of Wyn with her eyes and her hands where she could. She fumbled at her side for a pouch, but Kyn stopped her and took the pouch from her.

"Tell me what you need, and I will get it for you."

"Thank you," she replied, and proceeded to list the various herbs she wanted to make a compress for some of the burns on Wyn's back. The youngling expertly collected the herbs and placed them into a small bowl that he pulled from his pouch. He then started to mix them. The onlookers stared at their fellow villager in amazement. This was not the quiet, shy merchant's son they knew. This was a very adept healer.

When Wyn was finally resting and healing, Carryl turned. She noticed the look of awe in the eyes of the villagers. The closest any of these people had been to a dragon was from the observation stands of a procession, and those dragons had only seen two winters. The villages had certainly never been this close to a dragon who had just fought a battle to protect them. They were not sure what they were supposed to do.

Her father bowed to her and said, "Thank ya, honored rider." The others followed suit.

Carryl blushed. She started to say something, but Kyn hushed her. He led her back to the general store where Meredyth prepared tea while the youngling did some minor bandaging.

"You were fortunate," he said. "How many were there?"

"Three. I don't think they had any experience, or else they were not expecting a dragon to be here to defend."

"They may have thought that the riders were all tied up with the other dragons."

"I wouldn't want to have to do that again, though. Is there any way to get another rider and dragon here?"

"I don't know, but you have as much contact with anyone as I do. I think the other dragons listen to Wyn better than they listen to Wylen. I assume it is because of his age," Kyn said ducking his head in shame.

Carryl smiled. "That could be. Has your father made it back yet?"

Kyn's brief smile disappeared. "No, and I'm worried sick about him. Is there anything we can do?"

"I'll see. I may be able to take Wyn out in a bit and look for him." A sickening thought came to her as she remembered those last brief spurts of dragon fire near Philippi Canyon. It couldn't have been! Kyn's father would be safely home in just a short while.

She sipped the tea that Meredyth had handed her. In a little while, she would go back to the real world. Right now, she was ready for a nap.

CHAPTER 17: FARM ATTACK

CARRYL WAS AWAKENED by a hand on her shoulder. She looked up to find Meredyth standing beside her.

"Kyn's father has not returned. He is wondering if you could go out and look for him."

Carryl sighed. She hadn't realized how tired she was. Her muscles ached from hanging on to Wyn.

She called to Wyn, "Are you ready for another flight, girl? Hopefully, there will not be any fighting, but I can't guarantee that."

"What's the matter?"

"Kyn's father left last night to warn some farmers out by Philippi Canyon. He hasn't returned yet."

"Oh," was Wyn's only reply. Carryl received an image of the last dragon fire before the three disappeared from view.

"Yeah, I know. I'm afraid of that, too, but we need to do this for Kyn."

"Let's go. Make sure that you eat first," the dragon advised. "That will help you regain your strength."

"I should have thought of that. I'll see what I can find. I should tell my father I am leaving, also."

Carryl went in search of her father and found him sitting near the stove in the general store. Several others were there talking. Whatever the conversation was, it stopped as soon as they saw her. Several of the men stood and bowed.

"Thank you, honored rider," they said.

She bowed back. "The privilege was mine." Turning she said, "Da, can I speak with you for a moment?"

Casey stood and bowed to the other men. Carryl could tell it was awkward for him to be so polite. He was accustomed to the ways of the farm, not traditional society. She walked with him back to the merchant's living quarters. There she found some stew that had been left on the stove. Scooping some stew into a bowl for herself, she started to talk.

"The merchant left last night to warn some remaining farmers out by Philippi Canyon." She sat down and continued, "He hasn't returned yet. Kyn has asked me to take Wyn and search for him and the others."

Casey looked at her. "That means ya halfta go up against those dragons again."

Carryl nodded. No more words were necessary. Everyone had heard the reports from Byran about his daughter and son-in-law.

Slowly he nodded. "Ya need ta go. You are a rider now, daughter. Go do as ya must. I wantcha ta know that I'm proud of ya."

Tears came unbidden to Carryl's eyes. "Thank you, Da." Her father gathered her to him in an embrace, then straightened and walked out to let her be the rider the village needed.

Carryl wiped her tears away and finished eating. Then she gathered her pouches and her cloak and headed out. Wyn greeted her when she rounded the canyon wall. Carryl knew she was where she needed to be. Climbing up on her dragon, she sent a thank you and a blessing on her father. She felt Wyn send it on, too.

They had been in the air about a tenth of a glass when they saw the scorched ground. It wasn't large enough to be a farm. Wyn lowered down to let Carryl see better. There were burnt sagebrush and scorch-marked rocks. No one seemed to be in the area. Carryl flew on and saw similar signs. It wasn't clear whether the dragons were chasing something or randomly frying the land.

She turned Wyn back toward the first marks they had seen. From this angle she noticed an outcropping rock with space under it. She asked Wyn to land so that she could examine it better. The space was too small for a dragon, but large enough for several men to fit inside. She cautiously walked over to it and called out a greeting.

Bending down, she thought she saw something light colored. She wasn't sure what it was, but it didn't look as if it belonged there. She crawled closer for a better look. A hand was reaching out toward her.

In a soft voice, she called out trying to ascertain if the person was awake.

A moan followed. She worked quickly and carefully to squeeze along the wall. She found it was a man. In the dim light, she couldn't see much more than that.

"I need to move you out into the light. Can you move on your own or do you need help?"

"Water," the man croaked.

Carryl did better than that. She unstopped the waterskin and helped him drink a bit of Meredyth's tea. Carryl had added some energizing herbs to it. The man drank as if he hadn't drunk in years. Carryl pulled it away.

With much pushing, pulling, and scraping, Carryl, with help from the man was able to edge him closer to the opening. Finally, she could see clearly. She saw burns covered his face and most of his torso. The hands somehow had escaped miraculously with just mild burns. She took in a deep breath.

"I can only do so much out here. Are there any others with you?"

"A boy," the man managed to say.

Carryl covered the man with her cloak and went back in search of the boy. She found him further back in the cave huddled and shivering.

"It's okay, little one," Carryl said, smiling at the irony of the expression that had escaped her. "I'm here to help. Can you come here?"

The boy shifted, wary of the situation.

"It will be okay," she repeated. "I need to get the man back to Woolpren. Then I will come back for you, but first I want to see that you are not hurt."

The boy moved closer, and together they crawled out into the light. The boy shied away from the man's burnt face. Carryl turned him around so that he didn't have to look at the man.

"Let me see you. Are you hurt anywhere?"

The youngling shook his head, but Carryl searched anyway. Not finding anything more than some abrasions from the rocky outcropping, she stopped.

"I see you are fine. What is your name?"

"Braidyn," he said looking at her. "Will he be okay?"

"I believe so, but the longer he is out here, the less likely he will heal. How long have you been here?"

"Since last night. He came to warn us, but the dragons caught us before we reached the village." Wind whistled around them.

"It is okay. We'll get you back to the village." She turned to Wyn. "How many can you carry? There is the man with all the burns, the boy, and me. Is that too much?"

"I could do it if I knew there wouldn't be a dragon attack. If an attack came, I could not fight back."

Carryl nodded. "Let's try it. I don't hear the dragons right now." Turning to the boy, she said, "I am going to ask you to be very brave. I know that a dragon did this to you." She paused trying to think. "If a man was mean to you and hurt your friends, would you assume every man was mean because of one bad one?"

Braidyn shook his head.

"Good. Just because one dragon is mean, does not mean that all dragons are mean. I have a dragon with me. She is willing to fly us back to the village. We will get there in about a tenth of a glass. If we had to walk it would be closer to a half a glass. The man would have less of a chance to live. Are you willing to be brave and fly on the back of a good dragon?"

The boy looked at her with very solemn eyes. "This is not one of those who killed my family?"

Carryl exhaled. "No, she just fought this morning against three dragons who are doing those kinds of things."

The boy nodded. "I would know which one it is. He was aqua colored and he had two other bluish-green dragons with him."

Carryl nodded. "Those would be the ones we fought. No, come look. This dragon is the color of the flowers in the canyons in the summer."

"Bluebells?"

"You know your plants. Good."

The boy turned and saw Wyn. His eyes widened. "She is big."

Carryl laughed. "Not as big as the older dragons. Come, let's hurry. I need to get the man up. Will you help me?"

Together they managed to get the man onto Wyn. Carryl climbed up to her normal spot, and the boy followed behind her. Wyn took off, circled to make sure there were no dragons and then headed for the village. When the canyon rim came into view, Carryl called to Kyn, "I have two people. A man who is badly burned and a boy, Braidyn. I'll need help moving the man."

They landed to find Kyn and Casey waiting. At their feet lay a stretcher. Kyn reached to help the boy down and Casey reached for the man. As Casey laid him on the stretcher, Kyn turned to help. His face went ashen.

"Kyn," Carryl called, "what is it?"

But Kyn did not respond. He bent down to the man and took his hand that was the least affected by the burns. Carryl watched puzzled until she heard a word escape Kyn's mouth.

"Da."

"Oh, no," Carryl cried. "Da, please help me get him to the general store."

Without another word, Casey picked up the stretcher with Carryl's help. Kyn walked wordlessly beside it holding his father's hand. The boy trailed behind them, confused.

Upon reaching the general store, Casey pounded on the door until someone answered. "Quick," Casey commanded, "move aside. We have the merchant." One look was all it took to clear a path.

"Take him to the warmest place in his abode. I will need light, heat, and water," Carryl instructed. The others cleared the way. Murmurs went up about how this had happened, but Carryl didn't stop to answer any of the questions. The boy found the stove and sat down in an empty chair close by, staring straight ahead and letting warmth seep into his body.

In the abode, Carryl found water and bandages and created a salve. She knew she was going to have to remove the burned skin, but she was afraid to do so. She wanted a second opinion. Kyn didn't know enough and was too emotionally involved to help with that decision. She needed Meredyth. As she waited for her friend to come, she applied the salve to the areas that needed it the most. The worst areas she gently cleaned. These were far worse than the burns Ruskya had received. The thought of her friends' welfare flickered through her mind.

Meredyth approached quickly and quietly, and then expertly felt the burns. She pointed to several of the worst ones and reached for the scissors. Carryl nodded. She was glad to let someone else take over for a while. When the burnt skin had been removed, Carryl applied the salve and the bandages.

The whole time Kyn sat there, staring at his father, holding his hand. When they were done, Carryl put a hand on his shoulder. The youngling did not look up. "Kyn," she tried, but received no answer. She looked to Meredyth.

"I'll stay," Meredyth said. "He'll be okay. He doesn't seem to be in shock; he's acting more like Duskya does when she's talking to Wryn or another rider."

Understanding dawned on Carryl. "He's helping. He's healing from the inside. Just make sure he doesn't overdo it. The healing energy has to come from somewhere, and I am afraid it may take all of Kyn's reserves if he isn't careful."

Meredyth nodded. "Right. I'll be sure to have plenty of tea and food on hand."

Carryl went to find the boy, Braidyn. She needed to hear his story. She found him staring at the stove.

"Braidyn," she called softly, "Braidyn, can you come with me to get a bite to eat?" Braidyn looked up and nodded. He followed quietly after her. She served them both some stew and found a chunk of bread to share. The boy wolfed the food down. When was the last time he had eaten?

"Braidyn, when did the man arrive yesterday to warn you?"

"He came after dark. He said he had been to several farms, but no one believed him. My Da believed him, but said we shouldn't leave until morning. The man pleaded, but Da said no. I came out this morning to feed the cow and found the man sleeping in the barn. That is when the dragons attacked. They spewed green fire on the house. The man pulled me out and we went running. I cried for Da and Ma, but the man kept me going. I turned back to see the aqua dragon drop my parents from the sky. I didn't watch anymore; I ran. The dragons must have seen us because they started chasing us. Their fire fell closer and closer. Finally, the man pushed me into the crevice where you found me. He tried to follow me in, but got stuck. The entry filled with aqua flames. I have never seen that color of fire before. It was scary. I choked on the smoke, but I knew I was safe inside. The flames died down, but the man didn't move. I waited a long time, and then he finally moved to where I could see him."

Braidyn took a breath and then ate some more stew. The boy must be in denial, Carryl thought. There was no way he could so casually recount what had happened.

"The man told me stories. He said there were good dragons. He said I needed to be brave like the good ones. He told me to keep going, even when I wanted to turn around and see my family. He wouldn't let me. When we waited, even when he could barely talk, he spoke of a good dragon who would beat the aqua dragon. He said the dragon's name was Wyeth and he was icy blue. The color seemed to bring cooling to the heat from the flames of the aqua dragon. Do you know him?"

Carryl stared for a moment, wondered about this, but knew she had to respond. "Yes, Wyeth and his rider are friends of mine. Wyeth is strong and brave. He fought a worse dragon than the aqua dragon. He fought the turquoise dragon. We have to defeat them if we want life go back to normal."

"Carryl," Wyn called, "they are back. We must go."

Carryl sighed. She realized she was doing that a lot lately. "Braidyn, I have to go. The aqua dragon is back. I will return when I can. In the meantime, the merchant's wife will care for you. I also have friends here: Meredyth, and my Da, Casey. They will help you."

Braidyn nodded his understanding. Carryl checked her pouch, filled her waterskin with tea, and pulled her cloak around her tightly. She was ready to end this fight. She wished there were reinforcements, but for now, she was it.

*   *   *

As Wyn tried to fly out of the canyon, she let out a squawk and landed firmly back on the ground. "There is a net over the canyon. I cannot get out that way."

Carryl looked up and her eyes could just barely detect some type of barrier up there. This felt wrong. She walked Wyn back toward the main canyon and found that every time they tried to fly above the canyon, they were either blocked by netting or by dragon flames. They slowly headed to the mouth of the canyon.

"Wyn, I have a feeling we are trapped."

"I know, but what else can we do? If we stay here, they will rain fire down on the villagers."

Carryl nodded. "Let's go. Just be careful."

They moved along the way until they came to the mouth of the canyon. It seemed clear, but there was not enough room to fly through the entrance. They would have to walk out and then leap into the air. Just as Wyn put her weight down on the canyon floor to take flight, the ground gave way. The dragon and her rider fell into darkness. Carryl lost her grip and fell off Wyn. The last thought as she hit her head was for Ruskya.

CHAPTER 18: THE SEARCH BEGINS

THE BATTLE BLAZED around Ruskya as it had for the last day. Had it only been a day? The stray thought filtered through the flames, talons, and mental communications he was having with Duskya and Glendyn. At first, the turquoise dragon sat back and seemed to orchestrate the battle, but a couple of hours ago, he had reentered the battle and seemed to have targeted Ruskya and Duskya. He delighted in battling through Duskya's defenses to wound her so that Ruskya's mind would be confused. It was working, too, at least when the dragon could get past Duskya's defenses. She was good. She had learned her lessons well. The twins made an excellent team.

In the middle of the battle, Ruskya heard Carryl's voice call his name and then go silent. He felt the heat from the flames as they broke through his defenses. He called to Glendyn to help back him up. He needed to get out of this battle and find out what had happened to Carryl. Surprisingly, the turquoise dragon also seemed to back away, allowing Ruskya to withdraw. The turquoise dragon slowly moved back, allowing other dragons to take its place. Ruskya watched. Halfheartedly he attempted to chase it, but only for show. He allowed others to take his place in the fight as he retreated to the ground.

Wyeth needed a rest, anyway. They had been up there for several glasses already. Duskya followed on Wryn, calling after him to find out what was wrong. He told her to wait until they were on the ground.

Upon dismounting, Ruskya held on to Wyeth for a bit to gain back his land legs. Flying that long always made his legs rubbery when he returned to the ground. He realized that he should have taken more food with him. He needed to eat. He found the abode that had been set up as a dining area and entered. Duskya was right on his heels.

"What are you doing?" she demanded. She seemed to notice the stares around her, and quickly switched to mental communication. "What happened up there? That last bit of fire didn't need to get past your defenses. It hurt!"

Ruskya continued to get his food and to sit down at a small table. He motioned for his sister to do the same. "Go get some food, and I'll explain."

Reluctantly, she went and came back with some bread and cheese. As she sat down, the stare she gave him could have skinned a deer.

"All right," he said, realizing her eyes were as hard as Wryn's silver scales. "Ease up. It's Carryl. I was up there and I heard her call my name; and then, nothing. I need to find out what happened to her. Wyeth has called to Wylen and is trying to contact Kyn."

Duskya nodded, brushing a stray piece of dark hair back behind her ear. "I'm sorry I was so abrupt. I don't like the side effects of being your twin! When you get hurt, it hurts me. I can understand the occasional stubbed toe or accidental injuries, but when you get hurt and you don't have to…" She let the thought hang in the air. He chose not to pick it up.

"Now what?" she asked.

"I wait to hear back from Woolpren. I will have to clear it with Glendyn, but I may be leaving for the village. I think you should stay to help defend the riders here, but the turquoise dragon was withdrawing. That might mean a break in this battle."

"I hope so. Our riders can only handle so much of this. We were not meant to be fighters."

"That's for sure, but we seemed to have risen to the occasion." He paused as he heard from Wyeth. His face hardened and grew determined the longer he was quiet. Finally he looked up at Duskya, his eyes as cold as the ice they resembled.

"The farms near Philippi Canyon have been attacked and Kyn's father was badly burned. Two families have all but been destroyed. They don't know where Wyn or Carryl are. I'm going to go find out what I can."

"Ruskya, wait," Duskya stopped him from rising any further. "Sit down. See if you can find her first. Then talk to Glendyn."

Ruskya nodded as he sat back down. He envisioned the newest rider with her red hair and green eyes. He saw the concern in them when he had been in battle with the turquoise dragon the first time. He let his dragon senses search for her, but it was just dead air. He wondered if he was too far away, but he doubted it.

He shook his head as he rose. "No use, Duskya. Thanks for the thought. I'll go find Glendyn."

"I'm coming with you." She grabbed the bread and cheese and made a sandwich. She handed Ruskya his food. "You'll be no good to her if you don't have your strength back. Eat as we go."

"Thanks, sis."

They found Glendyn tending to Wyden. The royal blue dragon's sides were heaving. Glendyn was washing him down with damp cloths.

"Greetings, honored riders," Glendyn said. "It looks like the dragons have withdrawn for now." He paused and noticed the grim look in Ruskya's eyes. "What is wrong? Who has been hurt? Do we need to send for Carryl or Kyn?"

Ruskya shook his head. "No, Glendyn, I believe Carryl is missing." He explained what had happened at the end of the battle and then added, "Kyn can't find her, and the dragons can't seem to locate Wyn. Kyn needs to stay in the village to help his father heal from dragon fire. He was attacked trying to help a farmer's family make it back to the village in safety."

Glendyn nodded. "So, you want to go find her and are looking for my permission." He searched the younger rider's face, and then probed a little deeper. He saw exhaustion and care written there. He also saw a feeling that he understood but had not felt in over fifty winters. He recognized it as love for a woman. He smiled.

"Go, with my blessing. Keep in touch with us. And, Ruskya, don't let your feelings guide everything you do. Think with your head, not your heart, to bring her back safely. We want you both to come back in one piece. Do you understand?"

Ruskya nodded, "Yes, honored rider. I will take care to bring us both back."

"In one piece," Duskya added.

"In one piece," Ruskya agreed. He quickly packed a bag with extra clothes, an extra cloak, a blanket, and some food. Then he headed out to Woolpren village, all the while searching for the redheaded rider.

As he came upon the village canyon, he noticed that most the side canyons had been filled with farm animals. He realized how easily a dragon could come by and spew fire into the canyon and the animals would be barbequed—literally. He found a side canyon wide enough for Wyeth to fit into; they landed, and Ruskya headed for the general store.

Walking the canyon path, he noticed that most people were inside. He decided that was good, but wondered at the lack of guards. He would have to change that. They needed to know when dragons were in the air.

"Kyn," he called mentally to the youngling.

"Ruskya, where are you?" came the immediate reply.

"I'm heading to the general store."

"Good. I could use some help. I'm no good with people. They still view me as a kid. I need someone to talk sense into them."

"What's wrong, Kyn? Why do you need help with people?"

"Byran is in here talking of revenge. I think Casey would like to go after the dragons, also. He's been cooped up too long. Carryl taking off and not telling him where she was going has caused some problems."

"It's not going to help when I tell him I think she's been taken by the dragons."

"What?" Kyn exclaimed, the mental shout ringing in Ruskya's ears, "How?"

"That's why I'm here. I need to find her and bring her back," after a slight pause, he added, "in one piece."

"Well, hurry here. I'll tell them you are coming."

"Don't bother," Ruskya said as he climbed the few stairs to the doorway of the general store. "I'm here."

Opening the door, Ruskya was greeted by the aroma of the general store. He had always liked the blend of smells that the place held. This time though, he thought he could sense something else. It wasn't an odor; it was more of a feeling. He tried to place his finger on it, but it eluded him. It came to him as he walked into sight of the men around the stove. It was fear.

The men were in a heated argument over whether to leave the canyon and go find the dragons. One villager was adamant about avenging the deaths of the farmers. Ruskya wondered why a villager would care so much when a hand was placed on his arm. He looked down and saw his mother. He bent and gave her a hug.

"That's Byran," Meredyth informed him. "His daughter and her husband were killed and their farm burned. The children watched from a distance but escaped."

Another farmer was talking now.

"We halfta be careful, though. Those dragons are tricky. If'n they can steal one of our own out from under our noses without our even knowin' it."

Ruskya looked to Meredyth for an explanation. "That's Carryl's dad, Casey."

"Who's ta say she's gone, Casey?" another voice piped up. "Sure, I don't want anything to happen to Carryl, but she could be out on her dragon lookin' for a way to get those other dragons."

"Davyd, ya know she has never left without sayin' somethin' to me," Casey countered.

"And that's why I say we form a group and go looking," Byran took control again. "We can at least scout the area and see what we can do with more information."

"I agree," Ruskya stepped forward.

All eyes turned to Ruskya, amazed that he had just appeared out of nowhere. Kyn hid a smile. Leave it to Ruskya to make this type of an entrance. He wondered though where his teacher was taking this. He was supposed to discourage them from doing anything rash. This didn't sound like discouragement.

"We need to do a few things. First, a guard should be set up along the canyon rim. Any threat could be seen and the village could be prepared for it. Anyone good with a bow and arrow or other distance weapons could be up there to help defend. Don't shoot just any dragon, though. The blue-green hued dragons are the enemies here. Defenders and lookouts could be on a rotating system.

"Secondly, I would like a small—I say small as in two, maybe three, other men—to go with me to look for Carryl. I don't want anyone who will not listen to authority or who will easily be afraid. I don't know what we will find.

"Do we have anyone who will help with these tasks? I will put

Honored Rider Kyn in charge of the guard setup. Those interested will speak with him. Those with the courage and ability to obey orders, come talk with me about a scouting party. I will choose who goes. Understood?"

A murmur of assent went around the room. Kyn stood amazed at Ruskya. Where had that come from? He had been away from his trainer for just a few short days, but already something had changed him. He had heard the title, honored rider, and was surprised when Ruskya used it for him. Yet, it seemed to do the trick, for the men were addressing him with respect. They seemed to have forgotten his age, and many were clamoring to help with the guard. Kyn realized he would have his hands full here without dwelling on Ruskya.

* * *

Ruskya had four men who were interested in the scouting party. He looked them over. There was Byran, Casey, the farmer called Davyd, and a boy about Kyn's age. There was something about the boy that said he had a reason to be here.

"I meant what I said about picking who goes," Ruskya began. "I will ask your permission to weigh you using rider abilities. Do you agree to that?" All of them solemnly nodded, the boy almost in awe.

"Go ahead, rider, do what ya must," the farmer named Davyd said. "We've all got a stake in this mission. I've known Carryl since she was a wee babe. Casey, here, is her Da. Byran had his family taken by these here dragons, and Braidyn, well, he saw the merchant burnt by the dragons and his family and farm destroyed."

Ruskya sighed. "I still want to make sure that you all will obey orders. I don't doubt your courage, I doubt the ability to stay on task when that task may be different from what you think is best. I promised I would bring Carryl back in one piece. That promise goes for all who are in the scouting party. We have to keep each other together." The others nodded.

Braidyn spoke up, "If we go searching, we must be careful on the desert floor. I can keep an eye out for rocks to hide us and keep us safe from dragon fire." Ruskya nodded, but the boy wasn't done. "The merchant told me about a dragon who would help us. This dragon might be able to find the healer."

Ruskya looked at him. "What dragon would that be?"

"He is an icy blue dragon named Wyeth. He can fight the aqua dragon. The healer said that Wyeth was a friend and so was his rider. Can you ask them to help?"

Ruskya smiled. "I don't know why the merchant told you about Wyeth, but come, all of you. I have changed my mind. All of us will go, but you must all do as I say."

As they left, Ruskya sent a message to Kyn. "I'm leaving. I have Casey, Byran, Davyd, and Braidyn with me. We're going to go to Wyeth first, and then see what we can find of Carryl." Kyn sent an acknowledgment but he was too busy to do more than that. Ruskya understood. He met his mother's eyes as they headed out the door.

"Take care of the merchant, please. I will see what we can find. I'll be careful," he added before she could say it.

"I know you will. Think through things; don't follow just your feelings."

"Glendyn said the same thing."

"Glendyn has been around awhile and knows well. Come see me when you get back and let me know what you found."

Ruskya nodded and left. The others were waiting on the canyon path for him.

"I first want to know where Carryl kept her dragon," Ruskya told them. "We will go from there."

Casey led them to the place where he had last seen the dragon. Braidyn followed close behind. When they came to the side canyon, Braidyn stopped abruptly.

"What's wrong, young one?" Byran asked, and then he too sucked in air.

There, almost as if he had planned it, stood Wyeth with his wings partially out showing the iridescence. The pose made him seem larger than he really was. Ruskya hid a smile. The dragon must have been listening to the conversation earlier.

"It's Wyeth!" Braidyn whispered. "It has to be."

"Yes, Braidyn," Ruskya replied. "This is Wyeth," to the dragon he added, "show-off," and to the others he continued, "and I am his rider,

Ruskya. I know that Carryl needs help because I heard her call my name while I was in a battle. That is rare."

Letting the others absorb that thought, he looked around the canyon. Earlier, he had just been looking for a place to land. Now that he looked more closely, he could see it would be the perfect place for a dragon. There was a small space large enough for a small dragon to roust about halfway up the canyon wall. The opening was large enough for dragon wings to launch and to land, yet it was secluded from the rest of the village. As he glanced up, he noticed something he hadn't seen before.

"Wyeth," he called, "can you tell what is up along the rim of the canyon?"

"Not without flying up there."

"Well, leave your admirers and go look."

With a flap of his wings, Wyeth took off. Ruskya still admired the dragon when he saw him take off. The wings almost glowed as the light hit them, and the hind legs showed their power best. He noticed the others looking on in awe and amazement.

"Is he going to go fight the aqua dragon?" Braidyn inquired.

"No, Braidyn. We only fight because we have to. If we can settle this without having to fight anymore, we will. He is looking at something up on the rim of the canyon."

"It seems to be some type of netting. There is enough here to have covered the whole opening," Wyeth called back.

"Thanks, Wyeth. Why don't you stay up there and look for more of it. We'll follow back along the canyon."

Turning to the others he explained, "It looks like someone placed a net over the canyon so Wyn couldn't get out. She must have left from someplace else."

They retraced their steps to the village's main canyon path. There, Wyeth said he found a small amount of the netting again, hidden from plain sight. They decided to head out toward the desert floor. Cautiously, they made their way to the entrance where the canyon emptied out to the desert. Almost like a river running to meet the sea, the canyon slowly opened wider to embrace the desert. It was in this widening area that Braidyn noticed that the ground was torn up. Ruskya kept the others back from disturbing it. Wyeth landed on the desert floor.

Finding what he was searching for, Ruskya called the others to look for tracks like the ones he had found. They were able to trace the tracks back into the canyon. Ruskya called them back after they had gone a ways into the canyon.

"We know that she came this way, then. Now we have to figure out how far she got. We know she wasn't able to fly out of the canyon like she normally could. The netting, the space in the canyon, or something else forced them to come here. We need to find out what was here waiting for them. Be careful not to disturb any tracks."

They spread out and looked. They covered the area until they reached the widest point of the canyon, but couldn't find any further trace of dragon tracks. Ruskya began to notice some things about the other members of the scouting party. Giving Casey something to do was good for him. The man seemed to come alive. He was diligently searching every square inch of sandy floor. Braidyn seemed to be able to sit back and watch from a distance and still pick up on things. Davyd also was a solid person, someone good to have at your back. Byran was the one Ruskya worried about. He seemed eager for a fight. He had pent-up energy that was waiting to get revenge.

The search brought them back to the original place where Ruskya had found the track and the torn up ground.

"The ground doesn't look right," Braidyn said.

"What do you mean, boy?" Byran asked. "How can the ground 'look right'?"

"It doesn't look natural," Braidyn explained. "See how the sand has blown every which way over there?" he asked, pointing. "It isn't doing that in this area here." Again, he pointed to the area where the tracks stopped.

"I think the boy's right," Davyd added. "There aren't any plants growing here either."

"Yeah," Casey agreed. "There's small sage or grasses all around here, but not there. Why?"

Ruskya walked over to take a careful look. Bending down, he put his hand on the sand. He found it was hard packed. The ground he was standing on had a layer of soft sand that shifted with his weight or with the wind. That layer was missing from this other area, which covered a rectangle about the width of a dragon. Ruskya stretched out his finger and tried to bury it in the sand at the edge of the rectangle. He wasn't able to get his finger through the sand.

"That's not right!" Braidyn exclaimed. "I can dig in this sand. Why can't ya get your finger inta' that sand?"

"I don't know. Let me try digging here at the edge. The rest of you choose a spot around the edge and see if you can dig into the sand."

Everyone soon found a spot and began digging away. They found they could dig down a few inches and then they were on the desert's hard surface. They also found what appeared to be a board laying on the surface covering the rectangle. The board was covered with sand, or what appeared to be sand.

"What is it?" Casey called.

"It looks like a door," Davyd answered.

"What would a door be doing on the ground?" Byran asked.

"Covering a trap." Ruskya's voice was cold and hard, as were his eyes. "You all saw how Wyeth took off. He had to put all of his weight on the ground and push off with his hind legs and his wings. If the ground underneath him was unstable, he couldn't take off. I think what we have found is a covering for a hole that someone dug for a dragon trap. Let's get it off."

The men moved to Ruskya's side and carefully hoisted the cover to one side, revealing a deep hole.

"Ya were right!" Casey exclaimed. "Do ya think she fell in there?"

"I'm going to find out," Ruskya said. "Hand me some rope from my bag and lower me down into the hole."

The hole was too small for a dragon to stretch her wings to fly, but not too small for a dragon to spin around. The bottom of the hole revealed that Wyn had done just that. She had tried to fight, but something had stopped her from fighting. The floor of the hole was bare, but in the middle where the light was brightest, Ruskya caught sight of a golden sheen. He bent down and found a few strands of red hair. They were right beside a bloody rock. That was all he needed to see. The rage that built up in him was almost uncontrollable. It overwhelmed him to the point where Wyeth had to step in.

"Ruskya, hold on. Think. Stop. If you go off like that, you will get all of us killed. Ruskya, listen to me," the dragon almost screamed the last sentence.

Ruskya stopped in his tracks. What was he about to do? He looked around and found he was still in the dragon trap, but his hands were clenched and hurting. He still held strands of Carryl's hair in one hand. He took a deep breath and called to the men to bring him up.

Only Braidyn had the courage to talk to Ruskya when he came up. One look at his face and the men backed away. Braidyn didn't have the experience to know not to bother a man when he was that angry.

"What did you find, Ruskya?" the boy asked.

Ruskya seemed to mentally shake his head to clear it then with great care and gentleness held out his hand. "These, and a bloody rock. I think Carryl hit her head on the rock."

"No!" Casey exclaimed, stepping forward. His concern for his daughter overpowered his fear of the angry rider. He reached out a tender hand and caressed the strands that his daughter had left behind.

Ruskya continued, "We don't know where or how they took them. They must have erased all traces of their departure. They would have had to fly, or use a wagon for a ways."

"Wagons leave trails," Braidyn said, "even when people try to block out the tracks. They disturb the grasses and plants. Can I go up on the canyon rim? I can find the wagon trails," he paused, and said in a softer voice, "My Da taught me how to find wagon trails."

Ruskya nodded. "Would you like to ride Wyeth? He could get you to the rim without any problems." The boy's eyes widened, but he nodded. Ruskya motioned him to mount Wyeth.

"Alone?" the youngling asked.

"Yes, he'll bring you back. Just be sure to hang on. I'll head back to the general store on foot. I will need to figure out what we are doing from here."

"We'll come with you," Byran said. "Besides, I should check in on my family."

Davyd placed a hand on Byran's shoulder. "We'll find them and bring justice—not revenge, Byran, justice." Byran nodded absentmindedly. Casey just shook his head.

CHAPTER 19: A DAY WITH THE ENEMY

THE FIRST THING Carryl heard was a cacophony of voices. At first she thought she was back at Three Spans Canyon, but she didn't recognize any of these dragon voices. Then a familiar voice cut in and she shuddered. She was with the blue-green dragons, specifically with the aqua dragon. As she listened to their conversations, a name kept popping up: Kyanos. Who was he? He was spoken of with fear in hushed tones.

Carryl reached out for Wyn but couldn't find her. She wondered what had become of her dragon. She kept her eyes closed and decided to feel around her before opening them. She felt a presence she recognized but couldn't place. It was beside her.

"I know you are awake, Carryl, so you might as well sit up and get a drink." The voice was cold and commanding, just as it had been that day in Caravan Canyon with Kyle and Ruskya. She opened her eyes to see the turquoise rider bending over her with a waterskin. His expression showed concern, even if his voice hadn't.

"I should have known better than to leave that job to Kyle. He convinced me he could do it. I think he has gotten a bit big for his britches. It's time I bring him down a notch or two, don't you think?" the rider asked her, as he helped her to a sitting position. "Sorry about the ropes, but I was convinced you would try to run away the first chance you had. I couldn't let that happen, now could I?"

Carryl didn't bother answering. She sniffed the waterskin he held to her lips and took a tentative sip. It tasted good to her dry lips. She had some more and then pulled away.

"Thank you."

"Now about those bonds. If you promise not to run away as soon as they are off, I will have Cerulean come watch over you. He'll see to getting you food and a little privacy. Will you promise?"

Carryl thought about it. A bit of freedom would be nice, and she didn't have to run away right this moment. Besides, she needed to find Wyn first.

"All right."

"You can't agree and then, when you find your dragon, go back on your promise," he said, reading her mind.

She stared at him. "Stay out of my head! You don't belong there. Do I make myself clear?"

He just smiled at her. "I like your spunk. If you don't want me there, then learn to keep me out. Otherwise, it is an open invitation to me to come see what is there."

He motioned to a rider that walked by. The rider paused listened to the instructions and headed off to obey.

Carryl realized that he was the head of this group of riders. She didn't have any time to contemplate anything more, for a tall blond rider came forward.

"Kyanos," he addressed the turquoise rider, "you sent for me?"

"Yes, unbind her. Give her the freedom necessary to take care of personal hygiene and then feed her. Watch her carefully. She won't go anywhere until she finds her dragon. Don't let that happen. If she leaves, I will hold you personally responsible."

The rider bowed. "Yes, Kyanos. I understand and accept the responsibility."

"Carryl," Kyanos turned to her, "I present Cerulean. Do as he says as if the orders came from me." With that, the turquoise rider turned and walked away.

Cerulean went behind Carryl and with a couple deft slices of his knife cut her free. He returned and gave her a hand. Upon standing, she found herself looking up into his strange colored eyes. They looked like the color of the sky just before a storm. The eyes bore into hers. He turned away first.

"I thought Kyanos said you were the rider of the dragon we brought back."

"I am," Carryl said. Why did this rider not believe her?

"Then why aren't your eyes the purplish-blue of the dragon?"

Carryl paused. Her eyes were the green they had always been, what was wrong with that? "What do you mean?"

"When a dragon chooses a rider, the rider's eyes become the color of the mature dragon."

Carryl considered this. Images of her friends came to her mind. First, Ruskya's icy blue eyes, then Duskya with her silver eyes. Glendyn's royal blue eyes, also, flashed in her mind. Even Kyn seemed to have eyes the color of the dragons.

"I see you agree with me. You know the icy blue dragon, do you? The one Kyanos calls the twin."

Carryl flinched back as if she was slapped. Did everyone here read thoughts?

Cerulean laughed. "You can relax. Not all of the riders are capable of reading thoughts. Kyanos says it has something to do with Calamadyn and our dragons. Come, do you need some privacy?"

Carryl nodded. He led her to the entrance of the cave. They walked down a long passageway that ended at an arch with some sagebrush off to the side.

"Don't go far. And remember, I can read your thoughts if you decide to try anything."

Carryl shuddered. She knew several of the riders back at Three Spans Canyon could do that, but they allowed people their privacy.

Again, she tried to reach Wyn. What had happened to the dragon? She found a flicker of her presence. No answer, but at least she knew Wyn was alive and near. It disturbed her thinking of what it would take to incapacitate a dragon. She knew of some herbs that would render a human unconscious. Is that what they had done to Wyn?

"Come on," Cerulean called, "time to get back inside."

Carryl obeyed. Her stomach grumbled. They had mentioned food. The two walked back down the passageway, which gave way to a large cave. It was almost like a bowl had been dropped upside down and they were underneath it. A hole up at the top, large enough for a dragon to fly through, allowed the smoke from the fire to escape. Various riders were around the outside edge with their dragons. Others were gathering around the center fire. Cerulean lead her toward the fire and handed her some food.

"Do you mind if I make some tea?" she asked. He nodded consent. She took the cup he handed to her and pulled the pouch from her side. As she opened the pouch, she breathed in the aroma of Meredyth. A longing for the village and her friends came over her. She took a pinch of the tea out of the bag and put it into the mug. Then, with great care, not knowing how long it would be before she saw her friends again, she closed the precious bag. With the tea made, she was ready to go wherever Cerulean took her.

A hand on her shoulder stopped her. She looked up into aqua blue eyes.

"So, you finally decided to come to the right side, huh?" Kyle's loud voice drew the attention of several around them. Carryl carefully removed his offending hand. She avoided his eyes; they reminded her too much of the aqua dragon.

"Hi, Kyle," she said trying to hide the disdain she felt for the man. She saw that others seemed to look up to him. Cerulean just sat back watching what would happen.

"Do you need a place to eat?" he asked. "I have a spot over here." He began to lead her, but she stayed put. "What's wrong, Carryl?" he continued, "we villagers have to stick up for each other. I hear there may be a dragon for you."

"I already have one," she managed. All the peace the tea had given her was gone. It had shattered with the first note of Kyle's voice.

"Well, then let me come with you," he said and placed his hand on her arm.

"Kyle, I would prefer to eat alone." This time her tone portrayed her feelings.

"Really," Kyle said looking at Cerulean. "And eating with Cerulean is what you call alone? Or do you have eyes for him already?"

Carryl felt disgust welling up inside of her. "Kyle, I meant what I said. I would prefer to eat alone. It appears that I have no say over what Cerulean does. I think I am stuck with him one way or another. Even if we found your nice little nook, he would still come with me. You wouldn't have me as alone as you would like."

Kyle glanced at Cerulean and held the stare, but something made him turn away.

"Fine, but I have Kyanos's ear. He trusts me. If you want out, come to me."

Carryl shuddered. Unwillingly, an image of Kyle striking Calyb's mother came to mind, followed by the aqua dragon dropping Braidyn's parents to the ground. She turned to Cerulean. She didn't know if he was any different, but at least he wasn't acting so creepy.

He led her back to where she had been tied up. She noticed the other riders avoided Cerulean. She was glad. He offered her a seat, and she sat down. As she ate, she observed the layout. There was only the one entrance through the passageway. She didn't count the hole in the roof as a possible exit since she didn't have a dragon.

"It was designed to keep things in," Cerulean stated.

"What?"

"This cave. It was designed to keep hatchlings in and protect them from the outside."

"What do you mean?" Carryl repeated.

"This is where Ardyn kept the hatchlings. He said it was perfect for them. He could protect them from wandering eyes, and there was only one way people could get in. He forgot about dragons, though. The turquoise dragon surprised him."

This is where Ardyn had the hatchlings? She had heard of him among the riders and from Duskya. How did Cerulean know this?

"I knew Ardyn. We were friends until he decided to not use Calamadyn anymore."

"You knew Ardyn?" she repeated. She had learned not to judge riders' ages by their appearances, but she would have thought this rider was closer to her age.

"Ardyn and I grew up together. We were in the same procession. The dragon chose me and not him, but we didn't let that get in the way of our friendship. A dragon couldn't ruin our relationship, but a plant could. How ironic is that?"

"I'd say that it is sad. Friends are hard to come by," she paused and saw Kyle across the way glaring at her. Cerulean noticed her gaze.

"Yes, they are. He is not a friend, I take it?"

"Kyle? No. I only met him the night at the general store when he was offering people free dragons. Then we spent the day together in the trials. He didn't win me over." Carryl felt that was the safest way to put it.

"No, I wouldn't think he would. I don't know what Kyanos sees in him; unless it is someone to do his bidding without questioning, and with a penchant for the nasty side."

"You don't take to killing woman?" she asked before she could think better of it.

Cerulean glanced at her. She could feel him this time as he tried to find her thoughts. She didn't know what to do; so, helplessly she let him.

"He did that?" he asked with disgust.

"Did what? I felt you in my head, but I don't know what you saw."

"The farmers' wives. He killed them." This time it was a statement not a question. "I thought he was just boasting as men will do. I didn't believe him."

"I heard the children who watched it tell the tales of their mothers," she said in her quiet way. "When those tales reach all the villagers, you will have a war on your hands."

"Yes, we will. I will have to have a talk with Kyanos."

"You never answered my question," Carryl said boldly this time. Cerulean seemed to be a real person, someone she didn't need to be afraid of.

"Do I take to killing women?" he repeated. Then he shook his head. "No. Senseless killings are not right. Don't get me wrong, though. If you tried to escape, I would hunt you down. You would probably wish you were dead by the time I was through."

The coldness in his voice chilled Carryl to the bone. She remembered how Ruskya had been so tired after fighting Kyanos and wondered if part of that was in the threat from Cerulean.

Finishing her food, she set her plate down. She hoped that Cerulean would take it for her and give her some privacy. Instead he handed it to another rider. So much for that, she thought.

"Carryl?" a frantic voice called through her thoughts. "Carryl, little one, are you there?"

Trying not to show the surprise on her face, Carryl responded. "Wyn, I am here and safe. How are you?"

"I am here. I do not know what they have done to me. I cannot move my wings. My mind feels drowsy."

"I think they have given you some herb to keep you asleep."

"Carryl, there is another dragon here," Wyn said with fear. "The aqua dragon is here, and I cannot fight him. He laughs at me when I try to blow my fire at him."

"Is Kyle there also?"

"No, just the dragon, and another human. I do not know him."

"Where are you, Wyn?"

"In a canyon. There is no room to fly up and out. I would have to fly through the canyon to get out." Panic was starting to take hold of Wyn's voice.

"Easy, girl. Calm down. Is he hurting you?"

"No, but I don't want him around me."

"I understand. Kyle gave me the same feeling. Sometimes, though, we have to put up with what we don't like. Calm down, girl." Carryl was suddenly jerked back to reality, by two hands on her knees. Cerulean's storm green eyes gazed into hers.

"She is awake. What does she say?" Carryl tried to pull away, but Cerulean moved his hands to hold her from moving. "What does she say— this dragon you claim as yours, but who has not marked you."

"I don't have to tell you what she says to me," Carryl said fighting.

"You can do this easy, or you can do it hard. Which will it be?" Carryl tried to squirm away, but the rider was stronger. He held her head in his hands and pulled her head to his chest and held it there. Carryl couldn't move.

"Wyn, what is happening?" she called, trying to block out what was happening to her. "Wyn?" but there was no answer.

Carryl almost fell when Cerulean let go of her head and moved away. Rage was on his face as he stormed toward where Kyle had last been. Carryl was confused. She wasn't hurt, but she felt violated. What had Cerulean done to her, and why hadn't Wyn answered her? She reached out again to find her dragon. It was like before. Had someone given her more of the herb?

Her eyes searched for the outraged rider. They found him as he bent down and picked up Kyle.

"Get your dragon out of there!" His voice wasn't loud, but the authority silenced every conversation around him. All eyes were upon them.

Kyle pushed Cerulean's hands away from him. "I don't have to, rider. Kyanos told me I could let him in there. He wants to give her as good a chance as any of having one."

Kyle never saw what hit him. Carryl wasn't even sure what happened. One moment Kyle was standing there smug and cocksure. The next, he was on the ground holding his stomach.

"And if I ever see you harm an innocent woman, I will administer justice. This I vow by my dragon."

Kyle cowered on the ground holding his stomach. Others glanced away, afraid. They had never seen this type of rage before. There were always scuffles, but Cerulean usually stayed out of them. He didn't lower himself to the average rider. If he was swearing punishment on a rider, others knew to look out.

Cerulean turned and walked back to Carryl. She noticed his eyes seemed to be more of a storm, but they had calmed down compared to when he left.

"Is she still awake?" he asked.

Carryl wasn't sure if she should bring on his anger, and so decided to answer. "No. She went back to sleep as you left."

He nodded. "So someone else is with her, or..." he didn't finish the sentence.

"Or, what?" Carryl asked. "Or the aqua dragon has hurt her so badly she passed out?"

"That or she went there willingly so he would leave her alone," the rider admitted.

"If she was hurt that badly, wouldn't I know it? If she goes into grief when she loses her rider, wouldn't it be true the other way around?"

He shook his head. "No, the bond isn't as strong for the rider as it is for the dragon. You say that in the present tense as if she has lost her rider. You are still here."

Carryl cringed. Should she tell him? He didn't believe her anyway about being Wyn's rider. She decided to tell the whole story of how the turquoise rider had attacked and Marysa had died. She described how she was asked to be Wyn's rider.

When the telling was over, Cerulean just looked at her. "You are her rider," he stated.

Carryl nodded. "Please, don't let her be hurt."

Cerulean looked away. "I don't have a say in that."

"What do you have a say in?"

He didn't reply, just stared into space.

* * *

The rest of the afternoon passed uneventfully. Carryl went outside the nesting cave another two times. Each time she tried to think of a way to escape, but Cerulean seemed to know how to intimidate her. Besides, Wyn wasn't with her. Wyn woke up twice and then went back to sleep. Both times, she saw another dragon in the area with her. She was not as scared, but still she could not move her wings to escape.

The evening meal was being served when Kyanos entered the cave. Kyle met him first and held some sort of conference. Kyle must not have liked what he heard, for he hung his head. Later he lifted it and walked away with confidence. Kyanos came to where Carryl and Cerulean had just sat down to eat. He motioned for them to continue to eat and joined them.

"How goes it, Cerulean?" Kyanos asked.

"Fair. You know I would rather be with the dragon than with the rider."

"I know, but you also know I have no one else I can trust with her. The dragon is more easily subdued than the rider."

"What have you done to Wyn?" Carryl asked, her voice icy calm. She wasn't about to make a scene, but she was going to find out where and why her dragon was being kept.

"I am just keeping her safe for her own good. If she was free to fly around right now, she would hurt herself and other dragons."

"Why? What are you doing to her?"

"I am breeding her. We need hatchlings. If you notice, there are only male riders. Our riders and dragons pair by their gender. We have no female dragons. I wanted Calamadyn so that I could use it to increase our numbers. Since your riders have not consented, I have had to resort to this.

"What do you know about the herb?" he asked Carryl. She was still reeling from the news that he was trying to breed Wyn. She didn't hear his request.

"I said, what do you know about Calamadyn?"

Carryl debated what to say.

As she did, Kyanos added, "Ardyn tried to hide from me what he knew. He found out the hard way that I will find what I am looking for. I will search every last memory that you have if I must, but I will find what you know."

She felt a hand on her back and turned. It was Cerulean.

"Tell him. I don't like to watch when he drags things out of people."

If Ardyn had given all of his secrets away, what could her little bit of knowledge do to help or harm?

"I had not heard of Calamadyn until a few weeks back." She went on to explain what Glendyn and Ruskya had told her.

"Who was the rider who told you this?" Kyanos demanded.

It was said in such a way that Carryl almost immediately responded. She realized the rider was manipulating her. Instead, unbidden, Ruskya's icy blue eyes came to her memory.

"It's the twin, Kyanos," Cerulean answered.

Carryl turned on him, but he responded before she could say anything. "When you leave your thoughts open for the world to see, I will see them."

"You can control yourself," she said indignantly.

"He could," Kyanos said, "but then he wouldn't be any use to me. He's been with me for too many winters to go back to those nice traditional manners. Haven't you Cerulean?"

Cerulean bowed to Kyanos. "You know me too well, old friend." The word friend almost sounded wrong. It was as if the word was dragged out of the rider, and that he would have chosen a different word.

"That I do," Kyanos returned.

"You are doing what to Wyn?" Carryl asked, the reality of what he had said earlier sinking in.

Cerulean placed a hand on her knee as if to hold her there. "He won't hurt her."

"No, I won't hurt the only chance of keeping my dragon colony alive," Kyanos agreed. "I just want a chance to have the eggs, one for each of my riders."

"But, I thought it took dragons several moons before they laid their eggs to hatch," Carryl protested.

"Yes, that is the case."

"How do you intend to keep her with you that long? Are you going to keep her drugged the whole time?"

"Oh, my, no! There are much easier ways to keep a dragon with you than that. This is, just as I said, to keep her from hurting herself or my dragons. That often happens in dragon breeding, and I have learned ways to avoid it."

"And how do you keep a dragon when she doesn't wish to be kept?" Carryl demanded.

Cerulean, again laid a hand on her, as if in warning. "You keep the rider with you."

The air escaped Carryl as if she had been punched. "You expect me to stay with you?"

"No, Carryl," Kyanos replied, "I *know* you will stay with me. You will come with us as soon as your dragon can be moved without hurting her. Already some of my men are ready to return to our warmer climate. As soon as their dragons have a chance, I will let some of my men return home. We will leave in a few days."

The words 'leave in a few days' echoed in her head. This couldn't be happening. She couldn't be hearing this. And to think she had left without telling her father good-bye.

"We all have to make sacrifices, dear," Kyanos said. "I suggest you view yours as leaving your father behind."

Carryl almost laughed. A sacrifice to leave her father? She had spent many seasons wishing she was old enough to leave home, believing that he hated her. Now, when she knew better, she was being pulled away.

She buried her head hoping it would hide the thoughts swirling there. At the same time, she reached out to comfort Wyn. She envisioned herself smelling Meredyth's tea and the comfort it brought. She pictured herself serving Wyn that cup of tea, and the two of them being comforted by it. Amazingly, a peace came over her. She would do what was needed to escape and to bring Wyn with her.

"Thank you, little one," Wyn's weak voice cut in. "I needed that. This is not how it should be, but I know that we will escape together, and who knows, I may bring some eggs home to the colony."

"Oh, Wyn." A slight sob escaped her. "I am so sorry."

"Little one, do not fret. I am fine."

Carryl felt a soft hand on her back. She straightened, but the hand stayed there as if comforting her. Kyanos was gone, but Cerulean was still there.

"Don't cry, Carryl," he said so softly, she almost didn't hear him. "It will be fine. This twin," he continued, "is he really Ardyn's boy?"

Carryl nodded. That she knew for sure. "His name is Ruskya."

"And he rides the icy blue dragon that fights Kyanos as no one else ever has."

"Is that wrong?"

"No, I think it is good, because Kyanos was starting to think he could do whatever he wanted to, as with your dragon. That is not how it should be. She should have been given the choice of our dragons and left to decide who has the privilege of breeding her."

Carryl looked at him in awe. "You know about dragon breeding?"

"I was an apprentice to Ardyn." A bitter laugh escaped him. "Imagine that, we were friends, and I was the rider, but I was *his* apprentice."

"What did you learn?"

Cerulean seemed willing to talk. They talked of herbs and healing, of dragons and hatchlings, long after everyone else had gone to sleep.

Finally he turned to her and said, "You will need your strength. Rest now. I will not allow anyone to harm you." At her look of hesitation, he added, "This I vow by my dragon."

Carryl nodded and pulled her cloak around her. As she drifted off to sleep, she wondered who this rider was.

CHAPTER 20: IN SEARCH OF CARRYL

RUSKYA FOUND KYN beside his father. One look and he realized why these people wanted revenge; he was amazed the man was still alive. If dragons did this, then what would prevent them from returning? He laid a hand on Kyn's shoulder. The youngling looked up. Ruskya could tell the boy was discouraged.

"Come, Kyn, let's get something to eat."

Automatically, the boy moved. When he sat down at the table, it was as if he didn't see the food before him.

"Kyn," Ruskya quietly said, "What is wrong? You look like you haven't slept since I last saw you." Kyn just stared at the food in front of him. "Kyn, eat," Ruskya said.

As the youngling ate, Ruskya told him about what they had found, how Carryl had been chased into a trap, and how Braidyn had offered to find the wagon tracks. He explained the boy's wonder at being allowed to ride with Wyeth to the rim. Kyn smiled at that. Ruskya then asked about Meredyth.

"She's fine. She has helped a lot with Da," Kyn replied. "Da has been hurt badly, Ruskya."

Ruskya nodded, encouraging the boy to continue.

"I am trying my best to heal him, but I don't know if I will be able to do it. I'm scared he will not live, let alone have any kind of life after this."

"Kyn, I think you are doing too much. I don't understand how this healing works, but it looks like you are starting to wear yourself down."

"That's what Meredyth says. Ruskya, what is too much when it is your da?"

"You have a point there. I know if it was within my power to bring my da back, I would do it. What you need to keep in mind, though, is that we need you. You are rare, Kyn. No one else can heal like you do. You take the pain out of people's memories. If you are so worn out that you can't function, then we can't fight against these dragons who did this. Does that make sense?"

Kyn nodded. "I guess I forgot there was a bigger picture. How do I keep it all together?"

Ruskya laughed. "That, my youngling, is the question. If you can figure that out, then you can sell it to all the world. People have been trying to come up with an answer to that question for ages."

Kyn grinned. "Well, my financial problems would be solved, but I didn't think riders had financial problems."

"That's true, so there must be some reason these other dragons are coming. They want something, but what?"

"I thought they wanted Calamadyn."

"That's what the turquoise rider said, but why wage a full-blown war for a plant?"

"Good question. If you can answer that one, we'll both be prized by all."

Ruskya smiled. "Youngling, I don't think you are so young anymore. You have grown up."

"You would too, if you had read the memories of those young ones," he replied soberly.

They were interrupted by Braidyn running in.

"Rider Ruskya," the boy began, "they said I would find you here." He stopped short, realizing someone else was at the table. Ruskya noticed the glow the youngling had. Was that just from riding Wyeth? And how had Kyn's father heard so much about his dragon, anyway?

Ruskya realized the boy was waiting for an introduction. "Braidyn, this is Rider Kyn, the merchant's son. He was here helping his father heal while we were out looking for Rider Carryl."

Braidyn nodded. "I am sorry about your father," he began. "He," here the boy faltered, "he was good to me and protected me from the aqua dragon."

He turned to Ruskya, "Wyeth took me to the canyon's rim and I saw the tracks. They didn't bother hiding their tracks well. They abandoned the wagon not far from where the aqua dragon had found the merchant and me. Wyeth flew me out, and we saw the wagon hidden in the sagebrush. They were headed toward Philippi Canyon."

Ruskya held up his hands to stop the boy. "Wait," he commanded, "Wyeth flew you where?"

"Honestly, Rider Ruskya, I didn't ask him to. We took off from the rim, and I thought about looking, and all of a sudden, he was flying in that direction. He circled over where the wagon was hidden and then flew back. He landed in the small canyon where Carryl's dragon landed. I came here as soon as I could."

Ruskya calmed down. "It isn't your fault, but I will have to have a talk with Wyeth about flying off to other places unannounced."

"Don't scold him too badly, please," Braidyn requested. Kyn hid a laugh in his hands as if he was coughing. Ruskya glared at him.

"I won't, Braidyn," Ruskya assured him. "Would you be willing to take me to that place?"

"Sure. I don't know how far it was. Rider Carryl said that to fly from where we were was a tenth of a glass, but it would be more like half a glass to walk it. The wagon should only be just a fraction of a glass away by those reckonings."

"All right. Have you eaten anything?" The boy shook his head. Ruskya had him sit down and take his place. "I'll be back in a bit. I want to talk this over and see if any of the others are ready to go." Braidyn just nodded his head, since his mouth was full of food.

Outside the room, the two riders talked. "What do you think, Kyn?" Ruskya began, "Should it just be the three of us? It would be a bit much, but Wyeth could carry us."

"I think Casey should come. After all, Carryl is his daughter."

"You're right. This means we'll need to walk."

"What if we are out there and a dragon comes? We'll end up like my father."

"I can help protect us for a while, and Wyeth will fight them."

"That sounds good. It's times like this that I wish Wylen was old enough to fly. He could carry me and Braidyn, and Wyeth could get you and Casey."

"That would be nice, but give him time. He'll have his own adventures to be a part of."

* * *

It was mid-afternoon when the four set out. Braidyn searched the skies for dragons as he led the way to the wagon. After just a couple of moments, they caught sight of the wagon tracks. He had been right. The tracks sunk deep into the sand as if they were carrying a heavy load. Within a few moments more, they found the end of the tracks and the wagon hidden under some sagebrush just as Braidyn had said. A thorough investigation of the wagon turned up the pouch that Carryl used filled with healing herbs, some leather bindings riders use to create halters for young dragons, and a cloak.

"What're these?" Casey asked holding up the braided leather.

"Those are used when you are training a dragon to fly with a group," Ruskya explained. "Usually, the dragon is too little to be ridden, but the rider flies on another dragon, calling the dragon to follow."

"What would these riders need them for, though?" Kyn wondered.

"I don't know," Ruskya replied.

"Do ya think Carryl will need these herbs?" Casey asked next. The question hung in the air.

"Let's hope not," Ruskya said, swallowing the fear that was starting to build up in his throat.

"Why did they take her?" Braidyn asked in a quiet voice.

No one had an answer.

"And why stop out here in the middle of nowhere?" Kyn asked.

"Prob'ly so's we didn't just follow 'em straight to their hideout," Casey replied.

"That makes sense," Ruskya answered. "Where are they though?"

"The attacks have all been on farms near Philippi Canyon," Kyn said thoughtfully. "This is pointing right there, too. Is there a place where they could hide over in that area?"

"What's so special about Philippi Canyon?" Braidyn asked.

"Well, my father used to raise hatchlings there," Ruskya replied. "It has also been known to grow an herb that the turquoise rider wants. It's where Carryl found the Calamadyn."

"Who's the turquoise rider?" Casey inquired.

"Ruskya, the villagers have only dealt with Kyle's dragon, the aqua one," Kyn stated.

"That makes me wonder why the turquoise rider would divide his forces and send only a small group to hassle the villagers."

"Why hassle them in the first place?" Kyn asked.

"True. I don't understand."

"There's a whole bunch I don't understand," Casey admitted. "But one thing I do know. My daughter became a rider, and now other riders 'ave taken her."

Ruskya put a hand on the older man's shoulder, "Sir, I have made a vow to bring her back. If it is within my power, she won't be hurt." The lowering sun showed the determination in Ruskya's icy blue eyes.

"She's blessed ta have friends like ya, rider."

The four headed back to the village so that they would arrive before dark. The guard reported no dragons had been seen, other than Wyeth. Ruskya encouraged them to keep on the lookout.

After making the rounds, Ruskya ended up at his mother's abode. He had been invited to stay at the general store, but he thought it was getting a bit crowded. He needed a place where he could think and relax. His mother fixed him his favorite meal, and sat and listened as he told about the day. When he wanted to sit and quietly stare at the fire, she let him.

He tried to communicate directly with Glendyn, but the distance was too far. So instead, he sent a message through Duskya. The reply came back that all was quiet at Three Spans Canyon. Duskya sent her greetings and encouraged him to stay in one piece. He laughed at that.

Next, he tried to find Carryl. He focused on her face and her presence. He reached out toward Philippi Canyon. For some reason, the hatchling cave came to mind. He blended that with his thought for her. He saw her in his mind's eye. There were twenty riders spread out in the cave with about ten dragons. Most of them were sleeping, but others stood around the fire in the center of the cave. A tall blond man stood over Carryl. He appeared to be guarding her. She was sleeping peacefully. Ruskya started to call her, but thought better of it. For the moment, it was enough just to see her and to know where she was. They would go out to Philippi Canyon before dawn.

*   *   *

Before the sun was up the next morning, Ruskya was preparing for his day. Meredyth had arisen with him despite his protests and fixed breakfast. Ruskya had communicated with Kyn the previous night to round up the others and that they should all meet here before dawn. Braidyn, Casey, and Davyd joined them for the morning meal.

"Ya know where my daughter is?" Casey asked as soon as he saw Ruskya.

Ruskya nodded and motioned the four into Meredyth's small abode. They took seats around the table, and Meredyth served them.

"Carryl is in the hatchling cave at Philippi Canyon," Ruskya announced. The others stared at him blankly, but Meredyth gasped. "It's at the south end of the canyon," Ruskya went on. "Wyeth took me there after the three-day storm."

Meredyth regained her composure and poured tea all around.

"Kyn and I will fly there by dragon. The rest of you will need to come on foot. I want you to stay out of sight and avoid the dragons. If all goes well, we'll sneak in and out without drawing any unwanted attention. If that doesn't work, we may need your help in creating a diversion."

"How will we know where to go?" Davyd asked.

Ruskya thought for a moment. "I can draw you a map."

"Or," Meredyth put in, "if Kyn's father is stable enough to be left alone, I could show them."

All eyes looked at her.

"I know some quick paths to get there. I also know my way around the cave. There is a small opening that will lead out to the canyon. It is almost invisible from anywhere except right on top of it. Even then, you wouldn't know where it leads."

"Da is doing better. I think Ma can take care of him for now," Kyn answered.

"Then ya'll be our guide?" Casey asked.

Meredyth nodded. One look was all Ruskya needed. His mother's face had the same determined look that Duskya used.

"We will need provisions. I want to leave before the sun crests the desert floor," he said. The others agreed and headed out to gather what they would need.

When they reconvened, Byran had joined the group. Ruskya weighed him. He wondered if the man would chase revenge in place of obeying orders.

Byran just stared right back. "I'll obey, if that's what you're worried about," he said. "I won't go after him, unless the moment presents itself and Carryl is safe."

Ruskya nodded. "Let's go. We'll meet up with you at the north end of the canyon."

"Ma," he called mentally. She looked up at him.

"You will hear me call to you like this in the canyon. I will give you directions. You must tell the others what needs to be done."

Meredyth nodded.

"Men," Ruskya said, "when you get there, my mother is more than just a guide. I will be giving her directions. You must follow them to the letter. Do you understand?"

The four nodded.

"Blessings upon us all," Ruskya called as they left.

"We'll need them," Kyn mentally added.

"I know," Ruskya said.

"You're sure she's there?" the youngling asked.

"I saw her last night. There were about twenty other riders around the cave. One, especially, seemed to be watching her. I have no idea how many more are around."

"How do you know there aren't other riders outside?"

"I don't. That's why we are going now. We'll scout it out and see what we can find."

The ride to Philippi Canyon seemed longer than usual in their anticipation of what they would find. When they arrived on the north end of the canyon, they landed among sagebrush. Both of them stretched out to see what they could find. Kyn spotted ten dragons farther south of them. Ruskya looked for Carryl and saw that she was still in the cave. The same rider was watching over her. He searched around the canyon but could tell no more than Kyn. There were ten dragons somewhere around the mouth of the cave.

"Wyeth, can you figure out anything more?"

"Wyn," the dragon answered. "She's somewhere nearby, but I can't tell exactly where. She is awake, but she can't move freely. There are two dragons with her and one human. Oh, no," Wyeth flinched back physically as if dragon fire had been spewed all over him. Then he ducked down to become small.

"Wyeth," Ruskya asked, "What is it?"

Even the mental answer was a whisper, "The turquoise dragon is there with Wyn. I don't think he caught me, but I don't know." Ruskya nodded and conveyed the information to Kyn.

"Well, we will have to be very careful then," the youngling said. "We'll have to guard our minds."

Ruskya agreed. They would definitely have to be more careful.

CHAPTER 21: KYANOS'S CONTROL

CARRYL WAS AWAKENED by someone calling her name.

"Ruskya?" she asked turning over.

"No, Carryl," Cerulean's soft voice replied. "Wake up."

She sat up looking around the cave. It hadn't changed much. There were only a handful of riders up this early. She glanced up at the hole to see if it was daylight yet.

"It's still dark out, but I thought if you got up now, you could have a bit more privacy to wash and get ready for the day," Cerulean answered her unspoken question.

Carryl nodded and stood up. She noticed that he had a cloth in his hand and a waterskin hung from his shoulder. He motioned for her to follow him. He led her out of the cave, through the passageway, and out under the arched entrance to the hatchling cave. She wondered if Wyn had ever been in the cave as a little dragon. Cerulean handed her the towel and the waterskin. She almost dropped the skin in surprise when it touched her hand. It was warm!

"Thank you," she said.

"I thought you would appreciate it. If we were at our colony, you would have been treated as a guest. You should be a guest here as well."

Carryl didn't ask how a guest could be there against her will, but he looked at her as if he knew what she was thinking. His eyes said that he didn't like it any better than she did.

"Thank you," she repeated and headed off to the little privacy spot she had found yesterday. The canyon wall caved back a little from the archway. Carryl figured it was somewhere along the eastern side of the passageway. It created a small alcove filled with sagebrush, but also a lone tree. Finding a log, she sat down and started to wash her face with the tepid water. As she washed, she decided to check in on Wyn.

"Good morning, Wyn," she called. "How are you this morning?"

"Good morning, little one," came the reply. "Things are okay, but I am a bit scared. The turquoise dragon is here."

"Are you alone with him?" was Carryl's concerned question.

"No, his rider is here, and another dragon. This one is different. I feel like I have met him before, but I can't remember when or where. He is an odd color."

Carryl thought about it. Cerulean had been Ardyn's apprentice. Could Wyn have met his dragon as a hatchling?

"Wyn, what color is this dragon?"

"It is the color of the sky before a storm."

Carryl sucked in air. She wondered if Cerulean knew that his dragon was with Wyn. He seemed able to read her thoughts. She wondered if she could communicate with him as she did with Ruskya. She decided to try.

"Cerulean," she called tentatively.

"Carryl?" he replied immediately with an edge to his voice of concern.

"I am fine," she assured him. "There is no danger. I just wondered if you knew where your dragon is."

"What do you mean?" he responded cautiously.

"Wyn says there is a dragon the color of the sky before a storm with her, along with the turquoise dragon and Kyanos." There was a pause without any reply. "Cerulean?" she called as she tightened the stopper on the waterskin. "Are you still there?"

"I am here," he replied angrily. "Come, now. Let's go."

Carryl gathered her things and hurried back to where she had left him. Cerulean grabbed her arm and pulled her along. Instead of going back down the passageway, he led her to the right of the entrance. It appeared to be the end of a box canyon, but Cerulean found a path that led deeper back. Soon she was having to avoid plants and twigs both beside and above her. One moment she was ducking under a twig from sagebrush and the next she was in what felt like total darkness.

"Cerulean?" she whispered. "Where are we?"

"Hush," he whispered in her ear. "I don't want him to know we are here. Follow me without making any noise."

Carryl thought that would be unlikely since it was pitch black, but he motioned for her to place her hands on his shoulders, and they started to walk steadily forward. Soon her eyes grew accustomed to the dark, and she too could see enough to walk without tripping. Before long, a large cavern opened up before them lit by torches around the walls. Carryl dropped her hands from Cerulean's shoulders, just as he marched off to Kyanos.

"How dare you," he accused. "Kyanos, you said you would let me do it my way with Wymar. You said I could wait until we returned home." His statements and his long stride had brought him face-to-face with Kyanos. Kyanos's build gave him an advantage over Cerulean, yet Cerulean seemed to be on equal footing with the large rider.

"You feel I have offended you?" Kyanos said, his voice trying to soothe. "I was thinking of your honor, Cerulean."

"My honor? How?"

"I have stated that those whose dragons have had a chance at breeding will be able to leave first. I have decided to make the others wait until they return home. Yours will be the last dragon to have the chance to breed here. Then you can ride Wymar and lead the female back home as your own if you wish."

"How dare you!" Cerulean spat the words out. "As if one could own a dragon! You add insult to injury, my friend."

"Friend I am, and yet you do not accept the gift I am offering?"

"It is not yours to offer. It is the dragon's to offer. She has already given herself to her rider."

"Then take her rider with you, and the dragon will follow." He caught Cerulean's hand just before it reached his face. "I would not try that, Cerulean," Kyanos said icily, his eyes as hard as the stone they resembled. "I am trying to honor you. Yet you do not accept and try to strike me," he paused. "Do not try that again," he repeated with emphasis.

While the two argued, Carryl looked around. They seemed to have forgotten her. She saw the cavern was large; there was ample space for the three dragons inside and the riders were nowhere near the dragons. She saw the turquoise dragon as it turned on Cerulean's dragon. The two were almost like two bucks fighting over a doe. Carryl noticed that Wyn was not drugged as she had assumed. Instead, her wings were wrapped with some kind of cloth and then bound with braided leather. Another halter-like piece was secured around her nose.

Carryl looked back to see if they would notice her walking toward her dragon and stopped in her tracks. The sound of the blow rang in the cavern. Kyanos had struck Cerulean. Cerulean did not flinch, but Carryl saw blood start to trickle out of his nose.

"You will never say that again," Kyanos stated in a voice that made Carryl's blood run cold. "I am the leader, and unless you can prove otherwise, you will obey as I say." He paused and wiped his hands on his trousers, then continued, "So, later this morning, you will take the girl and the dragon along with the other dragons who have bred her and return home. You will be in charge until I return. I will follow with the last of the dragons. There is one last piece of business I need to take care of."

"And if he is stronger?" Cerulean boldly inquired.

Kyanos's hand stopped bare centimeters from Cerulean's face, "I will beat him, you mark my words. He is just a runt. I don't know how his father managed to do it but I am stronger."

At the mention of Ardyn, Cerulean's body straightened, "His father was a better man than you, Kyanos. I do not know why I did not see it before. I was foolish to have thought otherwise."

"Yes, but you did, and you willingly watched me kill him," Kyanos stated cruelly.

Cerulean hung his head a moment, then raised it again, "An act that I have regretted for twenty-two winters. You didn't need all of his information about Calamadyn, if you are going to ignore it when the time comes." He paused then continued. "Fine, we will leave later this morning. Come, if and when you can." He turned without another word. Kyanos's gaze followed him and saw Carryl.

"Cerulean," he bellowed. The other rider paused and turned. "You brought her here?" Kyanos said incredulously.

"You told me to not let her out of my sight. Where else would I keep her, if you have my dragon here and I wish to speak with you?"

Kyanos exhaled, unable to dispute the logic. "I see she has not touched her dragon, but who knows how much they have communicated."

"You forget, she can do that from anywhere."

"True, but she now knows how we have her dragon restrained. She will tell her dragon that information."

"And how is that going to help the dragon?"

Kyanos shook his head and waved his hand at Cerulean. "Just get her out of here."

Cerulean turned and stalked off. This time, Carryl was prepared for the rough arm that caught her and tried to drag her along. She willingly placed her hands on his shoulders as they headed into the dark tunnel. When they were out into the open, Cerulean collapsed on a log. After a moment of heavy breathing with his face in his hands, he motioned for Carryl to join him.

"Why did I not listen to my dragon and my own inner unrest?" Cerulean moaned.

Carryl was unsure what to do. She instead decided to make sure Wyn was still okay.

"I am fine, little one. The turquoise dragon has turned to his rider, and the other is quietly lying here beside me. He has tried to talk with me. He seems almost shy."

Carryl smiled at the description. So, unlike his rider, she thought. "Wyn, have you felt Ruskya's presence today?"

"Ruskya," Wyn repeated. "Funny you should ask. I thought for a moment that I had felt Wyeth, but it passed quickly."

"When was this?" Carryl inquired.

"A little before you called to me, this morning."

Carryl nodded. "I woke up and thought Ruskya was here."

She turned to the rider sitting beside her still holding his head in his hands. "Do you want to talk about it?" she asked. "And is this the best spot to talk? We could go over to where I was earlier. It is out of the way of anyone coming here to talk with Kyanos."

Cerulean glanced at her. "There is more beneath that red head of yours than Kyanos gives you credit for."

"Really?" Carryl answered. "Does he think I am dumb or something?"

"Or something," Cerulean replied. "He has a high estimation of what you did during the trials, but for some reason he thinks you are weak. Maybe it is the same thing I have fought with inside of me ever since I met him. He thinks I have a weakness in me, also." He stood and offered his hand to Carryl. She accepted his help up and led the way to the secluded spot. They sat down on the same log where she had washed her face.

"What does he have against Ruskya?" Carryl started the discussion.

"Ruskya?" Cerulean asked, puzzled.

"Ardyn's son," she explained.

"So, that's his name." He paused. "That's who you thought was waking you up, and that's who you called to in the trap."

She glared at him. "You were reading my thoughts then, too?"

He held up both hands in defense, "No, that one was a mental scream for all to hear."

Carryl felt the blood rush to her cheeks. She hated it when her face became as red as her hair, but there was nothing she could do about it.

"What does Kyanos have against him?" she asked again to divert the attention.

"I think hatred is the best thing to call it. Every time he tried to pry a memory from Ardyn that he would not give willingly, first would come the image of this son. Before Ardyn died, he swore that one day his son would avenge his death.

"Kyanos kept him alive," he continued, "I suppose I helped, there. I didn't want him to die, but deep down, I knew that was Kyanos's plan. I thought I could change Kyanos's mind if he got the information he wanted. In the end, getting the information is what killed Ardyn." Cerulean hung his head in silence. Carryl placed a comforting hand on him. She thought of the aroma of Meredyth's tea and felt herself relaxing. She sent a mental image of comfort to Cerulean. He looked up and smiled.

"Thank you," he said softly. "You are a healer." It was a statement. "What is Ardyn's son like?"

Carryl smiled. How could she explain Ruskya? A headstrong rider? One not bound by tradition? A compassionate man? Where did she begin?

He looked at her. "All that?" he asked.

She blushed. "I wish you would stay out of my thoughts," she said without anger.

"I told you to learn to keep me out. If it would be easier, I could look through your memories of him?"

"No," she shuddered. "I'll picture him as if I am telling Wyn about a place I am seeing." Carryl thought of Ruskya and all the intricate parts of him, including his connection with Duskya. There was no way of separating him from his twin. A few moments passed in silence.

"So, he is a twin," Cerulean stated.

Carryl nodded. "A Calamadyn twin."

"Is that why he can best Kyanos? He is the only one who has ever come close to doing that. I have tried these last few winters, and have not been able to do anything but look like a fool."

Carryl shrugged. "I don't know. Do you want Ruskya to beat Kyanos?"

"Yes!" came the adamant response. It was stated so fiercely that Carryl shrunk back as if she had been struck.

"Sorry," he said more softly, "Once he was my friend, or so I tried to make myself believe, but I know better now. A true friend would not ignore my wishes. I want him beaten, and if Ardyn's son can do it, then so be it."

"What if I told you I thought Ruskya was nearby, looking for me?"

"I would ask if you could contact him. We could go talk with him. Maybe together we could work to bring about Kyanos's downfall."

Carryl nodded. "I'm not very good at this mental communication—"

He cut her off. "You did just fine with me earlier. Try to reach out and call to him, as you would your dragon. He will hear you."

Taking a deep breath, Carryl called softly, "Ruskya?"

CHAPTER 22: A PLAN

"WHAT DO YOU THINK we should do?" Kyn asked Ruskya for what seemed like the fifteenth time.

Ruskya sighed. "I don't know, Kyn. If we can't move freely, then we may be stuck here. I don't want the turquoise dragon realizing we are here and sending his whole colony of riders and dragons after us, but I want to get in there and get Carryl and Wyn."

Kyn exhaled, trying to control his frustration. "I am sorry. I didn't mean to say you should have the answers. I'm just anxious sitting here doing nothing."

"I know. Wyeth is upset that he has to stay low and quiet up to the north of us. The others are still over a glass away."

Kyn nodded in the predawn light, then thought of something. "He doesn't know me, right? Should I go try to scout around?"

"It's an idea," Ruskya slowly agreed and then paused.

"Ruskya?" Kyn asked, then noticed the look on his face.

* * *

"Ruskya?" Carryl's voice cut across Ruskya's mind, drawing him to her.

"Carryl, where are you? Are you hurt?" he called back with concern.

"I am fine. I am with a rider who wants to see Kyanos's downfall. He believes that you are part of it."

"Who is Kyanos?"

"The turquoise rider." She paused, not sure how to say it, but deciding he needed to hear it. "Ruskya, he was responsible for your father's death." Instead of rage as she had expected, a deep resigned sadness filled Ruskya's reply.

"I know. I cannot do anything to bring him back, but I can keep him from harming you."

Carryl considered his reply as Cerulean cut in on her thoughts. "Have you found him? Let me talk with him."

"Ruskya," Carryl asked, "would you be willing to meet with a former apprentice of your father's? He was steered off track by Kyanos, but he now wants to bring justice where it is due."

Ruskya paused. "He is one of the other riders?"

"Yes. We have some time before everyone is awake, if you are in Philippi Canyon. We could meet up with you."

"I am here. What about Wyn?"

"It would just be Cerulean and me. We would have to make quick plans and come back for Wyn. What do you say? Will you meet with us?"

"Yes," came the decisive reply. "I am north of the hatchling cave. We are afraid that the turquoise dragon, or Kyanos, will sense our presence."

"Right now I think they both are preoccupied with Kyanos's plans for baby dragons. Don't worry about that right now," Carryl said quickly. "Where should we meet?"

A picture came to her mind of where they were. She turned to Cerulean and showed him. He nodded and then offered his own picture. She sent the reply back to Ruskya and they set out.

"Do you believe he will accept my help and look past my part in his father's death?" Cerulean seemed insecure now that they were moving.

Carryl laid a hand on his arm. "Cerulean, your kindness toward me will speak volumes. It is up to you to tell him the rest. He seemed at peace with his father's death."

Cerulean nodded. As they walked, the sun started to streak the sky above the canyon, and the pathway became clearer. With better visibility, they were able to make better time.

The canyon had a small stream that seemed to flow off-center. Along the stream bed, trees grew, shading and shadowing the land. It was into one such shaded spot that Cerulean led Carryl. They ducked behind the low branches and found a secluded, quiet place. They didn't have long to wait before Ruskya and Kyn appeared.

Carryl looked through the branches and saw the rider and his youngling. A lump formed in her throat at the sight of her friends. She had not realized that Kyn would come along, but she should have known. She quietly slipped out of the alcove and waved them over. The relief that she saw wash over Ruskya's face made her heart flip-flop. The next thing she knew, Kyn's arms were around her.

"You're okay!" he exclaimed.

"Kyn, quiet," Ruskya admonished, though his eyes echoed the youngling's words.

Carryl led them into the little hideaway. Cerulean stood with his back to a tree as the three entered. Carryl wondered if he was as nervous as he had been earlier. If he was, it didn't show on his face or in his body.

Cerulean stepped forward. "Son of Ardyn," he said addressing Ruskya, "welcome." Ruskya paused and looked at this other rider, weighing him. The salutation had caught his attention.

Cerulean bowed, then said, "You look as your father did at your age. I am Cerulean."

Ruskya bowed. "It is an honor to meet someone who knew my father. May I present to you my youngling, Kyn?"

Kyn bowed, as did Cerulean. "It is an honor," Kyn replied.

"Mine as well, youngling." He turned to Ruskya. "Can we talk about plans to bring Kyanos down?"

Ruskya nodded. "I am not after revenge. I will allow justice, but if his riders are willing to return home without harming any more villagers, I am willing to forgo any retribution."

Cerulean paused. "You say you do not want revenge, yet what will you do when you are face-to-face with the one who killed your father?"

"I have come face-to-face with him. I fought him on his terms, against his dragon, and his mind. I have some methods that help to keep me grounded." Ruskya cast a glance at Kyn. "I do not wish to kill him because he killed my father; I wish to have him removed from my home."

"What if he will not retreat?"

"If I must defeat him, I will, but I will not willfully kill him. If I killed him, I would be no better than he is."

"Your father was right about you. Defeat would be worse than death to Kyanos, especially in front of his riders. If we could bring a challenge of combat to him and guarantee that our riders would not interfere, would you fight him?"

Ruskya looked stunned. "Hold on, Cerulean. How was my father right about me?"

Cerulean chuckled, the sound softening his otherwise severe face. "Your father told Kyanos that his son would avenge his death one day. Kyanos is afraid of you! You have brought him down from the first. In the trials, he thought he had a good rider that he would be able to mold—two riders actually—and then you walked away, taking Carryl with you. When he met you in battle, he returned shaken both times. When he pulled away last time, it was because we had Carryl and her dragon, but the fatigue he carried with him was more than expected. I believe he was glad for the reprieve."

"What are his plans now?" Ruskya inquired.

Carryl answered, a fire lighting her green eyes. "He plans to have me go with Cerulean back to their home. If I go, then they will have Wyn and her eggs." Carryl was surprised to find that Ruskya did not react as strongly as she thought he would.

"If I was to challenge him…" Ruskya stated. "I said if…" looking at Carryl and seeing the fear there. "If I challenged him, I would want Kyn and Duskya within range of communication, yet out of his way. I would want Carryl and Wyn safe. Even if that means they are flying with you, Cerulean, back to your home."

"What?" Carryl exclaimed.

"I wouldn't entrust you to anyone in this colony but Cerulean. I have a feeling that Kyanos would not let you go unless I won. If you are where he can harm you, he will. He can read my thoughts, and he will see that he can use you against me."

"I would not let harm come to you or your dragon, Carryl," Cerulean stated. "I will fight any rider who would try to do you harm."

Carryl nodded, agreeing to their plan.

"How could I get the other two within range without him knowing?" Ruskya asked.

"I could have him help me prepare for our departure; then you could bring the challenge after we've gone," Cerulean offered.

"No, the challenge must come before you leave," Ruskya said.

Kyn, who had been quietly listening, offered his advice. "Why don't you have Duskya fly here or at least near the canyon, and your mother can bring her the rest of the way. Would we be close enough here?"

"That is a good idea, Kyn," Ruskya encouraged his youngling, "and speaking of Ma, she is bringing some farmers to the canyon." At Carryl's inquiring look, he added, "Your father is one of them, and Byran. I am afraid Byran is after revenge."

Cerulean looked puzzled. "Why would a farmer want revenge?"

"Not a farmer," Carryl explained, "a villager whose daughter and son-in-law were killed by Kyle while their children looked on from a distance."

Cerulean's face grew red with rage. "I told Kyanos not to accept him as a rider, but he wouldn't listen. The dragon he was given was twisted to begin with. The two seemed to fit, but I knew it would not be a good thing for anyone."

"Who would Kyle go with?" Kyn asked.

"I don't know. Kyanos may want him to come with me. In which case, I may have to be the one to fight him. If not, then you can hand him over to your farmer friends."

"So, who brings the challenge?" Ruskya brought the conversation back on track.

"Good question." Cerulean complimented Ruskya's thinking. "Should I tell him that I heard you and let him find you?"

"No, he will find Kyn, then. I will find him and bring the challenge. I will lay the rules out. If he wins, he may have Calamadyn, Carryl and her dragon," the last was said as if forced out of his mouth. "If I win, he will go home in defeat with all who wish to follow him. He cannot ever return to our territory."

Cerulean nodded. "Ruskya, if I am wrong about you, and you are defeated, I will protect her. This I swear by Wymar, my dragon."

Ruskya nodded his thanks. Carryl looked between them and wondered. Here were two leaders that would shape the future of the colonies they served. If they could unite the colonies as allies instead of enemies, they could do wonderful things.

Ruskya turned to Carryl. "It is time to return with him. Will you hold to the plan? I will not force you; you know that."

Carryl nodded. "I could not leave without Wyn. I will return, but Ruskya, please, defeat him. He is..." she paused, searching for the right word, "…evil. I do not want to have to face life in the same colony as him. Please tell my father that I am fine."

With that, she turned and headed back. As she walked away, she heard Cerulean promise Ruskya, "I will keep her safe, honored rider. Have no fear for her." She didn't hear Ruskya's reply, but knew that if she stayed she would do something to embarrass them both.

"Blessings on you, Ruskya," she thought to him through the tears coursing down her cheeks. She wiped them away furiously.

"Do not be ashamed to cry, my healer," Ruskya whispered into her mind. "Blessings on you. You were right to leave. When this is over, we will meet again."

She brushed the tears away. She felt Cerulean's presence beside her, but didn't look his way. He gave her the privacy she needed. They made it safely back to the entrance, and by then Carryl had gained control of her emotions. Halfway down the passageway, Kyle met them.

"There you are, Cerulean," he greeted loudly in his haughty manner.

"Kyle," Cerulean said flatly, without any trace of emotion.

"Kyanos wants me to go with you. He said to round up the other riders and their dragons. They're excited about going home. I just want to get out of this godforsaken land. When do we leave?"

"We will leave when Kyanos says we leave, and not a moment before," Cerulean said. Carryl noticed that his voice matched the color of his eyes—a storm was brewing. If Kyle couldn't hear it he must be completely ignorant. The aqua rider continued.

"So, do I get to carry Carryl for a while on my dragon?" he stage-whispered. Cerulean spun around, and before Kyle knew what was happening, his feet were off the ground, and his back was up against the wall of the passageway. Cerulean's eyes bore into the cold aqua eyes.

"I will only tell you once," Cerulean's voice was barely above a whisper. "If you so much as lay an eye on her, I will kill you. Do you understand?"

Kyle nodded, not able to breathe, let alone talk.

"Good, now go get your things ready and come back to me. Don't talk to anyone else. I will know if you do." He dropped Kyle back to the ground. Carryl had to give Kyle points for not collapsing on the floor. He held himself upright.

"You only had to tell me that you already had dibs on her," he muttered.

Cerulean's hand resounded off Kyle's face; then the rider turned, pulling Carryl after him. Absently, she noted that he did that a lot.

CHAPTER 23: HEADING SOUTH

THE FIFTEEN OTHER RIDERS were eager to leave. They had already gathered their things from the cave and had their dragons ready to go. Carryl noticed that most of them respected Cerulean. Only a few seemed to gather around Kyle. No one commented on the slight mark that Kyanos's blow had left on Cerulean's face.

"We wait until Kyanos gives us the all clear. I will then get the dragon and bring her out with Wymar. Any questions?"

"What about the other dragons?" someone called.

"If we meet resistance, then we fight. I will lead the way home, but those in back will be the rear guard. If anything happens to the dragon or her rider, we lose any hope of dragon eggs." That seemed to settle the group down. Carryl noticed Kyle eying her. She ignored him, but the aqua eyes seemed to bore into her wherever she was.

The call from Kyanos came sooner than either Carryl or Cerulean had expected. Cerulean led her out of the cave and around to the cavern. Carryl had the satisfaction of seeing Kyanos's face when they entered. It was pale.

"Cerulean, what do you know of this challenge?" He spat the word out of his mouth as if it gave him indigestion.

"Challenge?" Cerulean asked innocently. "I have been readying the men for our departure as you told me."

"About a quarter of a glass ago, I heard a voice call my name. It was the twin. I do not know how he learned my name, but he challenged me to a duel here and said that he would fight me to defeat. If he wins, the girl and the dragon go free, and we all leave. If I win, we keep them all, and he gives us Calamadyn."

Cerulean considered the offer. "That seems reasonable. "Did you accept?"

"Of course I accepted!" he screamed. "What do you think I am?"

"Kyanos, I did not wish to offend. I simply wondered when this challenge was to happen."

"In two glasses. You will leave, of course, although I am half-tempted to make you stay to witness his defeat. You think he can undo me, but you are wrong. You will take the girl and the dragon. Either way, we will have them to bring the colony back to life."

"But, I thought you just said—" Cerulean began, but Kyanos cut him off.

"Of course I will not abide by his rules. You will take her and leave. You will not turn around to help me. Kyle will go with you. If you try to double-cross me, he has my instructions."

Cerulean actually laughed. "And you think he is strong enough to stop me?"

"No," Kyanos said coldly. "But he will make you the established leader when he fights you. You will have to show your true colors to the group. If they accept you, then you will have the position you have always wanted, at least until I return. Then you will have to grovel at my feet, if you want to return to my colony. I will be out one poor rider and one thorn in my flesh. I will have gained a good rider and a female dragon. I think it is a fair trade." Carryl started to say something, but Cerulean stopped her with a look.

"Now, take these lariats, tie them to the halter on the dragon, and lead her out in triumph. Do not take the wing bindings off until you are almost ready to go in the air." Turning to Carryl he added, "You should warn her to not struggle. She will only hurt herself. My dragon is ready to set her straight, but I have held him back."

"Wyn, please, do as Cerulean asks of you. We will be together and safe if you follow directions." Carryl instructed her dragon, as Cerulean attached the lariats. He led Wyn past the turquoise dragon, who was poised to attack. When they were in front of Kyanos, he stopped them.

"Dragon," he addressed Wyn, "I have your rider. If you do not obey, I will hurt her. Not enough to kill her, because I want you alive, but enough that you will feel the pain. Do you understand me?" He raged when there was no reply, "Do you understand me!" A smile crossed his lips. "Yes, we agree," he said. "I bid you farewell until we meet in my home." He waved Cerulean on.

As Cerulean passed Carryl, he motioned for her to follow. She obediently fell in behind him. She didn't like what she had heard. How could they meet back up with Ruskya, and how would they know the outcome of the challenge? The questions swirled around her head annoyingly like flies in the summer time.

Upon reaching the canyon floor, they found all fifteen riders waiting for them. A cheer went up when they saw Wyn. Everyone seemed to know the female dragon when they saw her. She tried to look dignified, but with the wing binders on, she looked more like a caged bird than the magnificent dragon she was. Cerulean stood tall and proud with Wyn behind him. Carryl was at his side. He gazed down at the riders.

"This morning, we can fly home proud," he stated. "I will take charge of this group. Any who will not have my leadership, step forward now." No one moved. Kyle looked around confused, but held his ground. "Then we leave." As the words left his mouth, Wymar descended in front of them. He motioned Carryl up, warningly showing her the lead he had attached to Wyn. She knew it was for show, but her heart sank anyway. With leaden feet, she mounted the strange-colored dragon.

"Peace, little one," she heard. "Stand tall." Carryl's back straightened. She sat atop the dragon with all the pride she could muster. If Wyn wanted her proud, she would be.

The next thing she knew, Cerulean's arm was around her waist, and he whispered in her ear. "You've done well. I will not hurt her." To the rider on the ground, he said, "Unbind her. Let us see the magnificent dragon we will take home. Then call your dragons and follow me!"

The rider gingerly unbound the straps holding Wyn's wings. He let the blanket fall to the ground as she stretched out her wing. The second blanket soon followed and the gasp that escaped the crowd of riders made Carryl's heart soar with pride. "Wyn," she called, "it is your turn to be proud. Stretch those wings!"

"Yes, little one," Wyn replied as she stretched first one wing and then the other. She proceeded to clean them one by one.

Carryl felt Cerulean's discomfort. He was anxious to leave, but he felt he needed to let the dragon have her say. Yet, Carryl also felt his admiration for the creature. The mid-morning sun shone on her wings, bringing out the almost-lilac color. She turned to the second wing when Carryl felt a shift in the dragon under her. She looked down to see that he was taking off.

Wyn must have felt the change on the lead rope, for she laid the wing flat and prepared to leap. Simultaneously, the two took off. The wave of sound from the dragons around and the men below almost deafened Carryl. Whatever Wyn had just done, she had fifteen new admirers.

"Was that your idea?" Cerulean asked in her ear. "Or the dragon's?"

"A mixture of both. It worked. The men and the dragons love her."

"How can you know the dragons love her?"

Carryl faltered. She had forgotten he didn't know about her ability to hear dragons. She felt him start to reach for her thoughts. "Don't," she thought to him. He backed away shocked.

She sighed. "I don't know why, but I can hear the dragons. Any within a certain distance are in my head all day long. I can also talk with them, but I was told not to, for it was considered bad etiquette."

Cerulean chuckled. "That sounds like the riders from Three Spans Canyon, but this time they are right. Any rider here would be offended if he knew someone else spoke with his dragon. That is why Kyanos spoke with Wyn as you left. He was telling your dragon that she may have chosen you, but he has control of her."

"The dragons love her," Carryl repeated. "I don't know how long it will hold, but for now, they will protect her with their lives."

"Good. We will need them on our side when the time comes."

"Will you really kill Kyle?"

He sighed. "If I must, but there is something else bothering you, and it isn't Kyle or his aqua dragon. What is it?"

She was quiet for a little, then, finally stated her fear. "How will we know if Ruskya wins?"

"I will know," he replied in a quiet but firm way. "I have always wondered why I went with Kyanos in the first place, but it seemed to make sense then. Now, I know it makes no sense to follow him, yet, I can do no else. I am bound to him in some way I cannot explain."

"Have you ever tried to leave him?"

"Yes. My head hurts, and my heart races, I physically cannot do it. I am beginning to wonder if he has laid some kind of compulsion on me. When I wish to oppose him, I can only bring myself to try to hit him, when what I really want to do is punch him or put a knife through his chest. I cannot hurt him."

Carryl pondered that. "Perhaps Kyn could help."

"The youngling?" he asked in surprise. "What can he do?"

"He is a healer of minds. He was able to take away Ruskya's fear of Kyanos. Somehow, Kyanos had planted a thought in Ruskya's mind that he would kill him as he had Ruskya's father. Kyn was able to extract that thought and put confidence there instead." Carryl felt Cerulean's admiration, although he said nothing. "Does this bond between you and Kyanos respect distance barriers?" Carryl asked.

"No," he said quietly. "If it did, I would fight it until I had passed the limits of his control and I was free of him. I will know, young one. I will know," he said, as they continued to fly further south of Philippi Canyon and the only home Carryl knew.

CHAPTER 24: DRAGON FIGHT

MEREDYTH DID NOT LIKE Ruskya's plan one bit. Working with a rider that he didn't know, and challenging the turquoise dragon rider—what part of keeping himself in one piece was this? She shook her head.

Amazingly, Duskya had gone along with it. Meredyth had brought her daughter to the small alcove under the tree after she had landed at the north end of the canyon. Now Duskya and Kyn were neatly tucked beneath the tree beside the stream. They had enough furs to keep them warm, and the weather had started to improve. Meredyth now had to worry about getting Casey, Davyd, a young boy, and a man set on revenge to the cavern beside the hatchling cave. Any one of them could cause problems with Ruskya's plans. The others were to be in the background ready to help if it came to that, but what help could they be against dragons and their riders? One look at the boy's face and she knew he was scared. Should she use some of Wyeth's precious dragon courage? Not yet. It wasn't time.

As nimbly as a squirrel, she led them quietly and cautiously through the canyon. They crossed the creek on a fallen log. She took them to the end of the canyon, on the opposite side from where Cerulean had led Carryl. She found another hidden path and followed it alongside the cavern. Not much light seeped between the cavern wall and the canyon wall high above them, but it was enough to see by. They walked for close to a quarter of a glass before she found the crack in the rock wall. She motioned for them to be quiet and led them inside. It was dark, but she heard noises. She showed Casey how to place his hands on her shoulders and led the way. She hoped the others would get the hint and do likewise. With care, her feet found the way she had traveled so many winters ago. The path meandered around the enclosure toward the hatchling cave. They came within sight of light and stared down on the turquoise dragon and his rider. The man was talking to another rider.

"Do it right," the turquoise rider demanded.

"Kyanos, I can't with you moving around so. One would think this was your first fight." Meredyth watched as Kyanos struck the rider's face; a few seconds later the sound reached her.

"Don't you ever say that again, Kerean! Do you understand me?"

"Yes, Kyanos," Kerean said with resignation in his voice. "Here, I will tighten your gauntlet." Meredyth noticed that the rider was dressed entirely in turquoise-colored leather. He was intimidating even from this far away. She worried for Ruskya.

"Now, Kerean, hand me my dagger. I want it at my side where I can get at it."

"Yes, Kyanos." The rider handed the dagger to the turquoise rider. Like the rest of his clothes, the dagger's hilt was turquoise. The blade was a strange bluish-green hue that seemed to change in the torchlight as it was moved from side to side. Kyanos examined it and weighed it in his hand. He flipped it three rotations, caught it, and placed it under his pant leg.

"Now, I think I am ready. Has the other rider approached?"

"Not yet, Kyanos," Kerean replied. "There is a guard, he will notify us."

"Good, I want to be in place at the center of the cave on Cobalt when he enters. That will be the most intimidating. Now, get out of here!" Kyanos commanded.

When the rider had left, Kyanos turned toward the dark side of the cavern. A noise echoed up into the path Meredyth had chosen. She saw movement in the darkness, and then a turquoise dragon came into view. Even from her vantage point, she could tell this was an old dragon. She had never seen a dragon so big. As she watched, the rider mounted his steed, and they flew toward the exit of the cavern.

There was a muted gasp as the others let out their breath.

"Did you see that brute?" Byran asked. Meredyth nodded.

"That was larger than the aqua one!" Braidyn said.

"Yer son is goin' to fight that beast?" Casey asked with concern.

"Yes, and our job is to be there if he needs help. I can't think how we could go up against riders and dragons, but he seems to think we can.

So, let's keep going."

"I know I want to get my hands on a certain rider," Byran muttered.

"Ya just do as Ruskya said," Davyd warned him. "Ya don't want a rider mad at ya."

They made the rest of the trip in silence and without any problems. Meredyth led them through another crevice out onto the floor of the hatchling cave. There were some odd boulders that blocked them from view of the rest of the cave. They positioned themselves around the rocks where they could see over or around them, and yet they could not be seen by the others in the area.

Meredyth saw that there were ten riders positioned around the edges, but their attention was focused on the center of the cave where Kyanos sat atop his dragon. It was an imposing sight, Meredyth had to admit.

* * *

Ruskya wanted to set Kyanos on edge. If he could wait just until the other rider was feeling cocky, then, maybe, he would have an advantage. But if he waited too long or entered the cave too soon, he would not have the advantage. The problem was that he couldn't use Duskya, Kyn, or his own senses to observe the turquoise rider. Any of this would set off Kyanos. He pondered what to do, then he thought of his mother inside the cave with the villagers. Could he use her? They hadn't tried to communicate since his last battle with Kyanos, but Meredyth could hear Ruskya and dragons, now. He thought it was worth a try.

"Ma, I want you to try like you did at Glendyn's that day," he called to her. "If you can hear me, I want you to think of me, and then answer in your mind as if you are talking to me." He waited for the reply. It came quiet as a whisper and after much time.

"Ruskya, can you hear me?"

"Yes, Ma. Can you tell me what the turquoise rider is doing?"

"He is boasting to his riders that you are too scared to come to your own challenge. He seems to think he has won, but earlier, he was worried. He has a dagger hidden under his left trouser leg."

"Thank you, Ma. Can we try one last thing? Would you let me see the cave from your eyes? I will have to read your thoughts. Would you be okay with that?"

"You can do that?" she asked, amazed.

"Yes, I am careful when I do it."

"I trust you, son. Go ahead and try."

Ruskya concentrated and saw the cave with the turquoise dragon and his rider flying in the center. Kyanos was gesturing to his riders. There were ten riders who seemed to be grouped together with their backs to the villagers.

"Thank you, Ma," he called as he broke the connection.

"Well, Wyeth," he said. "What do you say about a surprise entrance through the hole in the top? We could come down raining fire."

"We would have to be careful of the onlookers," Wyeth said. "I think I could blow fire narrow enough just to reach Kyanos."

"Well, then, let's go." Ruskya mounted Wyeth and flew off. As he flew, he shared his idea with Duskya and Kyn. They were to mentally follow him as Duskya had done before in the battles and help any way they could.

All too soon, the hatchling cave appeared. Ruskya paused before the arched entrance and thought of Wyeth's memory of his father caught in the turquoise dragon's talons. Then he remembered his promise to Cerulean. He set his mind to bring justice—not revenge.

He motioned Wyeth up and over and found the hole in the cave. With a quick intake of breath, Ruskya lowered Wyeth down. The effect was perfect. One moment Kyanos was boasting, and the next icy-blue fire flared around him. Both the rider and dragon roared with rage and a bit of pain. Kyanos was good, Ruskya had to admit.

The battle raged on with both riders aware of the onlookers below. Ruskya deflected the turquoise fire, but the turquoise dragon's talon caught on Wyeth's flank. Ruskya knew the larger size of the other dragon would be to his advantage in a long-distance race, but here Wyeth's small size and agility would come in handy.

Finally, after much maneuvering, Wyeth was able to get a grip on the soft underbelly of the turquoise dragon. Here is a chance, Ruskya thought, but then something struck his mind like a physical blow to the head.

"You thought you could get away with it, you little runt." Kyanos's icy voice cut through Ruskya's head. "You were wrong. You are no match for me. I will kill you just as I killed your father. He squirmed before me, begging for mercy. I will see you do the same."

Ruskya shook his head. "You think I believe that my father begged for mercy? No, he was strong, and he passed that strength onto me. I will defeat you!"

Wyeth pulled away as the turquoise dragon dove for the ground. The two dragons circled each other. Ruskya couldn't see how he and Wyeth would have the advantage here, but they would need it. He felt renewed hope surge through him and wondered what Kyn or Duskya had done. He continued to block his mind from the rider, but wondered if he should try a mental attack himself. He decided to hold off for the moment.

The turquoise dragon came at them, and again Ruskya deflected the fire. He wasn't sure if the onlookers were being spattered with fire or not. There was no time to look. Instead, he focused his attention on the dragon. If Ruskya could foil the mental shield Kyanos had created, Wyeth could get through. He searched until he felt the barrier. He imagined a drill making its way through the barrier right where Wyeth would attack next. The moment Wyeth's talon hit the barrier, Ruskya pushed the drill deeper. Wyeth's paw pierced the mental shield and dove for the wing. Ruskya cringed as he heard the tender membrane tear and the dragon roar in pain. The dragon spun out of control and dropped to the ground.

Ruskya landed Wyeth and watched as Kyanos dismounted. Ruskya followed suit. Now it would get harder; it would be man-to-man. The turquoise dragon was out of the fight.

CHAPTER 25: KYLE'S DOWNFALL

CERULEAN CALLED FOR a break around mid-afternoon. They found a place to land on the desert floor and had a late lunch. Cerulean gave Carryl her freedom, explaining to the other riders that she wouldn't try to leave without her dragon. The riders understood and guarded Wyn closely instead.

Carryl was enjoying her newfound freedom, although it was limited by the sixteen riders milling around. After a leisurely lunch, she decided to take a short walk to stretch her legs. Many of the riders had already done so. She had never flown for such an extended period of time. How far had they traveled?

Suddenly, a rough hand grabbed her by the arm and spun her around. Before she could utter one word, another hand covered her mouth. She looked up into aqua eyes full of hatred.

"Don't make a sound. You're almost far enough from camp to not be heard, but let's not take any chances. All right?" Unlike every other time he had spoken, Kyle's voice now seemed quiet. He took his hand off her mouth, but the other hand still held her arm behind her back. "You're nothin' but a farmer's daughter. You don't deserve freedom, and when Kyanos gets here, you won't have it anymore."

"What do you have against farmers' wives and daughters?" she asked.

"I was a happy villager, up until I was orphaned and sold to a farmer. It was slavery. That is what a farmer is—a slave! I vowed I would never be a farmer. Now I am a rider, and I will be the one in control. I will mete out punishment where it is deserved."

"Really? How is that?"

"He's goin' to put me in charge, not that fool Cerulean."

Carryl stifled a laugh. "You really think Kyanos is going to select you over Cerulean?"

He pulled her arm up behind her back making her stand on her tiptoes. "I know so," he said. "You may laugh now, but I will rule over all of them."

"Kyanos will never let that happen. He knows Cerulean may not agree with him, but he is by far a better rider than you ever will be." Carryl didn't see the hand that hit her. The sound rang in her ears and she tasted blood. She held back the cry of pain, but tears came to her eyes.

"Never say that again," his voice changed to one so like Kyanos's that a shiver ran down Carryl's back. "How you treat me right now will determine your future. Kyanos thinks you're a rider, but I know better. Look at my eyes. They are the color of my dragon's, just like every other rider here. Yours are the same pathetic green they always were. You're not a rider. I am, and you will do as I please." Carryl tried to pull away, but he only wrenched her arm further.

"Don't want to face the truth? Let me help you. If you were a rider, your dragon would feel this." With a quickness that she had never seen in him before, he twisted her around and slugged her in the stomach. The air escaped her lungs, and she doubled over as he let her fall to the ground. She had no breath left, but her mind screamed for Cerulean to help. She barely had time to catch her breath before a kick connected with her kidneys. She tried to roll away from the next blow, and managed to avoid the primary point of impact. She flinched, anticipating the next attack but it never came. She lay there panting with tears running down her cheeks as she heard Cerulean's voice. It was low, cold, and deadly serious.

"If you so much as lay another hand on her, so help me, I will kill you. I should kill you, anyway, for the pain you caused the female dragon."

"I didn't hurt no dragon. I just had some fun with the girl." He was still trying to be the one in control. It must have been like this when he attacked the farms, Carryl thought. The difference this time was Cerulean was here.

"You call picking on someone half your size fun? Then here, have a go at me. Or are you a coward?"

Without bothering to answer, Kyle swung at Cerulean. Cerulean saw it coming and pivoted to avoid it. With a smooth motion, he sent Kyle away from him. Again Kyle came at Cerulean, and again Cerulean spun and sent Kyle's blow away. Carryl saw that the older rider was toying with Kyle, wearing him down. The other riders had gathered to watch. Kyle was getting weary but hadn't learned his lesson yet. With a force that would have knocked Cerulean to the ground, had it connected, Kyle aimed a punch at his midsection. Cerulean moved to the side, grabbed the hand and twisted it. The next moment, Kyle was on the ground. With a slight twist to the arm, Cerulean rolled Kyle over and held him in a wristlock, standing firmly in control from behind.

"Now, Kyle, are you ready to leave Carryl alone? Will you behave like a real rider?" Cerulean asked. Kyle muttered some inaudible answer. "What was that?"

"Yes," he said through gritted teeth. Cerulean stepped back and let go of Kyle's arm. Kyle slowly got up and brushed himself off. Carryl didn't see how it happened, but as Kyle turned, he sliced with a knife at Cerulean's arm. Bright red started to soak Cerulean's white tunic. There was a gasp from the riders in the circle, and several moved to stop Kyle. At a motion from Cerulean, they halted. Kyle and Cerulean slowly circled. As Kyle saw an opening, he lunged with the knife. Carryl had to admit, Kyle had more finesse with the knife than with his fists. Cerulean was able to dance around the knife despite his wounded arm. At last, Kyle made a mistake and came in with a thrust in the same way he had come with the punch. Again, in a matter of seconds, he found himself on the ground and disarmed.

"I gave you a chance, Kyle. Do you wish to throw it back in my face again?" Kyle lay there panting. A minute twist to the wrist brought a moan from him. "What do you say? Will you surrender?"

"Yes," Kyle said with reluctance.

"I didn't quite hear you." Cerulean pressed on Kyle's wrist, pushing the arm further up behind the young rider.

"Yes, I surrender."

Before letting him up, Cerulean stated for all to hear, "You have all heard that Kyle has surrendered to me. If there are any more problems, his life is forfeit." He backed away from Kyle and walked over to Carryl, who had been watching from the ground. Cerulean knelt down, but Carryl could tell that his body was primed to resume the defense if necessary.

"Let me look at that," Carryl said as she saw the cut. "I have some herbs here." She fumbled at her side, but came up empty. "I must have lost them at some point," she said disappointed.

"I have something back with Wymar. Come, let me help you up." His eyes were still on Kyle, who had started to rise. Kyle glared at the two of them and headed back to his dragon.

"We'll ride soon," Cerulean called to the riders. "Be ready."

* * *

A quarter of a glass later, Cerulean's arm was bandaged, and he and Carryl were on Wymar in the air. The other riders were behind them. Wyn followed along obediently on the lead. The air felt good after the dust that Carryl had swallowed on the desert floor.

They had been flying for about a half of a glass when Cerulean felt a pull on the lead rope. At the same moment, a horrendous roar filled their ears. Carryl covered her ears, but the sound was inside of her as well.

"Wyn!" she yelled.

Cerulean dropped the lead rope and spun Wymar around to see what was happening. The sight shocked them both. The aqua dragon was riding on Wyn's back, his talons cutting into her flanks. Before Cerulean could do anything, three dragons broke out of the formation and attacked the aqua dragon. The noise was awful—dragon cries, the roar of flames, and Kyle's screams. Carryl wanted to block the sight from her eyes, but it was burned onto her retinas. In a matter of minutes, it was over. Kyle had lost his seat on his dragon and their lifeless bodies both tumbled, separately, to the ground. The aqua dragon's wings had been shredded.

Cerulean found a mesa to land on. He immediately called the three riders over. "Did you have my permission to attack another rider?" he demanded.

"Cerulean," one replied for them all. "It was our dragons. They acted independently of us. They saw a dragon in despair and acted. They had sworn to protect her. Besides, sir, did you not say that if he attacked anyone, his life was forfeit?"

Cerulean nodded. "Nevertheless, he was a rider, and a dragon was killed. We need to give them an appropriate burial."

The others nodded, and slowly, several filed out to search for the bodies. Meanwhile, Carryl and Cerulean tended to Wyn. Carryl asked for Cerulean's herb bag and started to work on the dragon's wounds. She softly murmured to the dragon. She started to do what she had learned from Kyn, to help heal Wyn inside as well. Cerulean noticed her methods and she explained what Kyn had taught her.

"I will have to talk to this youngling. Perhaps he can help me, if your friend Ruskya doesn't end things."

Wyn's wounds were not bad, and when the others returned, she was able to fly. She insisted on being at the burial. All fifteen dragons created a circle above the downed rider and dragon. With a word from Cerulean, they blended their fire to create a funeral pyre of hues of blue, green, and a lone purple spectrum. The fire rose to slowly consume the dragon and his rider.

CHAPTER 26: ARDYN AVENGED

MEREDYTH WORRIED FOR RUSKYA as she watched as her son circle Kyanos. The other man was larger and seemed more adept at fighting.

The first blow came. Ruskya let it pass beside him and tried to land one of his own, but the larger man blocked it with his arm. The two returned blows and blocks for what seemed like forever before one landed. Ruskya peeled away and shook his head. Meredyth held her breath, but Ruskya seemed okay.

"Ruskya," Duskya called. "Think clearly. He's bigger than you, but you have an advantage."

"I can't get around his barrier. He not only blocks my blows, but he seems to have a mental barrier blocking me from reaching him."

"Then break it down!" she commanded.

Ruskya returned his attention to the rider. The man had been in more fights than Ruskya. Ruskya realized he would have to use not only what Glendyn had taught him about fighting, but also his mental advantages. Considering this, he thought about making two attacks at once. One would be the outward physical attack as a feint, and the other would be a mental attack.

He threw a roundhouse kick to Kyanos's head. At the same time, he imagined a punch to the belly. It worked! Kyanos backed away, gasping for air. Ruskya repeated this several times with success before Kyanos expanded his barrier. What now? How could he break the barrier completely? If it was a wall, he would have to knock it down. He envisioned a drill working on a specific spot near Kyanos's temple. He knew he could throw a kick that would disable him, if it landed and if there was no barrier to break the blow. He worked several other areas with his physical and mental attacks, before he saw that the drill could possibly have worked its way through the barrier. Before the hole could close, he sent a spinning hook kick to Kyanos's head. He added a hammer to his mental image and slammed through the barrier just before the kick made contact. Kyanos went down.

Kyanos's riders gasped in surprise. They backed away from the young rider who had bested their leader, but Ruskya had no interest in fighting them. He remembered his mother's warning about the dagger. He waited for Kyanos to get up, but he didn't.

"Rider," Ruskya called, "are you bested? Do you surrender?" Kyanos did not answer. He moved to get up. He made it to his knees.

"You think you have won, little upstart?" Kyanos called. "You do not know who you are dealing with. I am stronger than you think. It was I who killed your father, just as I will kill you."

Kyn, listening in, drew in a breath. These were the exact same voice and words that he had drawn out of Ruskya's memory after the first battle with Kyanos.

Kyanos stood, straightening to his full height. He stared down into Ruskya's eyes. "Your father squirmed and squealed," the hard voice went on, almost as if he was casting a spell. "Then he begged for mercy, but none came. So, too, it will be today. I will wrap you around my finger, and you will squirm and squeal. Then I will kill you and have my queen dragon, and a rider worthy of her."

Ruskya stared into his turquoise eyes. They were as cold as the gem for which they were named. "Kyanos," he said the name loudly for all to hear, "you do not frighten me. I no longer hear your lies. I know the truth." With each sentence, he came closer to the rider, seeming to become larger with each step. "My father may have died at your hands. That I do not dispute. You killed him as surely as you took him from this very cave in your dragon's talons, but he did not die a coward. Each time you tried to get information from him, he looked you in the eye, and he told you of this day. He told you that his son would exact justice. Today, that is happening. I, Ruskya son of Ardyn, demand recompense for the death of my father." The riders were spellbound. Meredyth's little group gave up hiding behind the boulders and had come out to better see what would happen.

"And how do you expect to get it?" Kyanos sneered. "Do you expect me to bring him back to life?"

"No, I expect you to tell every rider here why he would not willingly give you the herb Calamadyn. Tell them so that all may hear."

Kyanos looked strangely at Ruskya. "What are you up to, rider?" he asked in a voice only for the two of them.

"I am going to take you down, but not how you think," Ruskya replied in kind. Louder he said, "Tell them. Why did my father quit using Calamadyn?"

"He thought it was unsafe," Kyanos answered.

"How was it unsafe?"

"The bond it created was strong." It was like pulling weeds to get the answers out of Kyanos. All the while he watched to make sure that Kyanos did not pull the dagger and throw it at him.

"What kind of bond?" Ruskya asked.

"If the dragon was hurt, his twin was in equal if not greater pain." Kyanos said.

"Repeat that louder," Ruskya demanded. Kyanos grudgingly complied. The riders gasped and looked at one another. When quiet had resumed, Ruskya continued. "What did my father speculate would happen if one twin died?" Kyanos held his silence. "Kyanos, I asked a question. Answer it."

With a sigh, Kyanos answered. "He thought that if one twin died, the other would die as well."

"Riders, have you seen this happen? Did you have any wounds in your battle? Did any of your dragons seem confused or in pain when they were not hurt, but their twin was?" Ruskya called to the crowd, who nodded and affirmed that they had.

"Therefore, I say, since you now know the full implications of Calamadyn, I have defeated your leader. I will not humiliate him or even bring him to death, but I will not hand over one leaf of Calamadyn for the same reason my father sought to keep it secret. As for the rider and dragon that you have captured, they will be returned safe and unharmed within one day. Do I make myself clear?"

"And if I don't accept your terms?" Kyanos growled.

"Then we will continue this senseless fight. Shall I ask your men which it should be?"

Kyanos shook his head. "I accept," he ground out.

"Louder so that all may hear," Ruskya advised.

Kyanos turned to answer; then as if from out of nowhere, a streak of turquoise was flying through the air at Ruskya. Ruskya was prepared. He created a mental shield and then pushed the shield to redirect the dagger. Kyanos's eyes widened as he saw the turquoise streak head back toward him. Ruskya could feel him try to recreate a shield, but Ruskya blocked this effort. The knife was heading straight for Kyanos's heart. Kyanos dove to the side and the knife embedded itself into the wall behind him.

"Kyanos, your treachery betrays you," Ruskya said in a firm unwavering voice. "I call to your riders to cast judgment. Is the challenge over, riders? Has your leader lost?"

The riders were reluctant to answer, but in the end, they had to. "You have won, rider. Our leader has forfeited his cause." Kyanos glared at them, but his power seemed to be diminished.

"You have undone me, rider," Kyanos growled. "I will get you yet."

"Maybe, Kyanos, but I doubt it. It was your command that put Kyle in charge of capturing the dragon, wasn't it?"

Kyanos nodded. "He was mine to command. He willingly took the job."

"Therefore, the deaths that he was responsible for could be considered upon your head."

"So? What are a few farmer's lives? They were not riders. Those are the lives that are important; your life, and mine." He seemed to be spinning another spell. "In the grand scheme of things, we are the ones who wield the power; we will be the ones who are here a century from now."

"Kyanos, you may be right that we will be the ones here a hundred winters from now, but you are wrong about the other lives not being important. The others are our future riders."

"What? A rider from Three Spans Canyon breaking from tradition?" He paused. "I forget you are Ardyn's son. He always broke tradition."

"Sometimes traditions need to be broken," Ruskya stated.

"Well, I still say that the farmers and villagers don't matter. If one or two die, it isn't a big deal."

"Then we will agree to disagree. Take your riders and leave. Send Carryl back with a trustworthy rider." Ruskya turned to go, leaving his senses alert for any treachery. He sensed the movement, but didn't turn until he heard the gasp and realized that he should have intervened.

He hadn't sensed danger toward himself, but he hadn't thought to look out for danger toward Kyanos. Turning he saw the rider topple over with a turquoise hilt sticking out of his back. He looked around to see who the culprit was, but only saw riders staring in awe. A slight movement behind the boulders caught his eye.

"Ma," he called, "come out and bring everyone with you." The riders turned, startled to see a small group of villagers approaching.

Davyd had Byran by the shirt collar. "This is who yer looking for."

"Byran," Ruskya stated in a hurt, resigned voice, "why?"

"Why?" the man exclaimed. "Because he said my daughter and her husband were not important. They were important to my family. I did it for Braidyn, who watched his Ma and Da die at the hands of Kyle. This rider said they were not essential to the working of our world. He was wrong. I proved it by showing that a little nobody could make a difference in the life of a rider. If that was wrong, then I will face judgment."

Ruskya turned to the riders. "You heard his confession. Kyanos was your leader. You choose. Shall he face judgment or not?"

One rider stepped forward. "He has lost his family. We will not punish him further. Kyanos had slain others like him without a thought. It was right for him to be slain by one of them." The rider turned to the others. "We will leave. I will bring the verdict to Cerulean, for he is now our leader. Do you all agree?" Murmurs of assent passed among the ten riders. "I will return, Honored Rider Ruskya. Your rider and her dragon will be returned. I only ask that you do not leave us without any hope of a future."

"What do you mean?" Ruskya asked puzzled.

"Our dragons have no female. We were seeking a way to propagate. Several of our dragons have tried to breed with your female. I would ask mercy on any of her eggs."

Ruskya nodded. "We can discuss the matter when Carryl is returned safe and unharmed. Cerulean will have to make arrangements with me about that." The rider agreed, and the others left.

Ruskya sighed and called Wyeth. While he waited, he looked over at the turquoise dragon. The dragon had been silent this whole time. How could that be? The dragon should be partway dead by now from the grief of losing his rider. Instead he lay silent, his wings spread to show the shred that Wyeth had torn in the one. Wyeth landed at his feet.

"We will need to give him a rider funeral pyre, Wyeth. Will you do the honors?" Wyeth bowed his head and sprayed the icy blue flames to consume the rider's body. Ruskya carefully walked over to the turquoise dragon and quietly called to the dragon, but received no answer. Kyn ran past him and sat beside the dragon, placing a hand on the dragon's torn wing.

"I wish Carryl was here," the youngling muttered.

"She's not, but you can do it," Duskya replied following behind him. She turned and gave her brother a hug. The embrace said everything—thanks for staying alive, I'm proud of you for what you did, and don't you *ever* do that again—all at once.

Next, Meredyth came and hugged both of them. With tears in her eyes, she said, "You made your father proud today, Ruskya. Duskya, he couldn't have done it without your help. My twins are truly riders, and riders to be proud of."

Casey approached the group. "Ya really mean that Carryl will return soon?"

Ruskya put his hand on the man's shoulder. "Yes, sir, she will be returning within the next day. I had met with the rider they called Cerulean; he gave his pledge that she would not be harmed."

Their conversation was halted by a strange keening noise coming from the turquoise dragon. They turned to look at him. His head was cocked to the side and his eyes were unfocused. The dragon called again as if he were listening for an answer somewhere. When no answer came, he looked around bewildered. Seeing Kyn, he gazed into his eyes. He went on to weigh each one of them. Even Meredyth endured the dragon's penetrating gaze. When the dragon came to Byran, he paused longer than the rest. He let out a soft bellow of air that tousled the man's graying hair. Then he came to Braidyn. Looking at the boy, he trilled a series of calls that no one had ever heard before. Then he stood, bowed, and raising his wing, he tried to take off.

"Ho, boy," Kyn called. "I can help you with the wing, if you like, but you have to stay down here. Will you let me?"

They all heard the reply, "If the boy will stay with me, I will stay with you." Those who had never heard a dragon before stared with open-mouthed wonder. Braidyn looked around wondering who the boy was.

"Does he mean me?"

"Yes, little one, will you sit with me while I heal?" the turquoise dragon replied.

Braidyn nodded his dark head and swallowed, then stepped forward to see the dragon. He ever so carefully put his hand out to touch the dragon's flanks. The dragon shivered at his touch and then seemed to almost purr.

Braidyn smiled at the sound. "What is your name, Honored One?"

The dragon turned an eye to look at the boy at his flank. "My given name is Turqueso. I have not heard it in many winters."

They all watched in amazement as Kyn and Braidyn settled in to help the dragon heal.

CHAPTER 27: A NEW LEADER

CARRYL HAD ALMOST fallen asleep in front of Cerulean. They had been flying for close to a glass since Kyle's funeral pyre. She was jolted back to alertness by the simultaneous sound of dragons both in her mind and outside, and by Cerulean falling against her. The dragons were keening. It was a loud piercing sound echoing in her mind as well as through the sky. Cerulean slowly straightened.

"It is over." Then, firmer, "It is over!" Immediately, he led the dragons to land on the desert floor below.

"Cerulean," one rider called, "what is happening? Why are the dragons' calling out like this?" Another rider whose dragon had just stopped keening spoke up. "Cerulean, he seems to be telling me that he is now wholly mine. I don't know what he means. He says his master is dead," the rider said puzzled.

Cerulean nodded his head. "Yes, those who were owned by Kyanos are now free to go as they choose. I will not make anyone stay here, unless you wish to. I will return Carryl and her dragon to their home. I do not know about our future, but I will plead with the rider who bested Kyanos to show us mercy for our dragons' sakes. Who will follow me?"

A lone rider stepped forward. "I do not know about the rest, but I am willing to take the chance for my dragon's sake." Nods of agreement passed through the circle of thirteen riders.

"Then let's recover some ground yet today. We will not make it before dark, so we will have to camp tonight. Everyone look for a place that would be acceptable." Turning to Carryl, he said, "You may ride Wyn if you wish."

"Did you hear that, girl? Are you up for a rider?"

"Yes, little one. I am always willing to carry you."

Carryl turned to Cerulean. "Thank you for allowing me to ride Wyn. I accept your offer." Turning to Wymar, she verbally said, "Thank you, honored dragon, for carrying me this far." Wymar bowed his head in acknowledgment.

They took off shortly after that. It seemed by unspoken consent that the dragons avoided the spot where the aqua dragon had fallen. It was not long after they passed it that the sun started to set in the west.

A call came from a rider who had forged further ahead: he had found a cave that would house the riders comfortably; there were crags for the dragons to use for the night. They all landed near the man, and soon the riders were enjoying the warmth of a roaring fire. Carryl shared some of Meredyth's tea with the others. It was nearly gone by now, but she didn't mind using it, knowing that she would be home tomorrow. The men shared tales around the fire that night. Carryl noticed that they seemed more open and friendly than they had before. They regaled her with tales of adventures in their homeland to the south. She realized that not a single tale told of Kyanos.

The biggest change was in Cerulean. He had always been polite to her, but the cold, hard edge had disappeared and he seemed to walk taller and smile more often. He had a way of making the men feel important. Carryl thought he would make a great leader for this group of riders if they would have him.

* * *

The next morning, Carryl saw a tall man stride confidently into the cave. He called for Cerulean. Cerulean glanced up from the meal he was sharing with Carryl and motioned for the man to come over. He stood and bowed when the man reached them. Carryl noticed the man's teal eyes and realized that he was a rider.

"Carryl," Cerulean stated, "I present to you Honored Rider Tyrone."

Carryl stood and bowed. "It is an honor to meet you, rider."

"And you, honored rider," Tyron replied in a deep voice. "You are well respected among your colony. I now can see for myself why."

Carryl blushed as she ducked her head, her face turning as bright as her hair.

"Please, sit," Cerulean offered. He handed Tyrone the plate of cheeses and meats that they were sharing. The rider eagerly accepted.

"I flew all night to find you." Tyrone said after a few bites, "I came directly from Kyanos." He paused, took another bite and swallowed. "Kyanos was defeated by the icy rider, and the rider was letting him go. We were to leave and bring rider Carryl back to the cave." Again, he paused for a bite of food. Carryl could tell that Cerulean was getting impatient. She smiled, wondering if the rider was purposely dragging the story out. "There is no other way to put it than to say justice was delivered."

Cerulean nodded, encouraging the rider to continue.

"Cerulean, did you know that Calamadyn has harmful effects?" the rider asked.

Taken aback, Cerulean didn't reply at first. "Yes, I did. I argued with Kyanos about its use. I was apprentice to the man from whom Kyanos received his information. It was a dispute over the use of Calamadyn that led to our falling out." Cerulean was quiet and thoughtful for a moment.

"You were apprentice to the icy rider's father?" Tyrone said with amazement. Cerulean nodded. Tyrone sighed. "I do not know what our future will bring. Kyanos is dead. I assume you will be the new leader of our colony. We are to return rider Carryl and her dragon to the cave. Will you plead our case to the icy rider, Cerulean?" the rider almost begged.

Cerulean looked Tyrone straight in the eyes. "I am not the leader until every rider says so. I will plead our case to Ruskya, the icy rider, as you call him, but I will not take leadership without the agreement of the riders."

"Then, let us gather the riders. I brought the others with me. They are waiting outside with their dragons."

Cerulean was shocked. "You *all* flew through the night?"

"Yes, we all witnessed Kyanos's downfall. We wished to reach you before you got further south. I promised the rider his girl and the dragon would be returned to him within the day."

Cerulean noticed Carryl's blush at the mention of her being Ruskya's girl. He smiled. He had seen the spark between the two when they had rendezvoused at the creek in the canyon.

"Bring the riders in," Cerulean said. Turning to Carryl, "Would you mind waiting outside with Wyn while they discuss this?"

Carryl nodded and left. Wyn was glad to see her. Carryl rubbed her muzzle where the bridle had been. She noticed that a small sore had formed. She wished for her herb pouch to make a salve, but decided to try Kyn's way: she thought of the herbs and their potency, and then using her hands, she gently massaged the area pretending to work in the healing strength.

Cerulean soon joined them, and they talked for a while about his ideas for a colony, as the other riders deliberated. She could tell he was nervous, for he paced as he talked. She smiled at that. He did care about these riders, she realized. He had spent many winters with them and had grown to know them personally.

They did not have to wait long for the riders' decision. Tyrone came out and motioned for both of them to return. They found the riders seated in the cave. Everyone stood when the three entered.

"Honored Rider Cerulean," Tyrone started, speaking for all of the riders "we as a colony of riders have chosen you to be our leader. We swear loyalty to you." They all bowed to their knees. "Will you accept the responsibilities of being our leader, honored rider?"

Carryl noticed tears in Cerulean's eyes. He blinked and stepped forward. With a firm voice which hid the emotion that Carryl saw brimming underneath, he replied, "Honored riders, it is with mixed emotions that I stand before you. For many winters, I held Kyanos in great esteem. Unfortunately, in the last several, we started to disagree. I tried to reason with him, but he would not listen to reason. He listened solely to pure power and authority. I did not have that. I am sad that the man I had called friend is gone. I am overjoyed that you deem me worthy to take his place. I will tell you upfront, that I will not lead as he did. I will not hold you in our colony beyond your will. When you deem me unfit, please, come to me and talk. Show me where I have gone wrong. I will listen.

"Honored riders, today, I accept the leadership of the dragon riders of the south. I vow to honor your values, and to do all that is in the interest of our dragons. To this end, I will return Honored Rider Carryl and her dragon to their home. Any who wish may return with me. The rest may abide here until our return. I will also entreat the rider of Three Spans Canyon for mercy on our dragons. May the riders of the south endure and prosper." He then motioned for them to stand as he knelt to them.

A cheer went up from the riders as they stood. They knew they had chosen well. Carryl cheered along with them. She blinked back tears as her eyes met Cerulean's. He smiled at her. It had been worth it all to see this.

When the noise died down, Cerulean stood. "Now, who wishes from the bottom of their hearts to ride with me? No one is compelled to ride by my word. If you wish, you may join me."

Tyrone stepped forward. "I gave my word that I would see the rider and her dragon safely returned to the cave. I will go with you. I would suggest that the others wait here and rest your dragons for the return trip south." He turned to Cerulean. "My dragon has conserved his strength and informs me that he will fly at our earliest convenience."

"Then gather provisions, water, and whatever else you need. We will ride within one glass. I cannot guarantee that we will be back tonight. We may need to stay there awhile. We will return within seven days, or send a messenger to you here."

The other riders nodded their agreement and went about helping to gather food and waterskins for the three riders to take with them. Carryl and the other two riders were in the air in less than a glass.

CHAPTER 28: THE TALE OF DRAGONS

THE MOON HAD RISEN and was shedding its light through the smoke hole of the cave. Duskya had gone to retrieve Glendyn and give word to the villagers that their men were safe. Kyn and Braidyn sat beside Turqueso, who seemed to be sleeping peacefully. Ruskya, Casey, Davyd, and Byran sat near the fire with Meredyth's tea to warm their hands and the fire to warm their feet. Meredyth was lying down in the quiet spot she'd found by the boulders.

Suddenly, the moon was blocked, and the sound of dragon wings filled the air. Ruskya looked up to see the royal blue dragon descending through the smoke hole. He smiled at Glendyn's choice of entrance. Only earlier that day had he chosen the same route. He rose to greet his trainer, but his bow was cut short as he was enveloped in a huge embrace. Ruskya laughed and returned the hug.

"Ruskya, my son, I hear that I have reason to be proud of you today. You have avenged your da and made known the dangers of Calamadyn. You have also procured Carryl and Wyn's freedom. Not bad for a day's work." Stepping back, he held Ruskya at arm's length. "How are you? Are you unharmed?"

"I am tired, Glendyn, and have some minor bruises, but nothing compared to an afternoon of sparring with you," Ruskya replied.

"So, my lessons paid off, did they?"

"Very much so, honored rider."

Glendyn swung a halfhearted punch at Ruskya which he dodged. "Don't mock me, young one. I can still take you down." Ruskya laughed.

Casey entered the conversation. "If ya can beat him, sir, then ya must be one mighty rider!" Davyd and Byran agreed.

"I guess we may have to show them later, Glendyn."

"I don't know. From what I was told today, you might not fight fairly against me," Glendyn replied.

"I will always fight fairly, Glendyn. You taught me that. I knew I had to use the Calamadyn advantages with this rider. I do not know if he was a Calamadyn twin or not, but his mental abilities were strong."

"I know. I saw you after you first met him during the trials at Caravan Canyon. Duskya said the dragon was still living." Ruskya motioned over to Kyn and Braidyn with the resting turquoise dragon. "What is the boy doing with Kyn?" Glendyn inquired.

"The dragon asked for him." Glendyn looked askance at Ruskya, but Ruskya just shrugged. They walked over to Kyn.

"Kyn," Glendyn greeted him. "How is the dragon?"

"He seems to be resting, Glendyn. I do not think there were any physical wounds other than his wings. I have done what I can with those." Glendyn examined the bandages. They all stopped as the dragon moved. He turned his head and stared around him.

"Come closer, you three by the fire," Turqueso called. The men stared at each other in wonder. Byran kicked a stray pebble as he came with the other two villagers. When they were all near, the dragon spoke again.

"You are the ones who freed me? You, with the snow-in-the-spring hair," he said lifting his muzzle to Byran, "I owe you a debt of gratitude. If you had not slain my master, I would have continued to be a slave. For that, I thank you. May blessings be upon you and your family forever."

A light mist of turquoise sparkles fell on Byran. He slowly let out his breath. "Thank you, dragon."

The dragon turned now to Braidyn. "Little one, thank you for staying with me. I can see that you honor dragons."

With a slight tremble to his voice, Braidyn replied, "Only those who are kind to people, and don't go off killing or burning their homes."

"Ah," the dragon answered. "so you do not like all dragons, but what would you say, if a dragon was under the power of his rider and had no choice but to do some of those things?"

"I don't know. It would depend on whether the dragon still would do those things after the rider's power was gone."

The dragon seemed to nod his head. "Then, little one, I will make a promise to you. Never again will I willfully attack an innocent person or his home. Will that do?"

Braidyn thought about it. "I think so."

"Will you then accept me? Will you be my rider?" There was a large intake of breath, as the riders in the room realized what was happening, and the others understood the significance of being chosen by a dragon.

"You want me? Why?"

The dragon let out a small snort. "Why do dragons do anything? You seem to be an honest, just person with a sense of right and wrong. My former rider did not have that. I was one of many dragons he compelled to be his; he was not satisfied with just one dragon. I do not know how he did it, but he had power over many dragons and people—riders and others alike. This time I would like to choose my rider, and I choose you, if you will have me."

A smile lit up Braidyn's face. He stood up and reached for Turqueso's neck. He placed his arms as far around as they would go. "Will you let me be your rider?" he whispered against the dragon's neck. Again, the soft almost purring noise escaped the dragon.

Glendyn motioned the others away from the boy and his dragon. "That was different," he commented to Ruskya and Kyn as they drank tea around the fire.

"I've been thinking, Glendyn, if we are able to fix our dragon population problem, then we need to let those who wish to be riders—no matter their age—to come to the procession for a possible choosing. I know it goes against tradition, but I think the dragons will prefer it."

"You may have a point, Ruskya. I just wish we knew what to do about replenishing the dragon population."

"Well, we may have part of the problem solved for us," Ruskya answered. "Kyanos's plan was for his dragons to breed with Wyn. She could be carrying up to fifteen eggs. Cerulean will be asking for some portion of those, but our colony may be able to keep some, also."

"I thought of something," Kyn said. "I think the Calamadyn twin dragons don't feel the need for a mate because they have their twin to provide companionship."

Glendyn thought about that for a moment. "That would explain why our dragons haven't paired up; all of the dragons of mating age in our colony are Calamadyn twins."

Ruskya hid a yawn behind his hand.

"I think some sleep is in order for you, son," Glendyn said. "Go lay down. I doubt Carryl will be back tonight. I'll watch over and let you know if you are needed."

Ruskya nodded his head. As he stood, he laid a hand on his trainer's shoulder. "Thank you, Glendyn. For all you have done for me."

Glendyn caught Ruskya's hand with his own and squeezed it.

* * *

The next morning, Ruskya was impressed with the healing in Turqueso's wing. He wondered how Kyn was able to work such wonders. Kyn just shook his head, unsure of exactly what he had done.

The morning seemed to drag on without much to do but wait. Ruskya paced back and forth until the others drove him outside to pace. The villagers refused to go home, even though they had nothing to occupy their time either.

It was Braidyn who announced that Carryl was near. Turqueso felt the two other dragons' presence. Ruskya called Wyeth to see if he could feel Wyn.

"Yes! They are a ways out, but they are coming as quickly as they can."

Ruskya debated with himself on contacting Carryl, but finally decided to go ahead. "Carryl," he called beside himself with concern, "are you all right?"

"I am fine. We are coming as fast as we can. Cerulean was elected the leader of his colony. Tyrone told us that you killed Kyanos."

"He said that I killed him?" Ruskya asked.

"Well…" Carryl dragged out the word out in puzzlement. "He said that Kyanos was dead and that you had defeated him."

"Yes, I defeated him, but Byran killed him."

"Oh," Carryl said trying to take in the information.

"There's more," Ruskya called to her. "The turquoise dragon isn't dead. He was under some kind of compulsion from Kyanos and chose to live after Kyanos was killed. He asked Braidyn to be his rider last night. He also thanked Byran for killing Kyanos and blessed him."

"Wow!" Carryl exclaimed. "I have had a fairly uneventful time by comparison. I do have news, though. Byran doesn't have to worry about

Kyle or his dragon anymore." She explained what had happened.

"Is Wyn all right?"

"Yes. I'm riding her now. I can see the canyon!"

"Where does Cerulean want to meet?" Ruskya asked.

They decided on the cave itself. The three would land outside and let their dragons go. They would come inside and meet with Ruskya.

"Hurry," Ruskya thought toward them, not thinking anything of it.

"I am," Carryl replied.

Ruskya blushed. "You heard that?"

"Wasn't I supposed to?" she asked with a laugh in her voice.

When the three riders finally entered the cave, Ruskya came forward and met them at the entrance to the passageway. "Welcome, honored riders." To Carryl, he thought, "and welcome back to where you belong." She smiled at him.

"Thank you, honored rider," Cerulean stated. "We have brought back your rider and your dragon as you requested, and as I vowed. They are both fine, although we had some problems with one of my riders. He was dealt with by three of our dragons who were offended by his actions."

"I see, honored rider," Ruskya replied. "Come, we have prepared some food and drink and a place to relax." He led them back to the fire. Carryl noticed Tyrone's glance toward a small scorched area on the other side of the cave. She wondered but didn't ask about it. Meredyth served them cheese, meat, stew, and flatbread. She handed everyone mugs of her tea.

They all sat around and ate. Introductions were made all around, with Braidyn and Kyn introduced as younglings, and Glendyn as rider trainer. The villagers were introduced.

Casey saw Carryl and ran to her. She held out her arms and let him hug her. "Da," she said, "I am glad to see you."

"And I you, daughter." She noticed there were tears in his eyes and was surprised to find tears in her own.

After the meal, the villagers asked to be excused. They were ready to head back to the village and their homes. Casey paused and looked at Carryl.

"Can I leave ya, daughter? Will ya be fine with these riders?"

Carryl nodded. "I will come home to see you, Da, before I go back to

Three Spans Canyon."

Her father grinned. "Good, then I'll see ya at the farm."

After the villagers left, Meredyth passed the tea around one final time and then moved back to where she had spent the night.

Ruskya opened the conversation. "I think you should know that Braidyn has become a rider. Kyanos's dragon did not die with him. Kyn, our healer, worked on the dragon's wing, which had received tears during the fight. As he did so, the dragon searched each one of us and requested that Braidyn stay with him. He explained that he had been in bondage to Kyanos and asked Braidyn if he would be his new rider. Braidyn has agreed." The two riders from the south stared in amazement at the boy and then over to the turquoise dragon.

"It does not surprise me that Kyanos would have had a compulsion on the dragon," Cerulean commented. "He had such a hold on me, too. I believe there were several more dragons and possibly riders who felt the same."

Tyrone nodded. "They said as much when we voted."

"I am glad the dragon decided to live and choose a new rider," Cerulean stated. "There is one more item that must be dealt with. As you may know, Kyanos used Wyn to breed with sixteen of his dragons. I do not know how many eggs will result, but we would like to know if there is some way we could pay you for them."

Ruskya looked to Glendyn. "I do not know what the colony would say to that."

"I think the colony would look to the dragon and her rider. What does Wyn say, Carryl? What do you think would be proper payment and what does Wyn want done with her eggs?"

Carryl consulted with Wyn. The dragon definitely had a plan. "She says that Cerulean can have Wymar's egg. When the time comes, a message will be sent out to you. Any of your riders who desire a hatchling must return here. The rider must pass before the baby dragon, and Wyn will tell from the hatchling's response whether the rider may have the hatchling. If this is not acceptable, then return next winter and receive Wymar's egg alone. The rest will stay here."

Tyrone looked as if he was about to say something, but Cerulean laid a hand on the rider's leg. "She has judged us. Because of the circumstances of her breeding, she had no way of judging the character of the dragons who came to her, some of whom were under Kyanos's compulsion. If we return at the hatching, then the hatchlings can see the riders, and Wyn can meet the dragons on better grounds."

Cerulean paused. "Another thought comes to mind. Carryl, would Wyn accept it if we came together and celebrated the laying of the eggs? Then the dragons and the riders of both colonies could meet and get to know each other better. I could pick up Wymar's egg at that time. Then we will return at the hatching. The dragons again will have an opportunity to know each other, and the riders, also. Wyn will have better knowledge of those who desire a hatchling. We could all celebrate new life together."

Carryl smiled. "It sounds like you have a good idea, but let me ask Wyn."

The reply came back as a resounding yes. Wyn loved the idea. She did not want the defenseless hatchlings to go to a place where they would not be treated well. Getting to know everyone first would definitely help.

Braidyn spoke up. "Honored rider, if I went with them, then I could know where their colony is located. I could carry messages."

Cerulean smiled at the lad's courage. "It is far way, youngling. You could not travel it alone." He thought of something, "Ardyn always said give a mother dragon four seasons and an egg would be laid."

Glendyn agreed. "Yes, he did say that. Then next winter it is. We will celebrate at Three Spans Canyon. Bring all the riders. We will warn the villagers to expect your flight and that they have nothing to fear."

Ruskya noticed Braidyn's head hung down. "Youngling, did you wish to travel with the riders from the south?"

Braidyn looked up. "I would like to. Besides, it does not seem right to separate friends. When they were in range, Turqueso became happy. I don't want him to be sad. I think he would feel lonely, and maybe even bad, because he fought against Wyeth, Wryn and the other dragons from Three Spans Canyon."

Cerulean looked intently at the boy. "Where did you gain such wisdom, boy?"

Braidyn shrugged. "It just seems right. It sounded like the stories the merchant told me about Wyeth, and how the dragons work together and have real feelings."

Ruskya looked at Braidyn. "When did the merchant tell you those stories?"

"While we hid from the aqua dragon. We were in the rocky enclosure, and I could tell that he was burned from the way the aqua fire had come into the small opening. He told me stories so that I would not be afraid."

"What I don't understand, is how did he know these stories? I've never told him stories of Wyeth. I don't think I have even named him to the merchant. Kyn, did you tell your Da anything?" The young healer shook his head. "I guess, it will remain a mystery," Ruskya said.

"No, son," Meredyth spoke up. "I am wondering if Wyeth himself whispered those stories in the merchant's ear. The night he left, I saw that he would need courage. I used a pinch of Wyeth's dragon courage on him. I wondered if it is what protected him from the fire not burning as deeply as it could have." The riders looked at her with amazement.

"Dragon courage?" Glendyn replied. "There is much we do not know about it. That very well could be."

* * *

The riders from the south would have headed out that day, but Turqueso was not ready to fly. Carryl took a look at what Kyn had done and helped add her healer's touch to it. She asked Braidyn's permission to speak with the dragon and worked healing into his mind, while Kyn worked with his wing. In two day's time, the dragon was ready to fly. They waited one more day to test the wing. Carryl and Kyn wanted to see if it would hold up to a flight.

With the successful flight under his belt, the southern dragon riders decided to bid them adieu. Tyrone bowed to the riders from Three Spans Canyon and thanked them. Braidyn gave hugs all around with an extra long one for Carryl and Ruskya. Cerulean bowed to Glendyn and Kyn, shook hands with Ruskya and started to shake hands with Carryl. Instead, Carryl reached up and gave him a hug.

"Thank you, Cerulean for being you, and protecting me."

She heard the emotion in his voice as he responded. "I just wish I could have protected you better."

"You did what you could. You came when I needed you. You will make a wife a fine husband some day."

She was happy to see his blush, but it didn't last long, for he replied, "And you will be Ruskya's bride before the hatching, I would guess." Her blush matched his, but she smiled anyway.

The four from Three Spans Canyon waved their newfound friends good-bye and then turned to each other. Glendyn offered to take Meredyth back to the village, but she decided to stay and help with food. Ruskya said they could fly to Casey's farm and then return to the colony. He took Kyn with him, while Carryl rode Wyn.

Carryl enjoyed viewing the familiar desert. She found the farm and landed outside. Running up the porch steps, she knocked on the door.

"Look what the wind drug in," Casey exclaimed. "Ya are a sight fer sore eyes. Now, mind ya don't take so long in visitin' again. Ya hear?"

Carryl laughed. "I will come back more often, Da. I have a way of getting here easily with Wyn. Although, I don't know what rider responsibilities I will be strapped down with."

Casey turned to Ruskya. "Ya had better not keep her from me, young lad. I want her ta visit at least once every seven days. Ya hear?"

Ruskya grinned. "I think we can make that part of her duties. We probably should head back soon, though. We have a stop to make in the village."

Casey nodded and added, "Give the merchant my greetin's." He gave Carryl a hug and the others handshakes. Soon, they were in the sky again heading for the village.

Once there, Carryl was impressed with the difference. The riders were greeted by villagers out on the canyon pathway. There were no more animals in the side canyons, and the people seemed happier. They made their way to the general store. The atmosphere here was also changed. No longer were scared people huddled around the stove. Kyn's mother greeted them, eager to see them. She led them back to the abode where her husband sat up in bed.

"Da," Kyn greeted, "I'm glad to see you out of bed. How are you?"

"I am doing fine, except for some strange dreams. I keep seeing this icy blue dragon. Every time I am about to be had by the aqua one, this icy blue one comes along and blasts the aqua one."

Ruskya shook his head. "Sir, I think that may be my ma's fault. She sprinkled you with dust from my dragon. It was to help give you courage on your journey to warn the farmers. The icy blue dragon is mine."

"Now that's a relief! I was afraid there was another dragon I would
have to fight sometime."

"You also don't have to worry about the aqua one," Carryl said. "He was
attacked by three other dragons and died—along with his rider."

"Well, I sure am sad to hear about Kyle, but it's a load off my mind
to know that dragon won't be bothering the farms around here
anymore."

"No, Da," Kyn answered. "We made a treaty of sorts with the
remaining riders. Their new leader is a real man. You would like him.
He's older than Ruskya, but a lot like him."

The merchant nodded. "I think I owe my life to you, son, and to your
rider friend, Carryl. I never thought the girl who brought me herbs
would one day be a rider and save my skin."

Carryl grinned. "Life is interesting isn't it, sir?"

They said their good-byes and reassured the merchant's wife they
would check back in on him at least once a week while he healed.

The ride back to the canyon was short. Carryl relished the trip,
knowing it was familiar ground. She would soon be back at her place
with Duskya, and soon Ruskya and she would start building a room for
her plants. Her life as a rider was about to begin. It didn't matter that her
eyes had never changed color. Wyn had chosen her, and the talks that
she and Ruskya had in those two days waiting for Turqueso's wing to
heal had led her to believe that Cerulean may be right. She may one day
become Ruskya's wife. Until then, she had herbs to prepare and her next
patient was just around the corner.

EPILOGUE

THE SHARP CRY of a newborn rang through the still night air. Kyn sighed with relief when Meredyth sent him for a large bowl and more towels. He had never felt anything so intense. As he left the room, he found Glendyn pacing the floor. "Relax, you have a new nephew!" Kyn announced.

Glendyn grinned. "And Carryl? How is she?"

"Doing just fine."

Glendyn laughed, a full-hearted laugh that released the more than the half a day's worth of tension that had built up.

"I don't want to go through something like that again for many winters," Kyn exclaimed. "I don't know who was worse, Ruskya or Duskya. The two were so concerned, Meredyth threatened to kick them out! It was more intense than helping Ruskya beat Kyanos, or even healing my Da."

Glendyn chuckled. "Birth is usually like that."

Kyn was interrupted by Duskya. "Ma needs the bowl and towels, Kyn."

The youngling quickly washed his hands and headed back into the room with the necessary items. Duskya sat down on a chair with her head in her hands. Her fingers absentmindedly played with the dark strands of her hair. A tear forced its way past her hands. Glendyn noticed and sat down.

"Come here, girl," he said, drawing her to him. The floodgates opened and Duskya began to sob. He sat there rubbing her back until she was ready to talk, nestled into the shelter of his chest.

"It was beautiful. Ruskya looked at her so intently, so lovingly. He doesn't seem to need me anymore, Glendyn."

"There you are wrong, Duskya. He needs you now just as much as before. It is just a different kind of need. He needs his twin sister who will watch his back from the world. He needs his twin sister to help with her new little nephew."

"But Glendyn, the look he gave her! I wish someone would look at me that way."

"Then you are blind, girl. There is someone who looks at you that way."

Duskya pulled away to see his face. "Are you sure?" Glendyn nodded. "But he was my da's apprentice. He's the same age as my da. What..." She faltered. "What if he only sees me as a child?"

"Duskya, let me tell you something about being a rider," Glendyn said gently. "After a certain point, you forget about age. You see people in relation to how old you feel you are. With most riders, that's about their mid- to late-thirties. If someone looks as old as you appear to, then you think of yourself as the same age. When it comes to love and matters of the heart, you can't tell your heart what to do. If your heart learns to love a person, it often doesn't matter the age difference or how illogical it seems. Your heart will often tell your head otherwise."

Duskya heard an unspoken, "I know that as a fact," added to the end. She looked quizzically at Glendyn.

"Is that how it was with Caralyn and you?"

"In some ways, yes. Our true ages were about the same as you and Cerulean. By the time she was older than my physical appearance, I had already given my heart to her."

Duskya nodded. Although Glendyn had shared much of his life and opened up to them more in the last two winters, she still felt awkward trying to pry into his past.

"And how is this new nephew of ours?" Glendyn asked, changing the subject.

Duskya glowed. "He is a cutie. He has red hair like Carryl and a strong grip."

Glendyn smiled. "That's how Caralyn would have described a babe. I'll have to go see for myself."

Kyn emerged from the door carrying the bowl and some used towels. He glanced over at Duskya and Glendyn. "If this is what a midwife has to do, I would much rather be a regular old healer. I am exhausted!" The two older riders laughed.

"I should go knock and have a look at my new nephew and then head home so Kyn can go to bed," Glendyn said after regaining his composure.

"Bed sounds like I good idea," Duskya agreed, "but I will wait for Ma. She's spending the night with me."

As if hearing her name called, Meredyth exited Ruskya and Carryl's room and quietly closed the door. Glendyn met her at the stove as she poured herself some tea.

"How is everyone?" he asked.

"Doing well. Tired, but no more than to be expected."

Glendyn laid a hand on her shoulder. "And how are you doing?"

"I'm tired also, but glad to have a grandson. I miss Ardyn, now. He would be so proud of both the twins."

Glendyn nodded. "Can I go on in and see them?"

"Oh, goodness, yes!" Meredyth exclaimed. "I should have thought of that, Glendyn; forgive me."

"Don't worry, Meredyth. I'll go knock and take a look at my nephew. You go rest and get a good night's sleep. I'll see you all in the morning."

At Glendyn's knock, Ruskya called for him to enter. He opened the door and in the dim oil lamplight, he saw Ruskya sitting on the edge of the bed and Carryl sitting up with a small bundle wrapped in blankets in her arms. "So, is this my new nephew?" he quietly asked. Both nodded but didn't say any more. "How are you two doing? Did you both survive the birthing?"

"It was more than I ever thought it would be," Ruskya said. "I was never more proud of my Carryl as I was tonight. She did amazingly." Glendyn saw the glow and the look Ruskya gave Carryl that had made Duskya jealous. He didn't blame her. There was no connection as special as a husband and a wife just after birth.

"I won't stay long, but I wanted to at least get a look at the little fellow," Glendyn said.

"Here, Glendyn," Carryl said holding the baby out to him. "Come hold baby Ardyn."

"Ardyn, huh?" Glendyn said settling the little one into his arms. "I see your Ma and Da are thinking of your grandda tonight. I'll let you sleep, but in time, you'll hear all the stories of your family heritage from me, little Ardyn." He handed the baby back to Carryl. "You two did just great. Get some sleep if he'll let you. I'll see you in the morning."

Leaving the room, he found Meredyth and Duskya had already left. Kyn was half asleep in the chair. He put a hand on the boy's shoulder and woke him. "Head to bed, youngling. I'm going there myself."

"Thanks, Glendyn. I hope Ruskya doesn't wake early tomorrow."

The older rider laughed. "I think he just may give you a break."

* * *

The next few weeks were busy in the colony. The nestlings would begin hatching in about ten days, though some had already started. The riders from the south were scheduled to arrive soon. Several weddings had been planned to coincide with their visit.

In the last four seasons or so, there had been much coming and going between the two colonies. The riders from the south had met the Three Spans colony riders at the egg laying a winter ago. The friendships that had formed at the celebration had prompted various other meetings. In the process, three couples had decided to get married at the hatching, and wedding preparations filled up much of the time leading up to that time. If a rider wasn't involved in dressmaking, he or she was involved in preparing places for the extra twenty-five riders, or making the canyon ready for the visitors.

Duskya found herself counting down the days until the arrival of the riders from the south. Ruskya teased her that she was worse than the brides-to-be were. She would mumble something, but then he would break into her thoughts and tell her he knew differently.

One day, she decided to visit with baby Ardyn and Carryl. Ruskya was out fixing up one of the abodes for visitors. It would just be the women and the baby. Duskya brought some tea and a cake she had made. She was surprised when Carryl greeted her at the door.

"You're up," Duskya said with surprise.

"I haven't stayed down much, despite Ruskya's pleas. I would much rather be walking around the house than confined to bed," Carryl stated.

"I agree. I brought us something to eat with our tea. I'll set it by the stove. Where is baby Ardyn?"

"Finally asleep. He was awake almost all night."

"Oh, Carryl, then you should be in bed, too," Duskya said with concern.

"I would much rather have a visitor than a nap right now."

"Has it been terrible being confined to the abode? I think I would go nuts if I had to stay inside for that long."

"Oh, I've gotten outside, but it's more the lack of conversation. I hear the dragons all the time, but I am alone except when Ruskya comes home for meals and at night."

Duskya nodded. "Then let's talk. I don't care about what. You decide."

Carryl grinned. "Are you sure you want me to do that?"

Duskya glanced warily at her. "Sure, why not?"

"I've been talking with Ruskya," she stated. "His biggest concern besides Ardyn and me is you."

"So," Duskya answered still not sure where things were going.

"So, he talks about how you are counting days until the hatching, and it has nothing to do with new dragons, but with a certain rider."

Duskya hung her head. "I know, but sometimes, I think it is all in my head, or all one-sided."

"Why do you say that?" Carryl asked.

"I remember our times together and think there was something there, but then you say he was constantly reading your thoughts. I don't think he has even tried to read mine."

"Duskya," Carryl said choosing her words with care, "when Cerulean was reading my thoughts, I found it very intrusive. I would say he has learned his lesson and is being polite, if he hasn't even tried. Remember, he also knows you are Ruskya's twin. Calamadyn twins are supposedly the same strength. He remembers how strong Kyanos was, and Ruskya beat him."

"Does he even see me as a woman, or am I just Ardyn's daughter to him?" Duskya blurted out.

Carryl sighed. "You will just have to talk with him about it. But are you ready to leave Three Spans Canyon? Could you handle being away from Ruskya for moons on end?"

Duskya nodded. "I've thought of that, too. I don't know for sure, but I do know our link has weakened since your marriage. I know Ruskya still feels it, but it isn't as intense now that he has you. I feel left out a lot. Not that I begrudge your marriage, of course; I'm just saying what I feel."

"I understand," Carryl said. "Do either of you know what the Calamadyn bond will be like if you are that far apart?"

Duskya shook her head. "I assume it will still be there, but maybe I should go visit before any serious decisions are made."

"That's an idea," Carryl agreed. "Well, we still have a couple days until the riders arrive. I guess we'll have to wait."

Duskya nodded. They finished their tea before Ardyn awoke wanting to be fed. Duskya stayed around for another half a glass and then headed out.

Her feelings of being out of place seemed larger than ever. She decided that a flight with Wryn would help. The dragon always seemed to cheer her heart. The brisk air helped revive her spirits. Wryn flew fast, and Duskya let the wind whip her in the face and blow her hair behind her. When she landed, she felt better.

* * *

Ruskya finished the last abode and was heading home when he heard dragon wings above him. Although it had been two winters since Kyanos had attacked the colony, Ruskya still flinched and reached out any time he heard the sound beat overhead. This time he almost flinched at the mental contact. "Cerulean?" he called in surprise. "Is that you?"

"Ruskya!" the excited reply came. "I'm landing over by the crags. Would you have time to meet with me? I have Braidyn with me."

The walk to the crags was brisk and quick. Ruskya wondered what had happened to bring the rider in early. Hopefully there had been no complications with the hatching of Wymar's egg. Ruskya knew Cerulean had planned to wait for the hatching before visiting. He considered calling ahead to find out if all was fine, but decided against it. When he reached the crags, Braidyn had already dismounted. He came running to Ruskya, and the two embraced.

"I swear, young one," Ruskya exclaimed holding the youngling out to see him better, "you have grown an inch in the last two moons since I have seen you!"

Braidyn laughed. "Is Kyn around?"

"I'm not sure exactly where, but I think he had to go clean out the dragon crags for you all."

"Eww! That's a nasty job."

Ruskya laughed. The youngling definitely had grown in his knowledge of dragons over the last two winters. "Do you want me to call Kyn and find him for you?"

"No, I'll just go find him, if that's okay with you Honored Rider Cerulean," he added turning to Cerulean who had just dismounted carrying the luggage.

"Go ahead," Cerulean agreed with a grin. "Just make sure to check in before nightfall." The two older riders watched as the youngling ran off; then turned back to each other. They paused before simultaneously embracing.

"Cerulean, is everything okay? We weren't expecting you for another couple of days," concern shadowed Ruskya's voice.

"I am fine," Cerulean soothed.

"And the egg?"

"You mean the hatchling," Cerulean corrected.

"What!" Ruskya exclaimed.

"Yes, Nube is a gorgeous little thing. She reminds me of the clouds at sunset after a stormy day."

"Congratulations! That is so good to hear. Carryl will be proud."

"How is she?" Cerulean asked with concern.

"She is fine, along with baby Ardyn."

It was Cerulean's turn to show surprise. The emotions showed in his eyes. "Your da would be proud of you."

"I think of us both," Ruskya corrected. "You have brought life back to your colony."

Cerulean nodded and then looked serious. "Does Duskya know I am here?"

Ruskya glanced at him, "No, why?"

"I wasn't sure if you would have told her."

The twin smiled wistfully. "No, I think she has learned that not every emotion I feel is necessarily her concern. She hasn't kept tabs on me as much since I got married."

Cerulean laughed. "I see. Is there somewhere we can talk?"

Ruskya led the rider over to a small cave, and sat down on a log. "What's on your mind, Cerulean?" Ruskya asked sensing the man's seriousness.

The older rider sighed. Ruskya sensed a nervousness that he had never seen before in the man. He tried to figure out what it was, but realized Cerulean would tell him in his own time.

"Ruskya, has Duskya spoken to you about me at all?"

The younger rider grinned; he now understood. He had felt the same way when he went to talk with Casey. He decided to make it a little easier on Cerulean.

"You have nothing to be afraid of Cerulean. You need to talk with her, not me."

"But, Ruskya." Cerulean paused. "I would feel more comfortable knowing that I have your blessing."

Ruskya smiled. "May fortune shine on you, Cerulean. You have my permission and blessing."

Cerulean sighed with relief. "Now my biggest fear is trying to take her any distance from you."

Ruskya nodded. "I've wondered about that, too. I can tell you that since I have married Carryl, our bond has changed; it's not quite as strong. Perhaps it is like Carryl's ability to control or tune out the dragon's conversations. Duskya and I may have learned when to tune certain things out."

"That makes sense," Cerulean agreed. "I think I will try to go find Duskya."

The two left with a handshake. Ruskya was glad Cerulean was here early. Hopefully, his sister would be able to have a real heart-to-heart chat with the man.

* * *

After the evening meal, Carryl was nursing Ardyn when a knock sounded at the door. Ruskya went to answer it and found Cerulean and Duskya. He opened the door to invite them both inside. From the looks on their faces, Ruskya could tell that the conversation had gone well.

"Have you decided anything?" he mentally asked his twin.

"Oh, mind your own business," she replied.

"Aren't you part of my business?"

"Enough, you two," Cerulean said. "It's impolite to talk behind people's backs."

At his voice, Carryl came out of the bedroom carrying Ardyn. "Ruskya," she said then stopped, staring. "Cerulean?" she asked, then ran to him. Ruskya took Ardyn so the baby wouldn't be squished in their embrace. "When did you get in?"

"This afternoon. Braidyn is with me."

Carryl turned to Ruskya, "You didn't tell me!"

"He didn't tell me either," Duskya added. "I say we get him."

"Can't harm the man holding the baby." Ruskya laughed. "It was worth it to see the look of surprise on your face."

"Speaking of this baby," Cerulean said, "Can I see him? Then you two can have at Ruskya."

"I might not give him up," Ruskya joked, when Carryl lifted Ardyn from his arms and handed the baby to Cerulean.

As he held the little one, tears clouded Cerulean's eyes, reminiscent of rain in the clouds. "Your grandfather would be mighty proud of you, little one." The baby's tiny hand reached out and wrapped around Cerulean's finger.

"I'd say he likes you," Duskya said. Cerulean smiled.

After a few more moments of talking, Cerulean handed Ardyn back to Ruskya. "I need to get something from outside. I'll be right back." He stepped outside, while the others looked at one another, puzzled. He returned with a medium-sized crate with a towel wrapped over it. As he brought it into the living area, he was smiling. Carryl looked amazed and then wonder crossed her face. Ruskya was the next to catch on.

"When?" Carryl asked.

Cerulean nodded, "Two nights ago. As soon as she hatched, I knew it was time to return. Braidyn was willing and ready, and so we took off." He removed the blanket from the crate to reveal a small hatchling. The color was a muted purple, blue, and green. "I've named her Nube because she reminds me of the clouds after a storm."

"She is gorgeous," Carryl and Duskya said together.

"Can you let her out of the crate?" Ruskya asked, adding, "I agree, she will be a wonderful dragon." The hatchling perked up her head at his voice.

"Can she understand speech yet?" Duskya asked.

"Of course," Carryl said. "She is fully capable of communicating. You just have to be able to understand her."

The little dragon started to waddle toward Ruskya. The others continued their conversation, ignoring Nube's progress until the dragon stopped at Ruskya's feet and placed her muzzle on his knee. Ruskya glanced down. "Well, what do we have here?" With Ardyn in his arms, he bent over to look. The hatchling stretched up to see the baby boy. Ruskya brought Ardyn within the dragon's reach. Nube's muzzle gently reached for the baby's fuzzy head of red hair.

At a gasp from Carryl, Ruskya looked over. There were tears in her eyes. "Carryl? What is wrong?"

The next instant a picture came to his mind. A mature dragon the color of the clouds after a storm was flying through the air with a redheaded boy. Ruskya gasped.

"She's asking permission," Carryl replied, finally able to talk.

Ruskya nodded, swallowed and replied, "Honored dragon, it would be a blessing to accept your offer. May your flight be favored with blessings."

The little dragon drew in air and then slowly let it out. A small puff of air moved Ardyn's red hair and a few sprinkles of purple, blue, and green landed on the boy's forehead.

KEEP READING FOR A PREVIEW OF

DRAGON'S HEIR

BOOK 2 IN THE DRAGON COURAGE SERIES

CHAPTER 1: A CONTENTED RIDER

THE WARM SUMMER SUN beat down on Braidyn as he leaned
against Turqueso's flank. It was days like this that he enjoyed best: no
worries, a dragon at his side, and the heat of the day to relax in.

He turned and gave the dragon a hug. "Thank you, Turqueso."

"For what?" The dragon's sleepy voice replied.

"For choosing me ten winters ago."

"What else could I do? I needed a rider, and you needed a friend."

"But, there were others that you could have chosen."

"True, but none were exactly like you."

Braidyn thought back to his old home. He really didn't miss it. Yes,
at times he still missed his parents, but it had been ten winters since they
had been killed by the aqua dragon.

He reflected on how encounters with three dragons had changed his
life and thrown him into circumstances that had led him to this bluff
overlooking the Sur River. The aqua dragon had sent fear coursing through
him for the first time, and Braidyn had been happy to hear of his death.
After the aqua dragon had killed his parents, Braidyn had hid in fear
while the merchant had told him of the icy blue dragon called Wyeth.
This dragon had brought courage to his heart, and hope that there were
good dragons in the world. Later, he had learned that the merchant told
those stories under the influence of both his intense pain and the dragon
courage Meredyth had shared with him. Most significantly, Turqueso had
changed Braidyn's life, and his physical appearance, forever. Braidyn was
now a man of twenty-four winters. His sun-bronzed skin made his
turquoise eyes stand out, and he had let his dark hair grow to shoulder
length as was customary for several of the riders in his colony.

Braidyn sighed contentedly. "I wish afternoons like this could go on forever."

"I know, but if they did, we wouldn't enjoy them so much."

The young man nodded. "I suppose we should head home and see if Cerulean needs any help."

Braidyn stood, stretching to his full six feet. His tunic fell open to reveal a chest accustomed to physical labor. Drawing his tunic back around, he tied his belt tighter at his waist. It was a dark leather belt, which signified that he was no longer a youngling. He liked the freedom of being a mature rider. One day he would probably train a youngling, but he didn't have any aspirations to do so anytime soon. He bent down and shook out his knee length leather boots before tugging them up over his shins.

"Let's go, Turqueso. I need to stop at the market to pick up supper supplies."

The dragon stretched, allowing the rays of sun to soak into all the places that had been in shadow. Braidyn paused to admire him. He was a beautiful turquoise color with veins of darker greenish hues trailing along his belly and showing through his wings. The dragon was also large, since he had seen one hundred sixty winters. Normally, a dragon and rider were closer in age, but since Turqueso had chosen Braidyn after his former rider, Kyanos, had died, Turqueso was much older than Braidyn.

Arriving on the plain outside Boeskay, Braidyn dismounted and sent Turqueso back to the bluffs where he had his nest. Braidyn continued on to the town that sprawled over the top of the bluffs overlooking the Sur River. Even after ten winters, Braidyn couldn't get used to the houses spread out over multiple dragon spans. He had grown up around Woolpren a village where houses were practically stacked on top of each other in the canyon wall.

The center of town was reserved for the marketplace. Braidyn loved it there. He enjoyed the colors, smells, and sounds of the bazaar. He didn't like to be in the middle of the noise, but would rather sit back and let it all swirl around him. He came here each day to pick up his food. As he walked through the market, he tried to hold in check the disgust he felt toward the vendors who tried to pretend they were his friends just to get the sale.

"My friend, I have a deal just for you!" "A discount today, just for you!"

He didn't mind those who were honestly trying to sell their wares.

"Melons, fresh melons," the singsong voices called.

"Red, ripe tomatoes. The best this season!"

"Strawberries, two weights for three coppers."

The marketplace had both types of vendors; some took money while others accepted trades, but Braidyn had never gotten used to the idea of bartering. He approached a vendor toward the back of the square.

"Good day, my northern friend," the sturdy, graying man greeted Braidyn. "What will it be today? Some plump red peppers, or maybe some ripe, juicy tomatoes?"

"Greetings, Carvall. Those tomatoes look good, but I'll have to take a closer look."

"You always do, rider. How you can figure out what is on the inside of the produce by looking at the outside, I will never know. Must be some dragon ability."

Braidyn let the man think what he would. He hadn't told anyone down here that he had grown up on a farm. Most of his knowledge was the kind he couldn't verbalize, but just knew from instinct.

He considered the farmer's display. The red tomatoes contrasted with the greens of the peppers, lettuce, and cucumbers. The orange carrots brought a bright spot to the earth-tones of potatoes, ginger, onions, and garlic. The reds of the strawberries were surrounded by the pale yellows and greens of melons. He had always thought this vendor had more of an artistic arrangement than the others. That was what had caught his eye four winters ago, when he had first begun to prepare his own meals. Before that, he had lived with his trainers, Cerulean and Duskya.

The potatoes called to him, but so did the strawberries. Maybe a salad with nuts and strawberries complimented by fried fish and potatoes? That sounded good.

"Carvall, I'll take one, no, make that two, tomatoes; one carrot; a head of lettuce; three potatoes; two onions; and a measure of your chopped nuts. Do you have any bread today, my friend?"

"Sorry, I don't have any left. Had some this morning, but it goes awful fast these days. I can't keep it in stock. Besides, it's better when it's fresh and hot."

"Three measures of your flour, then, so that I can make my own bread. Now, wait a minute," Braidyn stopped the vendor. "Not that flour, the other one. It's better quality."

"Was that our deal?" the farmer inquired, hesitating as he turned to the bag indicated by the rider. "This is the best I have."

"Yes, and it wouldn't be worth anything if it wasn't for Turqueso and me."

The farmer hung his head. "You drive a hard bargain, rider, but you are right. All right, I'll give you the better flour, even though I could get two silvers for it."

"You wouldn't get those silvers if Turqueso hadn't come by this fall to burn the stubble off your land and fertilize the ground."

"Fine, I will gladly give it to you. I had to try bartering at least a little."

Braidyn laughed and thanked the man. He took his produce basket and started to weave his way back through the marketplace. Strident voices caught his attention. He paused and pretended to look at some produce while listening in on the conversation.

"But, sir, I didn't pay for rotten produce. I paid for the ones like those," the woman said, pointing to the bright vegetables in the vendor's display.

"Ma'am, I don't know what you are up to, but what you have in your basket couldn't have come from my booth. You can see I have nothing that resembles the garbage you have there."

"What am I to do? I can't serve these to my family!"

The woman was close to tears, Braidyn could tell. He had meandered to the booth where she was arguing with the vendor. The stench reaching his nostrils was overwhelming. He wasn't sure how no one else had noticed it, but then, he had always been able to tell when produce was going bad. His da had always relied on him to say when to harvest the potatoes before they turned rotten. Trips to the root cellar at the farm were not only for Braidyn to pull out the needed produce, but also to inspect for any possible rot. His nose told him that this vendor had rotten produce.

"Honored lady," he stopped the woman from walking away defeated, "what seems to be the problem?"

"This man claims that I did not purchase this basket from him. I did! He won't give me my money back or replace these rotting items with good produce."

"I see," Braidyn said calmly. He turned to the vendor. "Is this true?"

"She didn't get that garbage from me. You can see I only have fresh produce here."

Braidyn didn't comment, but started to remove the top layer of potatoes from the display in front of him.

"What do you think you are doing?" the man huffed.

Braidyn didn't answer. With great care, he picked up a potato from the second layer and broke it in half. He almost gagged. He held the potato out for the vendor, the woman, and the gathering crowd. The potato was black and putrid.

"This is what you call fresh produce? I don't think so."

"I-I," the vendor stammered. "I don't know how that got there."

"Then you don't know how this carrot got here, either?" Braidyn asked as he reached into the stack of carrots, took one from underneath the first layer, and proceeded to bend it in half. Instead of breaking crisply in two, it formed a limp, perfect arch.

"I am sure, honored sir," Braidyn continued, turning to another customer, "that if you look under that stack of lettuce you will find that it is almost a soup."

The man hesitated and then looked. He brought up a head of soggy lettuce. The crowd gasped.

For the finale, Braidyn reached for a tomato. He picked it up with care, but his fingers still sunk through the grayish-red skin. Placing the tomato on the table, he reached for the vendor's towel and slowly wiped his hands without a word.

The crowd was spellbound, Braidyn could tell. He felt a deep satisfaction. Since the aqua dragon had burned his farm and killed his family, he had vowed to defend the helpless at all costs. Now that he was a dragon rider, he could handle a bully, and he had the means to make sure his vow was kept.

"Honored lady, take your pick of his produce. Replace what is in your basket and take what your family will use—as much as you need."

The woman looked questioningly at Braidyn, but seeing that the vendors and farmers agreed, she started to empty her basket and fill it with the good produce from the top layers of the vendor's display.

"But—" the vendor started to protest.

Braidyn raised a warning hand and stared at the man. One look at the rider's turquoise eyes was enough to stop any complaint.

Murmurs ran through the crowd, and Braidyn heard speculation about how he knew about the rotten produce; they connected it to his being a rider. Let them think what they will, Braidyn thought. It will give them greater respect for the next rider they meet.

Braidyn stayed to make sure the vendor didn't go back on his word. He debated finding out the man's name and banning him from the riders' list of farms to fertilize each year, but decided against it. Public humiliation was enough for now. If the man continued to sell rotten produce, then Braidyn would reconsider. The young rider decided to keep an eye on the man and a nose in the air each time he passed this booth.

When the woman had filled her basket with fresh produce, she turned to him. "Thank you, rider. May blessings be upon you for looking out for my family."

"And may fortune shine on you and your family," he returned. "It was my duty and my privilege to help."

He bowed to her, and she inclined her head and left, leaving murmurs behind her. Braidyn wandered away, and then backtracked to watch. One of his favorite pastimes was to find a nook out of the way and watch the market activity. He kept his eye on the offending vendor, but saw no more trouble. Word seemed to have spread to avoid him, for no one else stopped and purchased anything from his booth.

Braidyn finally made his way to the fish market. Here, too, he had a specific vendor that he visited. He selected a few fish to receive in exchange for cleaning the fishmonger's nets each morning. It was a pleasure to clean the nets, since the man let Turqueso keep any extra fish that had gotten caught. Braidyn also liked the smell of the net and the river in early morning.

At last, Braidyn made his way back to his own little dwelling in Boeskay. There he started a fire and fried the fish with the potatoes and created a salad just the right size to finish off his meal. Duskya had instilled in him a love for tea; so while the fish and potatoes fried, he boiled water. When it was finished, he sat down to his small but satisfying meal, and relaxed. He would finish the evening with a book and then watch the sunset. In the morning, he would go clean the fishing nets and take care of his other business in the colony. Perhaps he would go for a flight with

Cerulean or Duskya tomorrow, or even offer to watch the children for them. But that was tomorrow. For now, he had a sunset to enjoy with his dragon.

Did you enjoy, *Dragon's Future*? Want to find out more about Kandi J Wyatt? Check out the following sites to connect with her. You can also sign up for a newsletter to be the first to know about new releases and other important happenings.

www.facebook.com/kandijwyatt/
www.twitter.com/kandijwyatt
http://kandijwyatt.com
http://plus.google.com/u/0/+KandiWyatt/posts

IF YOU ENJOYED *DRAGON'S FUTURE*, PLEASE CONSIDER LEAVING A REVIEW ON AMAZON.

ALSO IN THE DRAGON COURAGE SERIES

Dragon's Heir

Dragon's Revenge

MORE GREAT READS FROM KANDI J WYATT

The One Who Sees Me (Historical Christian Fiction) Follow Faru's tale in a retelling of a Biblical story found in the Old Testament book of Genesis, showing that when things don't make sense, God will guide the way.

MORE GREAT READS

The Beat on Ruby's Street by **Jenna Zark** (Middle Grade Historical Fiction) A strong-willed young girl's journey in to the heart of the Beat Generation and the complexities of family relationships shows Ruby Tabeata how to follow her heart, no matter what life throws at her.

Blast of the Dragon's Fury by **LRW Lee** (Young Adult fantasy) Ten-year-old Andy Smithson believes he is merely a kid too often in trouble with his overambitious parents--until his destiny as the Chosen One to break a 500-year-old curse is revealed. No pressure, but it's his skill alone that will save—or condemn—the kingdom of Oomaldee forever.

Made in the USA
San Bernardino, CA
26 August 2016